END OF AN ERA

Novels by Robert J. Sawyer

*Golden Fleece**
Far-Seer
Fossil Hunter
Foreigner
*End of an Era**
The Terminal Experiment
Starplex
*Frameshift**
Illegal Alien
*Factoring Humanity**
*Flashforward**
*Calculating God**

*published by Tor Books

(Readers' group guides available at www.sfwriter.com)

Anthologies Edited by Robert J. Sawyer

Tesseracts 6 (with Carolyn Clink)
Crossing the Line (with David Skene-Melvin)
Over the Edge (with Peter Sellers)

TOR®

A Tom Doherty Associates Book
New York

END OF AN ERA

Robert J. Sawyer

END OF AN ERA

Copyright © 1994 by Robert J. Sawyer
Revised edition copyright 2001 by Robert J. Sawyer

This book was originally published by Ace Books in 1994.

This book is printed on acid-free paper.

Design by Jane Adele Regina

A Tor Book
Published by Tom Doherty Associates, LLC
175 Fifth Avenue
New York, NY 10010

www.tor.com

Tor® is a registered trademark of Tom Doherty Associates, LLC.

ISBN 0-312-87693-9

First Tor Trade Paperback Edition: September 2001

Printed in the United States of America

0 9 8 7 6 5 4 3 2 1

For David Livingstone Clink

friend and brother-in-law
poet and punster

with sincere thanks and great admiration

ACKNOWLEDGMENTS

My profound thanks for years of encouragement go to Carolyn Clink, Ted Bleaney, David Livingstone Clink, John Robert Colombo, Terence M. Green, and Andrew Weiner. This book was unearthed with their help and the help of Dr. Dale A. Russell, former Curator of Fossil Vertebrates at the Canadian Museum of Nature; the late Nobel laureate Dr. Luis W. Alvarez, father of the asteroid-impact extinction model, who let me spend an afternoon with him at the Lawrence Berkeley Laboratory in September 1983; Roger MacBride Allen; Susan Allison; Kevin J. Anderson; Nick Austin; Asbed G. Bedrossian; Jerry Bokser; Richard Curtis; Peter Heck; Howard Miller; Dr. Ariel Reich; John Rose of Toronto's Bakka Science Fiction Bookstore; Robin Rowland; and Alan B. Sawyer. Thanks, too, go to paleontologists Michael K. Brett-Surman of the National Museum of Natural History, Smithsonian Institution, and Phil Currie of the Royal Tyrrell Museum of Palæontology, both of whom kindly embraced the first edition of this book, as well as my other novels about dinosaurs.

Special thanks to my agent, Ralph Vicinanza, and to David G. Hartwell, James Minz, Moshe Feder, and Tom Doherty of Tor Books for arranging for the publication of this revised edition.

END OF AN ERA

Prologue: Divergence

My father is dying. He's in the oncology ward at Toronto's Wellesley Hospital, cancer eating away at his colon, his rectum—parts of the body people think it's funny to talk about.

It's unfair having to see him like this. How am I going to remember him when he's gone? As I knew him from childhood —a temperamental giant who used to carry me on his shoulders, who used to play catch with me even though I couldn't throw for beans, who used to tuck me in and kiss me good night, his face like sandpaper against my cheek? I don't want to remember him like this, shrunken and old, an anorexic mummy with rheumy eyes and varicose face, tubes in his arms, tubes up his nose, drool staining his pillow.

"Dad . . ."

"Brandon." He coughs twice. Sometimes he coughs more, but it is always an even number. They rack his body in pairs, these coughs, like one-two punches from a wily heavyweight. "Brandon," he says again, as if the coughs have erased the earlier uttering of my name. I wait for the words that always come next. "Long time no see."

It's a little play we put on. My line is always the same, too. "I'm sorry." But I'm like an actor who's been in the same part too long. I say it without feeling, without meaning. "I've been busy."

He's been watching TV again. That forty-centimeter Sony mounted high on the hospital wall is a kind of time machine for him. Thanks to Channel Twenty-nine from Buffalo, which specializes in golden oldies, he gets to peek into the past. Sometimes he reaches back a full six decades for an *I Love Lucy* episode, flawlessly colorized and reprocessed in stereo. This afternoon he is casting back a mere twenty years for a rerun of *Roseanne*.

Rosie and Dan are standing in the kitchen talking about the latest trouble their daughter Darlene has gotten into. I'm used to the crispness of my flat-panel wall TV; this ancient set has ghosting and blurry edges. I pick up the remote from the table beside the bed. *Click*, and the Conners and their little neat world collapse into a singularity in the center of the screen. The dot lingers—a faint reminder of the former life, hanging on longer than it should. I turn to my father.

"How are you feeling?" I ask.

"The same." It's always the same. I put the remote down next to the crystal vase. The flowers I'd brought last time have withered. The once-bright petals have turned the color of dried blood and the water looks like weak tea. I take hold of the stems and, dripping on the stippled tile, carry the dead things over to the garbage pail and drop them in. "I'm sorry I didn't bring fresh ones."

I come back and sit beside him. The chair has a chrome-plated frame and vinyl cushions that smell like warm vomit. He looks old, older than anyone I've ever seen. He used to have a full head of hair, even in his early seventies. But he's completely bald now. Chemotherapy has taken its toll.

"Why don't you ever bring Tess with you?" he asks.

I look out the window. Toronto in February is a gray city, like a photograph printed in half-tones. The last of the snow, old and dirty, has been eroded by the first spring rains, forming hoodoos at the sides of the roads. Wellesley Street is streaked with white salt stains. It's three in the afternoon and hookers are already at the intersections, wearing heavy fur coats and fishnet stockings. "Tess and I aren't married anymore," I remind him.

"I always liked Tess."

Me, too. "Dad, I'm going away for a few days."

He doesn't say anything.

"I'm not sure when I'll be back."

"Where are you going?"

"Alberta. The Red Deer River valley."

"That's a long way away."

"Yes. A long way."

"Another dig?"

"Not so much a dig this time, Dad. But it *is* a dinosaur hunt. It may take a couple of weeks."

After a long, long time he says softly, "I see."

"I'm sorry to have to leave you."

Silence again.

"If you don't want me to go, I won't."

He rolls his crab-apple head to look at me. He knows I have just lied to him. He knows I am going anyway. What kind of son am I, leaving behind a dying father?

"I've got to be on my way now," I say at last. I touch his shoulder, a bony thing covered by thin pajamas. Once the color of summer sky, they've been washed and dried to the pale blue-gray of an old woman's hair rinse.

"Will you write? Send a postcard?"

"I can't, Dad. I'll be cut off from the rest of the world out there. I'm sorry."

I pick up my trench coat and head for the door, resisting the urge to look back, to say something—anything—else.

"Wait."

I turn. He adds nothing more, but, after a few eternal seconds, he beckons me closer, closer still, until I am leaning over him, his ragged breath pungent in my nostrils. Then, at last, he speaks, faintly but clearly. "Bring me something to put an end to all this pain. That stuff you've got in the lab. Bring me some."

In the comparative-anatomy lab at the museum we've got chemicals for killing wild animals: painless clear death for the rodents; amber death for the larger mammals; an incongruous peach-colored death for the lizards and snakes. I stare at my father.

"Please, Brandon," he says. He never calls me Brandy. Brandon was the name of his favorite uncle—some guy from England that I'd never met—and nobody had ever called *him* Brandy. "Please help me."

I stumble out of the ward, somehow find my car. By the time I realize what I am doing, I have driven almost all the way to the house where Tess and I used to live, where Tess still lives. I turn around, go home, and get very drunk, feeling no pain.

Countdown: 19

Professor Cope's errors will continue to invite correction, but these, like his blunders, are hydra-headed, and life is really too short to spend valuable time in such an ungracious task.

—Othniel Charles Marsh, paleontologist (1831–1899)

I will correct [Marsh's] errors, and I expect the same treatment. This should not excite any personal feelings in any person normally or properly constituted; which unfortunately Marsh is not. He makes so many errors, and is so deficient that he will always be liable to excitement and tribulation. I suspect a Hospital will yet receive him.

—Edward Drinker Cope, paleontologist (1840–1897)

Fred, who lives down the street from me, has a cottage on Georgian Bay. One weekend he went up there alone and left his tabby cat back home with his wife and kids. The damned tabby ran in front of a car right outside my townhouse. Killed instantly.

Fred loved that cat, and his wife knew he'd be upset when she told him what had happened. But when he got back Sunday evening, he said he already knew the cat was dead—because, according to the version of the story I eventually heard over my back fence, he'd seen his cat up at the cottage, two hundred kilometers away. The tabby had appeared to him one last time to say good-bye.

I always looked at Fred a little differently after I'd heard that. I mean, it was fantastic, and fantastic things don't happen in normal lives. Certainly they don't happen to people like me.

Or so I thought.

I'm a paleontologist; a dinosaur guy. Some might think that's glamorous, I suppose, but it sure doesn't *pay* glamorously. Oh, about twice a year, I get my name in the paper or five seconds on *CBC Newsworld,* commenting on a new exhibition or some new find. But that's about it for excitement. Or at least it was, until I got involved in this project.

Time travel.

I feel like an idiot typing those two words. I'm afraid anyone who reads them will start looking at me the way I look at poor Fred.

Sure, by now everyone has probably read about the mission in the papers, or seen the preparations on TV. Yeah, it really works. Ching-Mei Huang has demonstrated it enough times. And, yes, it's incredible, absolutely incredible, that she went from a first discovery of the underlying principle in 2005 to a working time machine by 2013. Don't ask me how she did it so fast; I don't have a clue. In fact, sometimes I don't think Ching-Mei has a clue, either.

But it works.

Or, at least, the first Throwback worked; the automated probe returned with air samples (a little more oxygen than to-day, no pollution, and, fortunately, no harmful germs), plus about four hours' worth of pictures, showing lots of foliage and, at one point, a turtle.

But now we're going to try it with human beings; if this test works, a bigger mission, with everyone from meteorologists to entomologists, will be sent back next year.

But for this attempt, only two people were going back, and one of them was me: Brandon Thackeray, forty-four, a little paunchy, a lot gray, a goddamned civil servant, a museum cu-rator. Yes, I'm also a scientist. Got a Ph.D.—from an American university, to boot—and I suppose it makes sense that it would be a scientist who'd go gallivanting across time. But I'm not an adventurer. I'm just a regular guy, with quite enough to deal with, thank you very much, without something like this. An ailing father, a divorce, a mortgage that I *might* be able to pay off by the beginning of the next geologic era, hay fever. Regular stuff.

But this was far from regular.

We were hanging by a thread.

Okay, it was really a steel cable, about three centimeters thick, but it didn't give me any more reassurance.

And I wished that damned swaying would stop.

Our time machine had been lifted up by a Sikorsky Sky Crane, and was now hanging a thousand meters above the stark beauty of the Badlands of Alberta. The pounding of the helicopter's engines thundered in my ears.

I wished that noise would stop, too.

But most of all, I wished Klicks would stop.

Stop being an asshole, that is.

He wasn't really doing anything. Just lying there in his crash couch, on the other side of the semicircular chamber. But he's so smug, so goddamned smug. The couch is like a high-tech La-Z-Boy upholstered in black vinyl and mounted on a swivel base. Your feet are lifted up, your spine tips at an angle, and a tubular headrest supports your noggin. Well, Klicks had his legs crossed at the ankle and his arms interlaced behind his head. He looked so bloody calm. I knew he was doing it just to bug me.

I, on the other hand, was gripping the armrests of my crash couch like one of those poor souls who are afraid to fly.

It was about two minutes until the Throwback.

It should work.

But it might not.

In two minutes we could be dead.

And he had his legs *crossed*.

"Klicks," I said.

He looked over at me. We were almost exactly the same age, but opposites in a lot of ways. Not that it matters, but I'm white and he's black—he was born in Jamaica and came to Canada as a boy with his parents. (I always marveled that anyone would leave that climate for this one.) He's clean-shaven and hasn't started to gray yet. I've got a full beard, have lost about half my hair, and what's left is about evenly split between gray and brown. He's taller and broader-shouldered than me, plus, despite having a job that involves as much time at a desk as mine does, he's somehow avoided middle-age spread.

But most of all, we're opposites in temperament. He's so cool, so laid-back, that even when he's standing he gives the impression of being stretched out somewhere, tropical drink in hand.

Me, I think I'm getting ulcers.

Anyway, he looked in my direction, his face a question. "Yeah?"

I didn't know what I had intended to say. After a moment, I blurted out, "You really should put on your shoulder straps."

"What for?" he replied in that too-smooth voice of his. "If the programmed stasis delay works, it won't matter if I'm standing on my head when they rev up the Huang Effect. And if it doesn't work . . ." He shrugged. "Well, man, those straps will slice you like a hard-boiled egg."

Typical. I sighed and pulled my straps tighter, the thick nylon bands reassuringly solid. I saw him smile, just a bit—but also just enough so that he could be sure that I would see the smile, the patronizing expression.

A crackle of static from the radio speaker fought to be heard above the sounds of the helicopter, then: "Brandy, Miles, are you ready?" It was the precise voice of Ching-Mei Huang herself, measured, monotonal, clicking over the consonants like a series of circuit breakers.

"Ready and waiting," Klicks said, jaunty.

"Let's get it over with," I said.

"Brandy, are you okay?" asked Ching-Mei.

"I'm fine," I lied, wishing I had a bucket to throw up into. The swaying back and forth was getting to me. "Just do it, will you?"

"As you say," she replied. "Sixty seconds to Throwback. Good luck—and God protect." I was sure that little reference to God was for the sake of the network cameras. Ching-Mei was an atheist; she only had faith in empirical data, in experimental results.

I took a deep breath and looked around the small room. *His Majesty's Canadian Timeship Charles Hazelius Sternberg.* Great name, eh? We'd had a list of about a dozen paleontologists we could have honored, but old Charlie won out because, in addition to his pioneering fossil hunting in Alberta, he'd actually written a science-fiction story about time travel, published in 1917. The PR people loved that.

Ching-Mei's voice over the radio speakers: *"Fifty-five. Fifty-four. Fifty-three."*

Anyway, nobody ever calls it *His Majesty's Canadian, Etc.* Instead, our timeship is almost universally known as the *Sternberger,* because to most people it looks like a fat hamburger. To me, though, it looks more like a squat version of the *Jupiter 2,* the spaceship from that ridiculous TV series *Lost in Space.* Just like the Space Family Robinson's vehicle, the *Sternberger* was essentially a two-level disk. We even had a little dome on the roof like they did. Ours housed meteorological and astronomical instruments; there was room enough for one person to squeeze into it.

"Forty-eight. Forty-seven. Forty-six."

The *Sternberger* was much smaller than the *Jupiter 2,* though—only five meters in diameter. Our lower deck wasn't designed for people; it was just 150 centimeters thick and consisted mostly of our water tank and part of the garage for our Jeep.

"Forty-one. Forty. Thirty-nine."

Our upper deck was divided into two halves, each semicircular in shape. One half contained the habitat. Along its curving outer wall was a kidney-shaped worktable, our radio console, and a compact laboratory unit crammed with geological and biological instruments. The straight back wall, marking the ship's diameter line, had three doors built into it. Door number one—does anybody remember Monty Hall?—led to a little ladder that angled up into the rooftop instrumentation dome and to a ramp that went down the meter and a half to the outer entrance door. Door number two led to the Jeep's garage, which took up the height of both decks. Door number three gave access to the washroom stall.

"Thirty-four. Thirty-three. Thirty-two."

Mounted against the central wall in the gaps between the doorways were a small stand with an old microwave oven on it, a large food refrigerator, a bank of three equipment lockers swiped from some high school demolition sale, and a small medical refrigerator with a first-aid kit on top. Bolted to the floor were the swivel bases for our two crash couches.

A time machine.

An actual time machine.

I just wish I knew exactly where it was going to take me.

"Twenty-nine. Twenty-eight. Twenty-seven."

The Huang Effect was accurate to one-half of one percentage point—a minuscule imprecision. But given that we were casting back from A.D. 2013 to 65.0 million years ago, a half-point error could plop us as much as 330,000 years into the Cenozoic, much too late to determine just what had caused the worldwide extinctions at the end of the previous era, the Mesozoic.

"Twenty-four. Twenty-three. Twenty-two."

My analyst says I'm going to excessive lengths to prove I'm right and Klicks is wrong. Thank God for socialized medicine—there's no way I could afford to stubbornly disbelieve Dr. Schroeder month after month if the government health plan weren't picking up the bills for my therapy. Besides, it's more than just me versus Klicks. If we don't miss our target, this trip might clear up an enduring scientific mystery, something that he and I and hundreds of others had argued for years through the pages of *Nature* and *Science* and *The Journal of Vertebrate Paleontology.*

"Nineteen. Eighteen. Seventeen."

The government of Alberta had wanted us to launch from Dinosaur Provincial Park, a UNESCO World Heritage site. But the fossils found there were from a time 10 million years before the end of the age of dinosaurs. We'd gone upstream along the Red Deer River to a formation from the latest late Maastrichtian—right at the end of the Cretaceous. But to make the government happy, Ching-Mei had established her control center at the Tyrrell Field Station inside Dinosaur Provincial Park.

"Thirteen. Twelve. Eleven."

The distance between the center of the Earth and ground level here in the Red Deer valley might have changed by several hundred meters in the last 65 million years. Unfortunately, the geomorphologists working on this project couldn't agree on whether the landforms would have shifted up or down during that timespan. To avoid the possibility of our ship arriving underground—killing us, of course, not to mention causing one hell of an explosion as matter tried to force itself inside of other matter—the *Sternberger* had been hauled a kilometer above the Badlands by the Sikorsky. Just before Ching-Mei threw the switch to activate the Huang Effect, we would be cut loose. The interior of the *Sternberger* would lock into stasis—a stopped-time condition, the first creation of which had won Ching-Mei a Nobel Prize in 2007—until ten minutes after we arrived in the Mesozoic. Plenty of time, supposedly, for us to come crashing to the ground and for the mountain of debris we would kick up on impact to rain out of the sky.

That's the theory, anyway.

"Seven. Six. Five."

I thought of something funny in those last few seconds. If I did die, my will still named Tess as my beneficiary. Not that I owned much of value—just a beat-up Ford and the townhouse in Mississauga—but it seemed strange that my ex-wife would get it all. I guess that would be all right if both Klicks and I died, but I didn't like to think of just me buying it. After all, since Tess had taken up with Klicks—just how long had they been seeing each other, anyway?—my estate would in essence go to him, too. That's the last thing I wanted.

"*TWO. ONE. ZERO!*"

My stomach lurched as the cable was released—

Countdown: 18

Look ahead into the past, and back into the future, until the
silence.

— Margaret Laurence, Canadian novelist (1926–1987)

● You pays your money, you takes your chances. We had
contingency plans for every possible outcome of the
drop: what to do if we landed in water; if we landed upside
down; if we couldn't get the door open; if for some reason we
came out of stasis too early and were damaged on impact. But
the worst of all, really, was if we landed at night, because for
that the contingency plan was simply to wait until morning.

My crash couch was swiveled to face the *Sternberger*'s curving outer wall. A glassteel window was built into it, giving a
full 180-degree panorama. Everything outside was dark. Actually it wasn't quite night: it just took my eyes a minute to adjust. More like twilight, really. Klicks must have been thinking
the same thing, because he whistled the *DOO-doo-DOO-doo*
signature from that old Rod Serling TV series.

"It's almost sunrise," I said, unstrapping myself, the aluminum buckle opening with a clang. I rushed over to stand in
front of the radio console and peered out of the center of our
window.

"And the glass is half-full," replied Klicks, also getting to his
feet.

"Huh?" I hated his little tests—cryptic phrases designed to
see just how much on the ball you were.

He came over and stood near me. We both peered into the
darkness. "You're an optimist, Brandy. I think it's just past sunset."

I pointed to my left. "That part of the window was facing
east when the Sikorsky dropped us."

He shook his head. "Makes no difference. We could have corkscrewed as we fell, or bounced on impact."

"There's one way to tell." I walked back to the straight rear wall of the habitat. I paused for a second to peer through the little window in door number two, the one that led into our Jeep's garage. The garage door was made out of glassteel panels, so it was completely transparent. I should have been able to see outside past the Jeep, but it seemed pitch-black. Oh, well. I opened the middle of the three equipment lockers and rummaged around until I found a compass. It was pretty beat-up, the veteran of many field expeditions. I brought it over to Klicks.

"No good," he said, not bothering to look at the compass's dial. "It'll only show us the north-south line; it won't tell us which is which."

I was about to say "Huh?" again, but after a second, I realized what Klicks was getting at. The polarity of Earth's magnetic field reverses periodically. We'd been aiming for about a third of the way down into 29R, a half-million-year-long chron of reversal that straddled the Cretaceous-Tertiary boundary during which the magnetic north pole was located near the geographic south pole. If we'd hit our target, the colored end of our compass needles would be facing south. But the Huang Effect's uncertainty was big enough that we might have landed well into the more recent 29N chron of normal orientation, or maybe just into the top of the more ancient 30N. If we'd landed in either of those, the colored end would be facing north instead. Klicks knew there'd be no easy way to tell, except by looking at the sun, which of course would still rise in the east and set in the west. Until we could see if it was getting brighter or darker along the glowing horizon to our right, we wouldn't know if it was dawn or dusk.

Except—hah! *Got him.* I looked at the compass dial, holding it very steady. The needle agitated for a few beats, then came to rest. "You can't tell which one is north," Klicks said.

"Yes I can," I said. "The end of the needle that dips down is pointing to the closest magnetic pole, following the curving lines of the Earth's magnetic field. Even with continental drift, the north pole will still be the closest."

Klicks grunted, impressed. "And which end is tipped down?"

"The unpainted one. The polarity is indeed reversed. So the good news is that we are indeed in 29R, and that *that* way"—I pointed back toward the flat rear wall—"is true north, toward the Arctic rather than the Antarctic."

"And the bad news," said Klicks, "is that it really is night-fall."

That wasn't going to dampen my spirits. I continued to peer through the glassteel window. Its central part was facing south. It was hard to make out exactly what we were seeing at first, but slowly our eyes irised open.

We weren't on flat ground. Rather, we seemed to be perched high up on a mound of dirt. A crater wall. Of course: while we had been in stasis, the *Sternberger* had plummeted out of the sky and evidently had hit some very soft material—mud or loose soil, perhaps. The shock of the impact had formed a crater with a diameter of thirty meters or so—six times as wide as the timeship itself. But the *Sternberger* had hit with enough force that it had bounced up out of the bottom of the crater and had plunked down here, high on the east side of the donut-shaped crater wall.

God, this was exciting. The past. *The past.* I felt light-headed, almost dizzy—practically floating. My heart pounded, an increasingly rapid one-two rhythm like a drummer warming up.

It would be folly to go outside in the dark. Who knew what creatures had been attracted by our explosive arrival? Still, until we actually saw a dinosaur, or some other piece of strictly Mesozoic life, we wouldn't know for sure that we'd arrived before the great extinction. Klicks and I moved to our right, away from the view of the crater wall.

To the south was a lake, looking like a vast pool of blood under the pink sky, its still surface broken at the perimeter by bulrushes, reeds, water lilies, and duckweeds. Straight ahead, running to the rose-colored western horizon, was a wide expanse of dried mud, cracked into a brown hexagonal mosaic, each piece curling up at the edges like a dead leaf. Dotting this mud plain were the ragged, ropy stumps of bald cypress trees, twisting and writhing toward the sky like tormented souls.

We both moved to the back wall. Klicks looked through the window in door number one, which led to the access ramp and ladder. He could see out the glassteel inlay in the main door. I looked through the window in door number two again. Although it was actually darker than when I'd first peered through here, my eyes had adjusted and I could see out better. Directly north, appearing almost like a wall, was a forest of broad-leaved deciduous trees, their upper branches intertwining about twenty-five meters up to form a thick canopy. Mixed in with these were a lesser number of bald cypresses and some eucalyptus-like evergreens. Some of the cypresses poked through the canopy like leafy flagpoles, stretching up an additional twenty-five meters.

With this backwoods-of-Louisiana setting, it certainly looked like the late Mesozoic, but I still harbored a fear that we'd arrived in the early Cenozoic, missing the dinosaurs altogether. We'd have to make the most of this trip, regardless of when we had landed—but with nothing over twenty kilograms surviving the Cretaceous-Tertiary boundary, the lower Paleocene was just plain boring. *Damn the Huang Effect and its half-percent uncertainty!*

"Look!" shouted Klicks. He'd moved back to the main curving wall, standing over our mini-lab and looking west. I hurried over to stand next to him and sighted along the khaki sleeve of his outstretched arm, following the cracked mud plain out to where it met the sky. A large object was moving at the horizon, silhouetted against the red glow of twilight.

Nothing over twenty kilos . . . This *was* the Mesozoic. It had to be! I dashed back to the equipment lockers and grabbed two pairs of binoculars, hurried back to the window, gave one pair to Klicks, fumbled the leather case for mine open, sent lens caps flipping through the air like tossed poker chips, and brought the eyepieces to my face. A dinosaur. Yes, by God, a dinosaur! Bipedal. A duckbill, perhaps? No. Something much more exciting. A theropod, stomping around on its hind legs like Godzilla pounding through Tokyo.

"A tyrannosaur," I said reverently, looking over at Klicks.

"Ugly mother, ain't he?"

I gritted my teeth. "He's beautiful."

And he was. In this wan light, he looked dark red, as if he had no skin and we were seeing the blood-soaked musculature directly. He had a giant warty head atop a thick neck; a barrel-shaped torso; tiny, almost delicate forelimbs; a thick, endless tail; corded, muscular legs; and bird-like triple-clawed feet. A perfectly designed killing machine.

We were getting the whole thing on video, of course. Each of us wore a Sony MicroCam, hooked into a digital recording system. The only flaw was that we had no way to play the imagery back until we returned to the future.

Suddenly a second tyrannosaur came into view. This one was slightly larger than the first. My heart skipped a beat. Would they fight? Animals that big, needing that much food, might well be territorial. How I wanted to see such a battle firsthand, instead of having to piece it together from mute bones. What a spectacle it would be! I felt buoyant, light as a feather.

The two hunters faced each other for a moment—an incredible tableau, straight out of a Charles Knight painting, a pair of multi-ton carnivores squaring off for a battle to the death. The smaller of the two opened its massive jaws and even at this distance the thing's sharp teeth were visible, giving a ragged, torn-paper look to the edge of the mouth.

But they did not fight. As one, both turned away from the twilight. A third tyrannosaur was arriving, this one even larger than the first two. It was followed seconds later by a fourth and a fifth. Each walked with a stooped gait, its body swinging forward from wide hips, the massive head balanced by the long, thick tail.

A pair of dark hills near the tyrant lizards shook and I realized that these were yet two more tyrannosaurs flopped on their bellies. They pushed with their hind legs, their tiny two-fingered forelimbs digging into the dirt, channeling the force of those mighty thighs into lifting their torsos instead of sliding them across the ground. Slowly the beasts rose to standing postures. One threw its head back and let loose a low roar that I felt even this far away through the metal walls of the *Sternberger*. Seven mighty carnosaurs banding together? It was inconceivable to me that there was any prey powerful enough to require these great hunters to combine forces into a pack.

By now it was getting darker. There were only a couple of dozen dinosaur genera left at the close of the Cretaceous, so identifying the genus, even in this light, was easy: *Tyrannosaurus*. Given this was Alberta, the species was probably mighty *T. rex* itself, but these were too small to be full-grown females; most of them were probably juveniles, the different sizes representing different hatching seasons, although the biggest might be an adult male. Amazing—

And then suddenly they began to move.

Toward us.

With purposeful strides, the largest of the seven headed toward our timeship, followed in single file by the others. They marched in unison, seven massive left legs pounding the ground, seven bodies tilting to the south, then seven right feet swinging forward, seven loaf-shaped heads tipping to the north. Left, right, south, north, like soldiers in rank and file. Cycads and ferns were pulped underfoot. Tiny creatures that had been hiding in the foliage—too dark to see precisely what they were—scampered out of the way.

It made no sense, this orderly procession of dragons. Granted, some fossil evidence suggested that certain dinosaurs had complex social hierarchies, but this goose-stepping was bizarre—a nightmare parade.

I thought briefly about the strength of the *Sternberger*'s walls. When locked in stasis, the ship was indestructible. But just sitting here, it was little more than a tin can. And tyrannosaur jaws could bite through steel.

As the seven hunters made their way closer to us, I saw through the binoculars that their bloody coloring wasn't just a trick of the twilight. They really were dark reddish brown, their skin a tightly packed matrix of round beads like Indian corn. Beneath each massive mandible a loose sack of skin, perhaps a dewlap, waggled back and forth. Their tiny double-clawed forearms, looking withered and useless, bounced like drumsticks against their massive guts.

When the reptiles got within thirty meters of us, they broke formation. The lead tyrannosaur headed to our right. The next went to our left, and so on, alternating, except for the last of the procession, who just stopped where it was, the tip of its tail swishing back and forth.

The beasts who had been near the front of the caravan tried to continue around back, but they seemed flummoxed by the crater wall upon which we were perched. One of them attempted scaling the steep sides, but its tiny forearms were useless for gaining purchase. The tyrannosaurs, now simply black shadows moving against the night, regarded us. They were apparently trying to make sense out of the squat metal disk that had invaded their stomping ground.

After a few minutes, the one who had tried to climb the wall backed off about twenty-five meters. It growled, a low, resonant thrumming, then ran forward, its legs pumping up and down like pistons. The creature's momentum, two tons of angry inertia, carried it up the crater wall toward us. The mass of blood-colored flesh hit hard, right in front of my face, the impact causing the *Sternberger* to teeter backward. The glassteel of the window deformed where the creature had hit, losing some of its transparency. The massive warty head, jaws snapping like castanets, tried to lock onto our hull. Serrated teeth, many of them fifteen centimeters long, scraped the glassteel with a sound like a dentist's drill. Several, presumably the ones that had been ready to shed anyway, popped from their sockets and went flying. Finally, unable to find anything to hold onto, the tyrannosaur slipped backward, stumbling down the crumbling crater wall to join its kin.

Then, just as they had come, they left, marching in single file back into the night, the pounding of their footfalls continuing long after they had faded from view. Overhead, in a sky clearer and blacker than any known to Earth after the Industrial Revolution, the Milky Way shone like a river of diamonds.

Countdown: 17

An obstinate man does not hold opinions, but they hold him.
—Alexander Pope, English poet (1688–1744)

Well, what were we to do? I mean, we'd only woken up four hours before; it was hardly time to go to bed. I was too excited to sleep, anyway. I felt light on my feet, almost giddy. After the tyrannosaurs had left, it was so dark that Klicks had turned on the overhead fluorescents. But after a few moments I asked him if he'd mind if I turned them off.

"Ready for beddy-bye so soon?" he said.

"I just want to look at the stars."

He grunted, but hit the switch himself. It took a while for my eyes to readjust, but soon the heavens were visible to me in all their splendor. In the southwest was a point of light brighter than all others. I thought I knew what it was and fumbled for my 7 x 50s, bringing the dual eyepieces to my face. Yes, the four Galilean satellites were visible, three on the left and one off to the right. The Galilean satellites? Strictly speaking, I was now the first person to see Jupiter's four largest moons. Maybe we should start calling them the Thackerayan satellites.

The rest of the sky was a mishmash. We'd gone back far enough in time that, even at their indolent pace, the stars had completely reconfigured themselves. None of the familiar constellations were visible. Knowing where the sun had set and where Jupiter was, I extrapolated the ecliptic. Scanning its length, I looked for Jupiter's siblings.

Venus would have dominated the sky had she been visible. Mars, too, should have been obvious because of its reddish glow. There *was* a colored point of light about thirty degrees above the horizon, but if anything it was more green than red. Another point shone higher up in the sky—Saturn, perhaps? I brought my binoculars up to check. I couldn't make out the rings, but that didn't prove anything. Even Hubble couldn't see them when they were edge-on.

I lowered the field glasses and simply drank in the night. And, as always of late, my mind wandered to Klicks and Tess.

We hadn't had much to say to each other lately, Klicks and me. It's not that there wasn't a lot I wanted to ask him. I wanted to know how Tess was doing, how their relationship was going, whether they were planning to move in together, how often they—well, a whole bunch of things that weren't any of my damned business, but that I wondered about anyway.

Klicks and I had been friends, dammit. Good friends. He'd been teaching assistant for Bernstein when I was doing my undergrad at U of T. We'd gotten along great and kept in touch after I'd left for Berkeley to do my graduate work. Years later, when I married Tess in that sprawling ceremony her parents had insisted on, it seemed natural to ask Klicks to be my best man.

May the best man win.

I don't know if it was just holding in my anger that made me feel congested or whether we'd actually been breathing inside this cramped tin can long enough for the air to begin to run out. Either way, it seemed awfully stuffy. "We'd better open the vents," I said.

Klicks grunted assent, and we each took hold of one of the red wheels that worked the louvers around the upper edge of the curving outer wall. My ears popped as pressure equalized. Cloying pollens wafted in and I was grateful I'd taken a Seldane before the Throwback.

The night was alive with weird insect sounds: zippings and chirpings and tick-tick-tickings and low, throbbing hums. There was wire mesh over the vents to keep the insects out, but I cringed at the thought of having to face the clouds of prehistoric bugs tomorrow.

"The moon's coming up," said Klicks. I turned and looked out the window. Fat and amber, waxing, about three-quarters full, the moon's pitted face reflected in the still waters of the lake to our south.

"Christ, look at that," exclaimed Klicks. It took me a moment to figure out exactly what was wrong with the moon's face. It had turned so that a good part of what was the backside in modern times was clearly visible. I could see some of what must have been Mare Moscoviense on the eastern limb. Librations do let us see a bit of the backside in the twenty-first century, but Moscoviense started at around 140 degrees east latitude, way around back. My first thought was that the moon must not yet be tidally locked, but I rejected that; its orbit was too close for it to be anything but. No, more likely this was the one side that faced Mesozoic Earth. I wondered what had caused Luna to twist in its orbit between now and my time.

"It looks small," said Klicks.

I thought about that. The moon did indeed seem smaller than normal. That was funny, since we'd assumed it would actually be closer to the Earth now, orbiting objects having a tendency to spiral away slowly over millennia. Still, the moon's apparent size normally changes by about thirty percent as it moves from perigee to apogee, but most people never notice that; the human eye is notoriously inaccurate at gauging such things. Still, the moon *did* look small.

Through the binoculars I could see other evidence that this was indeed a younger Luna. I looked at where Giordano Bruno should have been. Normally, that crater is right on the limb of the full moon, but here it should have been well in from the edge of the disk. As I suspected, its series of 500-kilometer-long rays was nowhere to be found. Five British monks in A.D. 1178, their faces tipped toward the heavens, had actually seen the meteor impact that had made that crater.

I thought about mentioning the missing crater to Klicks, but talk of meteor strikes always sparked the debate between us about whether one such had caused the Cretaceous-Tertiary extinctions. Klicks bought that theory. In the eyes of the general public, that made him right in line with mainstream thinking. After all, the newspapers and PBS shows in the 1980s had all concluded that an asteroid impact was indeed the culprit. I wasn't in the mood to rehash it all again—I'm more inclined to lock horns with Klicks after a few brews, and, sadly, there were none among our provisions—but then something happened that brought up the old debate anyway. Slowly, quietly, without any fuss, a *second* moon was rising after the first. It was smaller, only about a third the apparent diameter of Luna. Spherical, it too was waxing gibbous, looking like a white jelly bean.

"Klicks?" I said.

"I see it."

I brought my binoculars to bear on the tiny orb, but its face was too small to show any detail. "Trick," I said, surprising myself. "I think we should call it Trick."

"After Charles Trick Currelly, no doubt," said Klicks, wanting to demonstrate that he got the reference. C. T. Currelly, an early-twentieth-century archaeologist, was the founder of the Royal Ontario Museum, where I worked. One of my occasional forays into the world of popular writing had been a biography of him for *Rotunda*, the ROM's member magazine. Klicks did not dispute my choice of name and I was grateful for that small miracle.

We watched the two moons for some time. It seemed that Trick was catching up with Luna, meaning that it was in a much lower orbit. Since Luna is tidally locked, so that the same side always faces Earth, that would mean that Trick probably was also. It must be under a lot of gravitational stress being that much closer . . .

Aha!

"There goes the periodic extinction theory," I said, excitement in my voice.

The Alvarez Group at Berkeley published their asteroid-impact extinction theory in *Science* in 1980. About the same time, an interesting hypothesis was making the rounds concerning the Eocene-Oligocene extinctions, the ones that would come 30 million years after the demise of the dinosaurs. According to it, those later extinctions resulted from a general cooling caused by the breakup of an ancient second moon, leaving Earth with a temporary equatorial ring of orbiting debris that blocked enough sunlight to lower temperatures for a million years or so. The Alvarez theory, sexy because it dealt with dinosaurs and embraced by many pop-science communicators after Sagan had linked it to nuclear winter, eclipsed the ringed-Earth discussions.

Others, including Klicks, tried to push the Alvarez theory a step further, claiming that bolide impacts at regular intervals, caused perhaps by a dark star periodically disturbing either the asteroid belt or the Oort cloud, were responsible for a regular schedule of extinctions, including both the K-T and the E-O. That idea never washed with me, since to get the 26-million-year periodicity you had to use the late Ordovician dyings, which were obviously just the result of plate tectonics moving the supercontinent Gondwanaland over the south pole, causing an ice age.

Klicks knew my position on all of that, of course, so I simply pointed at the second moon. "Trick provides a one-of-a-kind explanation for the Eocene-Oligocene extinctions," I said. "There's nothing periodic about a moon breaking up."

To his credit, Klicks didn't contest that. But he did say, "Why link it to those deaths? Why not to the ones that are about to occur?"

"Tektites," I said, referring to the glassy, moon-like rocks found at various locations on Earth. "The age of the southeastern U.S. tektite field coincides with the E-O boundary. I bet they were caused by the impacts of the remnants of Trick."

Klicks was quiet for a minute or so, although I could hear

him grinding his teeth in the dark, the way he does when he's thinking—chewing over a problem, you might say. Finally he spoke. "We have sleeping pills."

"Huh?" I guess the change of subject meant I had won that round, but I couldn't see what he was getting at.

"I said, we could take something to get to sleep. We're going to be useless in the morning if we stay awake all night."

I never took sleeping pills. I knew I had an addictive personality—another one of Dr. Schroeder's little insights. That meant messing with any drug would be out of the question for me. Hell, I have a hard enough time avoiding pizza, and Schroeder swears that there's nothing in the old double-cheese-and-pepperoni that could cause a chemical dependency. Still, what Klicks said made sense. I could hear him moving around the dark cabin. When he opened our medicine refrigerator a small yellow bulb came on, illuminating its interior. Klicks found the bottle he was looking for and, leaving the door open so that he'd have some light, went to the sink and filled a couple of paper cups. We had more than enough water in the tank beneath our feet to last the eighty-seven hours we would be here, that being the maximum length of time the Huang Effect could hold a lock on us when casting this far back.

"Here," he said, offering me one of the Dixie cups and a silver caplet. I slipped the pill into my breast pocket. Klicks kicked the fridge door shut and all was darkness for a moment, until he turned the overheads back on, their brightness making us both squint. He turned the crank on the side of his crash couch, and it ratcheted around from its normal sitting configuration into a flatbed position.

I moved away from the window, from the odd spectacle of Trick slowly chasing Luna through the forest of stars, and converted my couch to sleeping mode, too.

Next, I changed into my pajamas. While doing so, my eyes kept being drawn out the window to the sight of the two moons. Even if the existence of Trick disproved the periodic extinctions theory, I was sure Klicks would stick to the asteroid model for the death of the dinosaurs.

It's frustrating being a paleontologist. My neighbor Fred—the one with the dead cat—once said to me, hey, now that they know what killed the dinosaurs, guess your job is pretty much over. That seems to be the public's attitude. But, really, it's all because a couple of astronomers and physicists who knew nothing about dinosaurs and a couple of glib talkers from the paleontological community who wanted some limelight pushed the idea so vigorously that it got, quite literally, more popular-press coverage than any scientific theory since World War II.

But it's just a theory, and not a very good one at that. Yes, there's no longer much doubt that there was an impact of a ten-kilometer-wide asteroid at or near the end of the Mesozoic. But the Mesozoic lasted 160 million years, and during it there were at least *seven* other large-asteroid impacts. Each is at least as well documented as the supposed dinosaur-killer (one formed the 100-kilometer-wide Manicouagan crater in Quebec), and there's zero turmoil in the fossil record associated with any of them.

It's what Bob Bakker calls the frog problem: frogs, notoriously sensitive to climactic change, survived the end of the age of dinosaurs just fine, but big animals, which should have had more resistance, were all killed off. An asteroid impact is the wrong sort of scenario to explain the selective extinctions we see in the fossil record.

Sure, there's a buried crater called Chicxulub half on land and half beneath the sea near the northern coast of Yucatán, Mexico. And, yes, by the early 1990s, a series of tests had dated it to very close to the K-T boundary. But with so many con-firmed and possible Mesozoic craters, it surprised me that the impact-extinction theory continued to have any legs. Beside Chicxulub and Manicouagan, the later dated at 214 million years before the time I'd been in when I'd woke up this morning, there's also the 175-million-year-old Puchezh-Katunki crater in Russia, the 145-million-year-old Morokweng crater in South Africa, the 144-million-year-old Mjölnir in the Barents Sea, the 128-million-year-old Tookoonooka in Australia, the 117-million-year-old Carswell in Saskatchewan, and the 74-million-year-old Manson in Iowa. I mean, heck, if large bolide strikes really did have staggering biological effects, we'd have seen a constant series of massive extinctions throughout the age of dinosaurs; it'd be a wonder that the terrible lizards had survived as long as they did.

Nonetheless, to this day, people ask me about the asteroid that killed the dinosaurs. I explain that from time to time the Society of Vertebrate Paleontology surveys its members about the Alvarez theory. The first time such a survey was done, in 1985, only four percent believed that an asteroid impact had caused the extinction of the dinosaurs. In a separate survey in 1991, Mike Brett-Surman at the Smithsonian found those paleontologists who didn't believe in an impact-extinction correlation outnumbered those who did by four to one. The figure has fluctuated a lot in the intervening two decades, but a show-of-hands at the last SVP meeting indicated support was currently hovering at around twenty percent.

Really, many paleontologists see two separate issues. One is what caused the interesting geology at the K-T boundary—there's a clay layer rich in iridium there. The other is what caused the extinctions. The geology may or may not have anything to do with the dyings.

Klicks believed the asteroid had killed off the dinosaurs; I vehemently disagreed. I wasn't even convinced that Chicxulub was the source of the iridium layer; like Officer and Drake, I think it's mostly volcanic in origin. Yes, iridium is rare on the surface of the Earth but plentiful in some kinds of meteors. But Earth *does* have the same iridium content as most rocky bodies in the solar system; ours is just fractionated into the deep mantle. There's lots of evidence for volcanism at the end of the Cretaceous. The Deccan Traps in India, for instance, represent at least one million cubic kilometers of basalt that date from the K-T boundary. And volcanic material shows the same concentrations of arsenic and antimony found in the boundary-layer clay, concentrations that are three orders of magnitude greater than what's normally associated with meteorites.

Indeed, the largest known impact craters on Earth, including the huge crater remnant off Nova Scotia, show no evidence of iridium deposition. Comets, sometimes named as an alternative culprit, are even less likely: there's no direct evidence at all for iridium in cometary material.

Klicks and I had argued these issues many times in person, in print, and once when I was visiting scholar at the Royal Tyrrell Museum in Alberta, where Klicks worked, on a phone-in show on the local community-access cable-TV channel. Klicks had been adamant during that debate: the impact of an asteroid had killed the dinosaurs. It was clear by the calls we got that those members of the public who didn't have their own crackpot theories almost exclusively sided with Klicks. They wanted to know what all the fuss was about; hadn't this issue been settled years ago? Everybody *knew* an asteroid impact had wiped out the dinosaurs.

Well, we were here.

And we were going to find out, one way or another.

I've been keeping this diary for years, and tonight, the most exciting of my life, I'm certainly not going to miss making an entry. Someday perhaps I'll turn these notes into a book about our voyage (editing out the private stuff, of course), so I think I'll add a little more background detail than usual.

I typed silently in the dark on my Toshiba palmtop for about an hour, its keyclick shut off and the brightness of its screen turned way down so as not to bother Klicks. When I was done, I swallowed the silver sleeping caplet dry.

Soon morning would be here. Soon we would step out into the Mesozoic.

Boundary Layer

I never travel without my diary. One should always have something sensational to read in the train.

—Oscar Wilde, Irish playwright (1854–1900)

Klicks always took his vacations in Toronto. Partly it was because his parents, both in their seventies, still lived there. Partly it was because his sister and her two sons, whom Klicks doted on, lived just east of the city in Pickering. And partly, I liked to think anyway, it was because he enjoyed spending time with Tess and me—although he did always turn down our invitations to stay at the house, preferring his sister's luxury condo overlooking Lake Ontario.

But the main reasons for his frequent trips to the mighty T.O. were the culture and the food, both as good as New York's. Klicks relished the finer things, and there weren't a lot of them in Drumheller, Alberta. Tonight we were going to see Andrew Lloyd Webber's latest musical, *Robinson Crusoe*, touted by the critics as his best since *Phantom of the Opera*. Even the most pathetic road company of a major show like that wouldn't make it out to a small town in the middle of the Prairies.

It was an 8:00 P.M. curtain. That gave us time for a leisurely dinner at Ed's Egalitarian, the new hot spot in the heart of the theater district.

"I hate menus like this," I said, my eyes running up and down the three panels of steaks, poultry, seafood, salads, and soups. "Too much selection. I never know what to order."

Tess, seated next to me, sighed that I-married-him-despite-his-faults sigh she was getting so good at as the years went by. "You do this every time we eat out. It's not like you're making a lifetime commitment." She gave me a playful poke in the belly. "Just pick something that isn't too fattening."

That was sound advice. My weight usually started going up around Thanksgiving and continued to rise until the good weather came back in March. I always managed to take it off over the summer, and, if I was doing any fieldwork, I could get reasonably thin by late August, but right now I was up a good seven kilos. I glanced across the table at Klicks, who looked more like an athlete than a scientist, then turned my attention back to Tess. "What are you going to have?"

"The petite filet," she said.

"Hmmm. I just don't know . . ."

Klicks looked up from his menu. "Well, while you agonize over what to eat, I've got some news."

Tess, always a devourer of any gossip, smiled that radiant smile of hers. "Really? What?"

"I'm moving to Toronto for a year. I'm taking my sabbatical at U of T."

It was a good thing that the waiter hadn't yet brought us our drinks. Otherwise, I might have spluttered gin and tonic all over the fancy lace tablecloth. "You're doing what?" I said.

"I'm going to be working with Singh in the geology department. He's gotten a small grant from—what do they call it? Whatever that new, scaled-down thing that replaced NASA is. Anyway, the money's to study satellite photographs. We're going to see if a technique can be worked out for identifying fossiliferous locales from space, as a prelude to an eventual Mars excursion."

"If they ever get enough money together to do one," I said. "But, Christ—that might put you in line for the mission. I'd heard they were considering having a paleontologist go with them."

He made a dismissive motion with his hand. "It's too early to speculate on that. Besides, you know what they say: the reason Canadians have an inferiority complex is that we're the only country that routinely has to lay off our astronauts."

I laughed, the better to hide my envy. "Lucky stiff."

Klicks smiled. "Yeah. But now we'll be able to spend a lot more time together." He turned to my wife. "Tess, see what you can do about dumping Brandy."

"Ha ha," I said.

Our bow-tied waiter returned with our drinks, the aforementioned gin and tonic for me, an imported white wine for Klicks, and mineral water with a twist of lime for Tess. "Are you ready to order?" he asked in the requisite obscure European accent used by all waiters at Ed's various restaurants.

"You go ahead," I said. "I'll decide by the time he gets round to me."

"Madame?"

"A small Caesar salad, please, and the petite filet wrapped in bacon, rare."

"Very good. Sir?"

"To start," said Klicks, "the French onion soup—please make sure the cheese is cooked." He looked over at Tess. "And the lamb chop."

My heart skipped a beat. I wondered if he knew that "Lambchop" was my pet name for her. I tried never to use it in public, but I suppose I might have slipped from time to time.

"And for you, sir?" the waiter said to me.

"Hmmm."

"Come *on*, Brandy," said Tess.

"Yeah," I said. "The lamb chop sounds good. I'll have the same thing as him."

"Good night, Dr. Thackeray."

"'Night, Maria. Try not to get soaked."

Another strobing flash of lightning sent wild shadows sprinting around the room. Even when it wasn't storming out, the Paleobiology offices at the Royal Ontario Museum were a wonderfully macabre place—especially in the evening after most of the lights had been turned off. Bones were everywhere. Here, a black *Smilodon* skull with fifteen-centimeter-long saber teeth. There, the curving brown claws of an ornithomimid mounted on a metal stand, poised as if ready to seize fresh prey. Sprawling across a table, the articulated yellow skeleton of a Pliocene crocodile. Scattered about: boxes of shark teeth, sorting trays with thousands of bone chips, a small cluster of fossil dinosaur eggs looking as though they were about to hatch, and plaster jackets containing heaven-only-knows-what brought back from the latest dig.

From outside, the claps of thunder were like dinosaur roars, echoing down the millennia.

This was my favorite time. The phones had stopped ringing and the grad students and volunteer catalogers had gone home. It was the one opportunity in the day for me to relax and get caught up on some of my paperwork.

And, when all that was done, I took my old Toshiba palmtop out of the locked drawer in my desk and wrote my daily entry in this diary. (I normally wouldn't run a computer during an electrical storm, but my trusty Tosh was battery powered.) I executed a macro that jumped to the bottom of my diary file, inserted the current date—16 February 2013—boldfaced it, and typed a colon and two spaces. I was about to begin today's write-up when my eyes were caught by the tail end of the previous entry. *I let my tears flow freely*, it said.

Huh?

I scrolled back a few pages.

My heart pounded erratically.

What the *hell* was this?

Where did this entry come from?

Living dinosaurs? A journey back through time? An attack by—? Was this some kind of joke? If I ever found out who'd been messing with my diary, I'd kill him. I was so pissed off, I barely noticed that the freak lightning storm had stopped almost as suddenly as it had begun.

I jumped to the top of the document. I'd begun a new diary file on January 1, about six weeks ago, but this file started with a date only five days ago. Still, there were pages and pages of unfamiliar material here. I began to read from the beginning.

Fred, who lives down the street from me, has a cottage on Georgian Bay. One weekend he went up there alone and left his tabby cat back home with his wife and kids. The damned tabby ran in front of a car right outside my townhouse. Killed instantly.

Those weren't my words. Where was my diary? How did this get here in its place? What the hell was going on?

And what's this about Tess and Klicks—? Oh Christ, oh Christ, oh Christ . . .

Countdown: 16

To really understand a man, you have to get inside his head.
—Rudolph L. Schroeder, Canadian clinical psychologist (1941–)

Mesozoic sunlight shone through the glassteel window that ran around the curving rim of the *Sternberger*'s habitat, stinging my eyes and casting harsh shadows on the flat rear wall. I woke up still feeling strangely light-headed and buoyant. I looked around the semicircular chamber, but Klicks was nowhere to be found. The bastard had gone outside without me. I quickly shed my PJs, pulled on the same Tilley pants that I'd worn yesterday, fumbled into my shirt, jacket, and boots, and opened door number one, bounding down the little ramp that led to the outer hatch. Much to my surprise, I hit my head on the low ceiling as I went down the ramp. Rubbing my bruised pate, I opened the blue outer door panel and looked down at the crater wall. In the brown earth, I could clearly see the skid marks made by Klicks's size twelves. To their right, there were giant triple-clawed tyrannosaur tracks, made by the beasts that had reconnoitered us last night. Also visible: tiny two-pronged marks made by the minuscule tyrannosaur finger-claws.

I took a deep breath and walked forward. The first step, as the saying goes, was a doozy. The hull of the *Sternberger* jutted out from the crater wall, and I fell close to a meter before my boots connected with the crumbly, moist soil. Still, it was a surprisingly gentle fall, and I skidded with ease down to the mud flat, brown clouds of dirt rising behind me. At the base of the crater, I fell back on my bum; a rather ignominious first step into the Cretaceous world.

It was hot, humid, and overgrown. The sun, just clearing the tops of the bald cypresses, was burning brighter than I'd ever experienced. I looked everywhere for a dinosaur, or any verte-brate, but there was none to be seen.

None, that is, except Klicks Jordan. He came bounding around from behind the crater wall, jumping up and down like a madman.

"Check this out, Brandy!" He crouched low, folding his knees to his chest, then sprang, the soles of his work boots clearing the dark soil by a meter. He did it again and again, leaping into the air, a demented rabbit.

"What the hell are you doing?" I said, irritated by his child-ishness and perhaps a little envious of his prowess. I certainly had never been able to jump that high.

"Try it."

"What?"

"Go ahead. Try it. Jump!"

"What's gotten into you, Klicks?"

"Just do it, will you?"

The path of least resistance. I crouched down, my legs stiff from just having awoke, and bolted. My body went up, up, higher than I'd ever jumped before, then, more slowly, more gently than I'd ever experienced, it settled back to Earth, land-ing with a dull thud. "What the—?"

"It's the gravity!" said Klicks, triumphantly. "It's less here—much less." He wiped sweat from his brow. "I estimate I weigh just over a third of what I normally do."

"I've felt light-headed since we arrived—"

"Me, too."

"But I thought it was just excitement at being here—"

"It's more than that, my friend," said Klicks. "It's the grav-ity. The actual fucking gravity. Christ, I feel like Superman!" He leapt into the air again, rising even higher than he had be-fore.

I followed suit. He could still outjump me, but not by much. We were laughing like children in a playground. It was exhila-rating, and the pumping adrenaline just boosted our abilities.

You can't avoid building up some decent leg muscles doing fieldwork, but I'd never been particularly strong. I felt like I'd drunk some magic potion—full of energy, full of power. *Alive!*

Klicks set off leaping around the crater wall. I gave chase. The donut of dark, crumbling earth had been providing some shade, but we came out into the fierce sun as we moved around back. It took us several minutes of mad hopping to circumnavigate the thirty-meter-wide crater, returning to the part of the wall upon which the *Sternberger* was perched.

"That's amazing," I said, catching my breath, my head swimming. "But what could possibly account for it?"

"Who knows?" Klicks sat down on the dried mud. Even in less than half a *g*, leaping up and down like an idiot is enough to tire you out. I crouched about ten meters away from him, wiping sweat from my soaked forehead. The heat was stifling. "I'll tell you one thing *it* accounts for, though," said Klicks. "Giantism in dinosaurs. Matthew of the AMNH asked the question a century ago: if the elephant is the largest size our terrestrial animals can now manage, how could the dinosaur have grown so much larger? Well, we've got the answer now: they evolved in a lesser gravity. *Of course* they're bigger!"

I saw in an instant that he was right. "It also explains the extensive vascularization in dinosaur bones," I said. Dinosaur bone is remarkably porous, which is part of the reason it fossilizes so well through permineralization. "They wouldn't need as much bone mass to support their weight in a lower gravity."

"I thought that vascularization was because they might be warm-blooded," said Klicks, sounding genuinely curious. He was, after all, a geologist, not a biologist. "Haversian canals for calcium interchange, and all that."

"Oh, there's probably a correlation there, too. But I've never bought the idea of warm-blooded brontosaurs, and even they have bones that look like Swiss cheese in cross section. I'm sure you've seen the studies that say they'd break their own legs if they tried to walk faster than three kilometers an hour. That figure assumed normal gravity, of course. And, say, speaking of odd bone structure—it never quite seemed possible to me that *Archaeopteryx* and the pterosaurs could really fly. Their skeletons are weak for normal gravity, but they should be more than adequate in this."

"Hmmm," said Klicks. "It does explain a lot, doesn't it? We'll have to have a good look at dinosaurian heat production while we're here. I seem to remember that another argument in favor of warm-blooded dinosaurs was that their fossils have been found inside the Cretaceous Arctic Circle, where the nights would be months long."

"That's right," I said. "The idea was that dinosaurs must be warm-blooded because they couldn't have possibly migrated far enough to avoid the long nights."

"Hell," said Klicks, taking off his boot and shaking it upside down to get rid of a pebble that had found its way inside, "*I* could walk to here from the Arctic Circle in this gravity."

"Yeah," I said. "But I'd still like to know *why* the gravity is less. I guess the gravitational constant could have increased in value over time."

"That would mean it's not much of a constant, then, wouldn't it?"

"Well, I don't know a lot of physics," I said, ignoring his smart-ass comment, "but didn't Einstein more or less pull the value for G out of the air to get his equations to balance? We've only been measuring its value for a century, and measuring it precisely for only a few decades. A general tendency for it to increase over time might not have shown up yet."

"I suppose, although I'd expect to find—" Suddenly he fell silent, his head swinging around. "What was that?" he said.

"What?"

"*Shhsh!*"

He pointed to the deciduous forest, the sun now well above the trees. There was a rustling as something man-sized pushed aside fronds. I caught a flash of emerald in my peripheral vision. My heart began pounding and my mouth went dry. Could it be a dinosaur?

We didn't have much of an armament. Hell, we didn't have much of a budget. Someone had suggested we bring modern automatic assault weapons to protect ourselves, but no corporate donor came through with any of those—bad PR to be associated with killing animals, after all. All we had were a couple of old elephant guns, each holding two bullets at a time.

Klicks had brought his elephant gun with him when he'd come out this morning. It was propped up against the crater wall, about a dozen meters away. He sauntered over to it, casually picked it up, and motioned for me to follow. It took about forty seconds for us to reach the dense wall of trees. Pushing foliage aside with his hands, Klicks made his way into the forest. I was right behind him.

We heard the rustling again. Breath held tight, I strained to listen, scanning the dense growth for any sign of an animal. Nothing. Branches and leaves stood still, as if they, too, were frozen in anticipation. Seconds ticked by, heartbeats added up. Whatever it was must be nearby, either to my left or in front of me.

Suddenly in a flurry of motion the thick vegetation parted and a green bipedal dinosaur leapt into view, the top of its head coming to no more than the height of my shoulder.

It was a slender theropod, using a stiff, whip-thin tail held parallel to the ground to balance a horizontally carried torso. At the end of its darting neck was a head about the size and shape of a borzoi dog's, drawn out and pointed. Two huge eyes, like yellow glass billiard balls, stared forward, their fields of vision overlapping, providing the kind of depth perception a predator needed. The creature opened its mouth, revealing small, tightly packed teeth, serrated like steak knives along their rear edges. Long, thin arms dangled in front of its body, the three-fingered hands ending in sickle claws. The animal flexed them in anticipation and I saw that the third finger was opposable to the other two digits. Bobbing and weaving its head, it cut loose a sticky sound like a person trying to kick up phlegm.

I recognized this creature in an instant: *Troödon*, long hailed as the most intelligent dinosaur, a carnivore armed not only with slashing claws and razor dentition but also with a hunter's keen senses and—perhaps—with cunning. Although the best troödon skeletons were known from a time 5 million or more years before the end of the age of dinosaurs, fossil troödon teeth were found in beds right up to the close of the Cretaceous. These specimens were on the large side for troödon, but the shape of the skull was unmistakable.

Klicks had already brought up his elephant gun, its wooden butt resting against his shoulder. I don't think he intended to fire unless the animal attacked, but he was aiming along the gun's shaft, finger on the trigger. Suddenly he pitched forward. The gun went off, missing the troödon, the thunderclap of its report startling a flock of golden birds and a smaller number of white-furred pterosaurs into flight. A second troödon had kicked Klicks in the small of his back, its slender claws shredding the khaki material of his long-sleeved shirt. Two more troödons appeared from the brush. Each was hopping rapidly from foot to foot for balance, like shoeless boys on hot pavement. Klicks rolled over, trying madly to reach his gun. A three-clawed foot slammed into his chest, pinning him. The dinosaur let loose a sticky hiss, showering him with reptilian spit.

I ran toward Klicks and, approaching from the left side, brought my steel-toed boot up and under the creature, kicking it in the center of its yellow gut. I made no dent in the lean, muscular belly, but, much to my surprise, my kick lifted the thing clear off the ground. It must have massed less than thirty kilos and the reduced gravity magnified my strength. Freed, Klicks scrabbled for the gun again, his fingers clawing dirt.

The recipient of my kick turned on me, moving with surprising agility. I held my arms in front of my body, trying to grab its scrawny throat. Hands shooting forward in a green blur of motion, it seized my wrists with sickle digits. My spine arched back like a limbo dancer's, trying to avoid the jaws at the end of that dexterous neck. The creature wasn't built for fighting something more than twice its mass with muscles, such as they were, accustomed to more than double the gravity. I held my own for a good fifteen seconds.

Still gripping my arms, the troödon crouched low, folding its powerful hind legs beneath it, and kicked off the rich soil. The force of its leap knocked me backward and I hit the ground hard, rocks biting into my spine. Straddling my body, the crazed reptile arched its neck, opened its lipless mouth wide, exposing yellow knife-like teeth, and—

Kaboom!

Klicks had found his elephant gun and squeezed off a shot. He'd hit my attacker in the shoulder, sending the beast's neck and head pinwheeling into the sky. Twin geysers of steaming blood shot from the torso's severed carotid arteries. No longer balanced, the body tipped forward and the cavity of the open chest, sticky and wet, slammed into my face. Revolted, I rolled away, dirt clinging to the dinosaur blood that covered my face.

Klicks was taking a bead on another dancing troödon when the remaining two descended on him from opposite sides. One, balancing on its left leg, slashed out with its clawed right foot. The curving digits grasped the gun's barrel. Using the leverage provided by its long, stiff tail, the dinosaur twisted the rifle free from Klicks's hands and, with a deliberate movement, tossed it into the brush. In unison, it and its partner jumped on Klicks, pinning him to the ground again.

The remaining troödon, five meters away from me, crouched

low, its slender legs folded at an acute angle. I had made it to my knees when it leapt, knocking the wind out of me with its impact. The creature stood over me, its long arms bent like less-than and greater-than signs. They reached forward, the crescent claws grabbing the sides of my head. If I'd made the slightest movement, those strong hands would have shredded my face, tearing my eyes from their sockets. I felt, for the first time in my life, that I was going to die. Panic gripped me like a shrinking sweater, binding my chest, constricting my breathing. The drying blood on my cheeks cracked as my face contorted to scream my final scream.

But death did not come.

Something was happening to the troödon. Its face convulsed, the tip of its muzzle twitched, and, much to my amazement, sky-blue jelly, faintly phosphorescent, began to ooze from the dinosaur's close-together nostrils. I watched in horror, unable to move, thinking that the creature must be allergic to my strange twenty-first-century biochemistry. I expected the monster to sneeze, its clawed hands convulsing shut on my face as its body racked.

Instead, more of the jelly began to ooze from around its bulging eyes, rolling slowly along the contours of its face. The thick slime also began to bead up on the skin halfway down the reptile's long snout, over the top of its preorbital fenestrae, those large openings in the sides of dinosaurian skulls. The thing was looking down at me, so all the jelly flowed toward the tip of its snout. It slowly ran together, joining into one viscous lump.

The mass continued to grow, seeping out of the creature's head, until a glob the size of a baseball had collected at the end of its long face. It hung lower and lower, taking on a teardrop shape, until finally, horribly, the glistening, trembling lump dropped off the creature's nose, hitting my face with a soft, warm, moist *splat*.

I had slammed my eyes shut just before the glob of jelly hit, but I could feel it on me, oozing like worms through the whiskers of my beard, pressing down on my cheeks, heavy on my eyelids. The mass was pulsing and rippling, almost as if probing my features. Suddenly it started to flow up my nostrils and then, a moment later, *through* the cartilage of my nose. I felt completely stuffed up, as though I had an awful cold. The mass within my nasal passages undulated back into my head. I felt pressure on my temples and, painfully, through the curving channels of my ears. The sounds of the forest muffled and finally faded away as the jelly pressed against my eardrums. All I could hear now was my own heartbeat, booming at a rapid pace.

Suddenly a burst of blue light appeared in my right eye and then, a second later, in my left. The phosphorescent slime had seeped through my clenched lids and was now sliding around my eyeballs. My lungs were burning with the need to breathe, but I fought the sensation, terrified to open my mouth.

And then, mercifully, a reprieve was granted—or so I thought. The sickle troödon claws that had been holding my head let go. I waited for the hands to swipe back, julienning my face. Five seconds. Ten. I dared open one eye a slit, then, astonished, popped them both wide. The dinosaur was walking away with docile meter-long strides. It stopped, then turned around, its stiff tail clearing a wide arc. The thing's cat-like eyes fell on mine, but there was no malice, no frenzy, no cunning in the dull gaze. Every few seconds, the creature shuffled its bird-like feet to keep balanced. I brought my hands to my face to wipe away the blue jelly, but there was nothing there except drying flakes of dinosaur blood, left over from the troödon Klicks had decapitated earlier.

My lungs were pumping like blowfishes in heat. Indeed, still panicky, I feared I was going to hyperventilate. I fought to bring my breathing under control. I tried to rise to my feet, my one wish being to get out of there as fast as possible, to find some solace from this madness. But instead of obeying my command, my right leg went rigid, the muscles locking like ossified tendons. Then my left leg began flexing at the knee, the foot pivoting at the ankle. I felt as though I was having a seizure. My jaw slammed shut, biting into my tongue, and my eyes pulled in and out of focus. Then my left eye irised wide, the Cretaceous sunlight feeling like a hot lance as it stabbed into my cornea. My heart raced. Suddenly, incongruously, I found I had an erection. And then, just as suddenly, my whole body went limp.

I caught a glimpse of Klicks, although the image kept blurring and I seemed unable to control the direction in which my eyes looked. The pair of troödons that had pinned him had also backed off and he was thrashing around facedown in the dirt.

Throughout, my ankle kept swiveling, my foot tracing out a small circle in the air. *Such a contrast to the simple hinge of dinosaurian ankles.* That didn't seem to me the sort of thing I should be thinking at a time like this, but before I could wonder about that further, I lost control of my brain. It began running through emotions, feelings, sensations. Incredible transorgasmic joy, greater than any sexual pleasure I'd ever dreamed of, as if I'd become a mindbender, with a battery hooked to my pleasure center. No sooner had it started than it was replaced by searing pain, as though my very soul was on fire. Then deep depression—death would be a reprieve. Then giddiness, child-like giggles escaping my throat. Pain again, but of a different sort—a longing for something irretrievably lost. Anger. Love. Hatred, of myself, of everybody else, of nothing at all. A kaleidoscope of feelings, constantly shifting.

Then memories, as though the pages of my life were blowing in the wind: being intimidated by a bully in public school, him pushing me to the pavement, the skin on my kneecaps shredding, the dust jacket on the picture book Dad had lent me for show-and-tell ripping; my first awkward kiss, dry lips pressing together, then the delightful shock as her tongue pushed into my mouth; having my wisdom teeth removed, the unforgettable cracking sound as the dentist twisted each one free of its socket; the thrill of seeing my name in print on my first published paper, and the subsequent depression when Dr. Bouchard's scathing letter about it was printed in the journal's next issue; the sense of loss that just wouldn't go away when my mother died, with me having left so many things unsaid, undone; the wonder of the first time Tess and I had made love, the two of us melding together into a single being with one breath, one thought.

And things long forgotten, too: a childhood camping trip in Muskoka; the only time I'd ever been stung by a bee; helping a blind man cross the street when I was four—a street my parents wouldn't let me cross by myself. Spilling my Super-Size Pepsi at a football game and Dad throwing a fit over it. Humiliations, joys, triumphs, defeats, all jumbled together, fading in and out.

And then—

Images that weren't mine; memories that weren't my own. Sensations beyond senses. Weird, false-color views. Tints without names. Bright heat. Dark cold. The loudness of blue. The gentle susurration of yellow. A long sandy beach, running to a too-near horizon. A cool sea that I somehow knew was salt-free and shallow, waves lapping against the sandy shore heard not with ears but as vibrations throughout my entire body. My lower surface tasting the sweet flavor of rust. Differing electric potentials in the sand making sounds like Ping-Pong balls bouncing across a table. An easy sense that north was *that* way.

And more—

A pleasing awareness of thousands of others calling out to me and me calling back, gentle greetings carried on something more attenuated than the wind. A feeling of belonging like I'd never had before, of being part of a greater whole, a community, a gestalt, going on and on and on, living forever. I felt my individuality, my identity, slipping away, evaporating in the cool sunlight. I had no name, no face. I was them and they were me. We were one.

Slam! Back to the past. Yorkview Public School. Miss Cohen's class, her mane of gold hair fascinating me in a way I didn't then understand. What did I learn in school today? Facts, figures, tables—rote memorization, harder to dredge up as the years go by, but never totally forgotten. *A, E, I, O, U,* and sometimes *Y. I* before *E* except after *C.* Nouns are people, places, or things. Verbs are action words. A bomb in a bull. Abombinabull. Abominable! I run. You run. He runs. We run. You run. They run. See Spot run! *A* is for apple. *B* is for ball. Adjectives modify nouns, adverbs modify verbs, advertisers modify the truth. Don't split infinitives. *Out, out, brief candle! Life's but a walking shadow . . .* Avoid clichés like the plague. Place the emphatic words of a sentence at the end. *Our Father, who art in heaven, hallowed be thy name . . .* A participial phrase at the beginning of a sentence must refer to the grammatical subject. Alpha, beta, gamma—no, irrelevant. A, B, C . . .

And then, at last, it was over. My brain came back under my control slowly, numbly, like regaining use of a limb that had fallen asleep. I opened my eyes. I was flat on my back, a black cloud of tiny insects buzzing above my face. I tried to lift my head, but failed. In this reduced gravity, even weakened by a fight, I should still be able to do that. I contracted the muscles in my neck again. This time my head did rise from the dirt, but it had taken an extra effort to get it moving, as though . . . as though it had acquired some additional mass.

Klicks had also finished his bout. He had already regained a sitting position, his head propped up by arms resting on his bent knees. I sat up, too. After a moment, though, I felt something in my mouth like warm, wet cotton. Soon my mouth was full of sickly sweet jelly. I bent my head and opened wide, letting it ooze from between my lips. Klicks, too, looked as though he was throwing up blue Jell-O.

The stuff I was ejecting collected into a rounded mass on the ground in front of me, somehow the brown earth failing to stick to it. I had an urge to stomp on it, to bury it, to do anything to destroy the damned thing, but before I could act, a troödon walked over to it. The beast tipped its lean body down, the rigid tail sticking in the air like a car aerial. It laid its head on the ground next to the gelatinous lump, then closed its giant eyes. The jelly throbbed and pulsed its way, like a sky-blue amoeba, onto the dinosaur's snout and settled into its head by percolating through the reptile's leathery skin. Over by Klicks, a second troödon was likewise being entered.

I'd avoided the word, revulsed by the very idea, but the blue thing was undoubtedly a *creature*. Although I knew consciously that it was gone from me now, my body evidently wanted to be sure. I doubled over, my stomach muscles knotting, and racked with convulsions as vomit—what little was left of my last meal back in the future—burned its way up my throat and out onto the fertile Cretaceous soil.

After I'd stopped retching, I wiped my face with my sleeve and turned to face the troödons. The two that had been assimilating the jelly things had straightened and were now shrugging their shoulders. One threw back its curving neck and let loose a bleat; the other stamped its feet a few times. I had a brief picture of my father, back when he was well, stretching into his old cardigan after supper, trying to get it to sit comfortably. The third troödon hopped over to stand near the other two.

I looked at Klicks, raising my eyebrows questioningly.

"I'm okay," he said. "You?"

I nodded. There we stood, face-to-snout with three crafty hunters. Shafts of sunlight pierced the leafy canopy over our heads, throwing the tableau into stark relief. We both knew the futility of attempting to outrun creatures that were mostly leg. "Let's try backing away slowly," said Klicks casually, presumably hoping a soothing tone wouldn't alarm the beasts. "I think I can find the elephant gun."

Without waiting for my answer, he took a small step backward, then another. I sure as hell didn't want to be left there alone, so I followed suit. The troödons seemed content to watch us go, for they just stood there, shifting their weight between their left feet and their right.

We made it perhaps eight or nine meters back when the one in the middle opened its mouth. The jaw worked up and down and a raspy sound issued from the beast's throat. Despite my urge to get out of there, I was fascinated and stopped backing. The creature produced a low grumbling, followed by a few piercing cries like those made by hawks on a hot summer's day. I marveled at its vocal range. It then started puffing the long cheeks of its angular snout, producing explosive *p* sounds. Was this a mating call? Perhaps, for a ruby-colored dewlap beneath the thing's throat inflated with each puff.

Klicks had noticed my dallying. "Come on, Brandy," he said, a nonthreatening lilt to his voice, but still retaining a certain quiet edge conveying the message "Don't be a fool." "Let's get out of here."

"*Wait up.*"

It was an expression from my youth. To an adult, "wait up" means to refrain from going to bed until someone returns home, but to a child, especially one who was a bit on the pudgy side, as I had been, "wait up" was the plaintive call made to friends who were running faster than he could. Only one problem here. I hadn't said those words and neither had Klicks. They had come, hoarse and booming, as though from a person who had been deaf since birth, from the carnivorous mouth of the middle troödon.

Impossible. Coincidence. I must have heard it wrong. I mean, get real.

But Klicks had stopped backing, too, his mouth agape. "Brandy—?"

Everything I knew about troödon came rushing back in a flood of memory. First described by Leidy in 1856, based on fossil teeth from the Judith River formation of Montana. Back in 1987, Phil Currie proved that troödon was the same as *Stenonychosaurus*, whose particulars were first published in 1932 by Sternberg, the man after whom we had named our timeship. I'd only been a kid at the time, but I remember the big fuss the media had made over the suggestion by Dale Russell, then of the Canadian Museum of Nature, that, had the dinosaurs not died out, stenonychosaurus-troödon might have eventually evolved into intelligent human-like "dinosauroids" who would have become the lords of creation. Russell even had a life-size sculpture made of his proposed reptile-person, a fully erect tailless biped with a braincase as big as a large grapefruit, three long surgeon-like fingers on each hand, and an incongruous-looking navel. Photos of it had appeared in *Time* and *Omni*.

Could troödon have been more advanced by the final days of the Cretaceous than anyone had previously thought? Could an elite few dinosaurs have had spoken language? Were they on the way to civilization, only to have their tenure on the planet cut short by some catastrophe? For me, a lifelong lover of dinosaurs, the idea was compelling. I wanted it to be true, but I knew in my bones that even the best of the terrible lizards, although not as desperately stupid as once thought, was still no better endowed mentally than a shrew or a bird.

A bird! Of course! Simple mimicry. Parrots do it. So do mynahs. We knew that birds were closely related to dinosaurs. Granted, our feathered friends hadn't shared a common ancestor with troödon since the avian line split from the coelurosaurians in the mid-Jurassic, 100 million years before the time I was in now. Still, troödon was remarkably bird-like, with its keen binocular vision, quick movements, and three-toed feet. That's it, of course. It must have heard me call "Wait up!" to Klicks and simply imitated the sound.

Except.

Except that I hadn't called "wait up" or anything else to Klicks. And Klicks hadn't said anything remotely like that to me.

I must have heard wrong. I *must* have.

"Wait up. Stop. Stop. Wait up."

Oh, shit . . .

Klicks recovered his wits faster than I did. "Yes?" he said, astonished.

"Yess. Stop. Go not. Wait up. Stop. Yess. Stop."

What do you say to a dinosaur? "Who are you?" asked Klicks.

"Pals. We pals. You pals. Eat an ant and I'll be your best friend. Pals. Palsy-walsy."

"I don't fucking believe this," said Klicks.

That did it. The thing launched into George Carlin's list of the seven words you never used to be able to say on TV. The troödon's speech was still difficult to understand, though. Indeed, it would have been incomprehensible if it weren't for the fact that it put a brief pause between each word, the obscenities coming out like the sputters of a dying muffler.

"How can a dinosaur talk?" I said at last, to Klicks really, but the damned reptile answered anyway.

"With great difficulty," the troödon rasped, and then, as if to prove its point, it arched its neck and hawked up a ball of spit. The gob landed on some rocks at the base of a bald cypress trunk. It was shot through with blood. The effort of speaking must be tearing up the creature's throat.

That the beast could speak made no sense, and yet the words, although not clear, were unmistakable. I shook my head in wonder, then realized what was doubly incredible was not just that the dinosaur was speaking, but that it was speaking English.

Now, in retrospect, it seems obvious that it wasn't the dinosaur talking. Not really. It was just a marionette for the blue jelly thing inside it. I'd had a hard enough time accepting that some weird slime had crawled into my head. The thought that the stuff had been an *intelligent* creature was something my mind refused to accept, until Klicks said it out loud. "It's not the troödon, dammit. It's the slime-thingy inside it."

The talking dinosaur clucked like a chicken, then said, "Yess. Slime-thingy me. Not dinosaur. Dinosaur dumb-dumb. Slime-thingy smarty-pants."

"That one must have learned English from you," said Klicks.

"Huh? Why?"

"Well, for one thing, it sure didn't get phrases like 'palsy-walsy' and 'smarty-pants' from me. And for another, it's got your snooty Upper Canada College accent."

I thought about that. It didn't sound to me like it had any accent at all, but then again it certainly didn't have a Jamaican accent, which is what Klicks spoke with.

Before I could reply, the three troödons stepped forward, not menacingly, really, but they did manage in short order to form the vertices of an equilateral triangle, with Klicks and me at the center. Klicks nodded toward the dense undergrowth, a mixture of ferns, red flowers, and cycads. There, sticking up, was the barrel of his elephant gun, quite out of reach. "Enough said by me," rasped the reptile, now standing so close that I could feel its hot, moist breath on my face and smell the stench of its last meal. "You speak now. Who you?"

It was insanity, this being questioned by a baby-talking dinosaur. But I couldn't think of any reason *not* to answer its question. I pointed at Klicks, but wondered if the hand gesture would have any meaning to the beast. "This is Professor Miles Jordan," I said, "and my name is Dr. Brandon Thackeray." The troödon tilted its head in a way that looked like human puzzlement. It didn't say anything, though, so I added, "I'm Curator of Paleobiology at the Royal Ontario Museum. Miles is Curator of Dinosaurs at the Royal Tyrrell Museum of Palaeontology, and he also teaches at the University of Alberta."

The reptilian head weaved at the end of that long neck. "Some words link," it said in its harsh voice. "Some not." I could hear an undercurrent of clicking as it spoke, the sound of its pointed teeth touching as its mouth made the unaccustomed movements. It paused again, then asked, "What is name?"

"I just told you. Brandon Thackeray." Then, after a moment, I added, for no good reason, "My friends call me Brandy."

"No. No. What *is* name?" It tilted its head again, in that puzzled gesture. Then it brightened. "Ah, word missing—indefinite article, yess? What is *a* name?'"

"What do you mean, what is a name? You *asked* me what my name was."

Klicks touched my shoulder. "No. What it asked was, 'Who you?' That's not necessarily the same question."

I realized that Klicks was right. "Oh. I see. Well, a name is . . . it's, uh, a—"

Klicks chimed in. "A name is a symbol, a unique identifying word, that can be rendered either with sound or with written markings. It's used to distinguish one individual from another."

Clever bastard. How did he think up such a good definition so quickly? But the troödon made that puzzled face again. "'Individual,' say you? Still not link. No matter. Where you from?"

Well, what do I tell this thing? That I'm a time traveler from the future? If it doesn't understand *name*, it's not going to understand that. "I'm from Toronto. That's a city"—I looked up at the sun to get my bearings, then pointed east—"about twenty-five hundred kilometers that way."

"What kilometer?"

"It's—" I looked at Klicks and resolved to do as good a job as he had at making things explicit. "It's a unit of linear measure. One kilometer is a thousand meters, and a meter is"—I held up my hands—"this much."

"And what is city?"

"Ah, a city is, um, well, you could say it's the nesting place for herds of my kind. A collection of buildings, of artificial shelters."

"Buildings?"

"Yes. A building is—"

"Know do we. But no buildings here. No others of your kind, either, that we have seen."

Klicks's eyes narrowed. "How do you know what a building is?"

The troödon looked at him as though he were an idiot. "He just told us."

"But it sounded like you already knew—"

"We did know."

"But then"—he spread his hands imploringly—"how did you know?"

"Do you have buildings?" I said.

"*We* don't," replied the troödon, with an odd emphasis on the pronoun. Then all three of them moved in closer to us. The leader—the one doing all the talking, anyway—reached out with its five-centimeter claws and slowly brushed some dirt from my shirt. This one seemed to have a diamond-shaped patch of slightly yellowish skin on its muzzle, halfway between its giant eyes and the tip of its elongated snout. "No cities here," Diamond-snout said. "Will ask again. Where you from?"

I glanced at Klicks. He shrugged. "I *am* from a city called Toronto," I said at last, "but from a different time. We come from the future."

There was silence for a full minute, broken only by the buzz of insects and the occasional *pipping* call of a bird or pterosaur. Finally, slowly, the dinosaur spoke. Instead of answering with the disbelief a human might express, its tone was measured and calculating. "From how far in the future?"

"Sixty-five million years," Klicks said, "plus or minus about three hundred million."

"Sixty-five million—" said Diamond-snout. It paused as if digesting this. "A year is the time it takes for—what words to use?—for this planet to make one elliptical path—ah, one *orbit*, yess?—one orbit around the sun?"

"That's right," I said, surprised. "You know about orbits?"

The creature ignored my question. "A million is a number in . . . in base-ten counting? Ten times ten times ten times ten times ten times ten, yess?"

"Was that five 'times tens'?" I said. "Yes, that's a million."

"Sixty . . . five . . . million . . . years," said the thing. It paused, then hawked blood onto the ground again. "What you say difficult to comprehend."

"Nevertheless, it's true," I said. For some reason, I took a perverse pleasure in impressing the thing. "I realize sixty-odd million years is an impossibly long time to conceive of."

"We conceive it; we remember a time twice as long ago," the troödon said.

"My God. You remember, what, a hundred and thirty million years ago?"

"Intriguing that you own a god," said Diamond-snout.

I shook my head. "You've got a history of a hundred and thirty million years?" Dating back from here at the end of the Cretaceous, that would be around the Triassic-Jurassic boundary.

"History?" said the troödon.

"Continuous written record," said Klicks. He paused for a moment, I guess realizing that the jelly creatures couldn't possibly have writing as we know it, since they didn't have hands. "Or a continuous record of the past in some other form."

"No," said the troödon, "we do not that have."

"But you just said you remembered a time a hundred and thirty million years ago," said Klicks, frustration in his voice.

"We do—"

"So how can you—"

"But we not aware that time travel is possible," said Diamond-snout, overtop of Klicks. "Last night, that black and white disk that crashed into the ground. That was your vehicle for time displacement?"

"The *Sternberger,* yes," said Klicks. "Its technical name is a Huang temporal phase-shift habitat module, but the press just calls it a time machine."

"A time machine?" The reptilian head bobbed. "That phrase appeals. Tell how it works."

Klicks appeared irritated. "Look," he said. "We know nothing about you. You've crawled around in our heads. What the hell are you?"

For the first time, I noticed the way the troödon blinked, an odd gesture in which it closed its left eye, opened it, then briefly closed its right. "We entered you only to absorb your language," Diamond-snout said. "Did no harm, yess?"

"Well—"

"We could enter you again to absorb additional information. But time-consuming process. Clumsy. Language center obvious in brain structure. Much mass devoted to it. Specific memories much harder to faucet. Faucet? No, to *tap.* Easier you tell us."

"But we could communicate better if we knew more about you," I said. "Surely you can see that a common set of references would make it simpler."

"Yess. See that and raise you—No, just see that. Common reference points. Links. Very well. Ask questions."

"All right, then," I said. "Who are you?"

"I am me," the reptile said.

"Great," muttered Klicks.

"Unsatisfactory response?" asked the theropod. "I am this one. No name. Name not link."

"You're a single entity," I said, "but you don't have a name of your own. Is that it?"

"It is that."

"How do you tell yourself from others of your own kind?" I asked.

"Others?"

"You know: different individuals. One of you is inside this troödon; another is inside that one. How do you distinguish yourselves?"

"I here. Other is there. Easy as 3.1415."

Klicks hooted.

"What are you?" I asked, annoyed at Klicks.

"No link."

"You are an invertebrate."

"Invertebrate: animal without a backbone, yess?"

"Yes. What are your relatives?"

"Time and space."

"No, no. I—Damn. I want to know what you are, what you evolved from. You're unlike any form of life I've seen before."

"As are you."

I shook my head. "I'm not too dissimilar from the dinosaur you are now inhabiting."

"Dinosaur is efficient creature. Strong. Keen senses. Yours are dull by comparison."

"Yes," I said, irritated. For years, I'd explained to people that dinosaurs weren't the sluggish, stupid creatures so often portrayed in cartoons, but somehow I didn't enjoy hearing the same sentiments expressed by a reptilian mouth. "But we are more similar than different. Each of us is bipedal—that means we each have two legs—"

"Bipedal links."

"And we each have two arms, two eyes, two nostrils. Our left sides are nearly perfect mirror images of our right sides—"

"Bisexual symmetry."

"Bilateral symmetry," I corrected. "Clearly, the dinosaur and I are related—share a common ancestor. My kind did evolve from ancient reptiles, but there are other creatures about, tiny mammals, that are even more closely related to us. But you—I've studied the history of life since it began. I don't know of anything similar to you."

"Its body is completely soft," said Klicks. "Creatures like that might go undetected in the fossil record."

I turned to him. "But intelligent life arising millions of years before the first human? It's incredible. It's almost as if—"

I'd like to claim that I was about to state the correct conclusion, that at that instant I had pieced together the puzzle and had realized what was going on. But my next words were drowned out by a great roaring clap, like thunder, followed by several bellowing dinosaur calls and the cries of flying things startled into flight. I recognized the noise, for my home was due south of Pearson International Airport and, despite the complaints from me and my neighbors, it had become part of the background of our day-to-day lives ever since Transport Canada had approved inland supersonic flights of the Orient Express jetliners. High overhead, three tawny spheres moving at perhaps Mach 2 or 3 streaked across the sky. At the least, they were aircraft, but I knew in an instant that they were much more than that.

Spaceships.

"You under a misapprehension operate," said Diamond-snout once the sky had stopped rumbling. "We are not from this planet."

Klicks was flabbergasted, which pleased me no end. "Then where?" I said.

"From—home world. Name I not find in your memories. It's—"

"Is it in this solar system?" I asked.

"Yess."

"Mercury?"

"Quicksilver? No."

"Venus?"

"No."

"Not Earth. Mars?"

"Mars—ah, Mars! Fourth from sun. Yess. Mars is home."

"Martians!" said Klicks. "Actual fucking Martians. Who'd believe it?"

Diamond-snout fixed Klicks with a steady gaze. "I would," it said, absolutely deadpan.

Boundary Layer

I can be expected to look for truth but not to find it.
—Denis Diderot, French philosopher (1713–1784)

The traveler's diary—the one that purported to tell the story of a trip back to the end of the Mesozoic Era—had to be a fake, of course. It had to be. Oh, it superficially resembled my writing style. In fact, whoever had put it together had obviously read my book *Dragons of the North: The Dinosaurs of Canada*. In preparing the manuscript for that book, I got sick of all the italics. See, Linnaeus established that biological naming would be in Latin, and non-English words are usually italicized in modern typesetting. Plus, Linnaeus said the genus part of the name should always be capitalized: *Tyrannosaurus rex*. Since there are no common English names for individual types of dinosaurs, popular books on the subject have slavishly followed this convention so that almost every tenth word is italicized or capitalized, bullying the reader's eye.

I'd taken some flak from my colleagues for it, but in *Dragons of the North* I chucked out that convention. The first time I mentioned some Mesozoic critter, I'd use the Linnaean standard, but thereafter I'd treated the name as if it were a common English term, just like "cat" or "dog," uncapitalized and unitalicized. Well, whoever had cobbled together this bogus diary had copied at least that much of my style.

Although I never used it, my palmtop had come bundled with a grammar-checking program. I had my diary from last year still stored on the Toshiba's built-in optical wafer, so I called that up alongside the fake traveler's diary. With each document in a separate window, I let the grammar checker run a stylistic comparison between them. The program produced a dozen charts—including "Flesch-Kincaid grade level," "average number of words per sentence," and "average number of sentences per paragraph." The conclusion was inescapable: both diaries, mine and the supposed time traveler's, were in almost identical styles.

The grammar checker had a feature that I'd never before found a use for: the ability to output an alphabetized list of all the words in a document. I had it do that for both diaries, then filtered and piped between the two lists until I had a new file containing only the words in the traveler's diary that did not appear in my own diary from last year. I thought perhaps the forger would have tripped up by using words that weren't part of my vocabulary.

I scanned down the list. There were a lot of words, including "archaeopteryx" and "hawked," but almost all were ones I could see myself using. There were one or two—such as "firmament"—that didn't sound like me at all, but, then again, I did have *Roget's Thesaurus* loaded onto my optical drive.

No, it was clear. Without one of those new Japanese AI style replicators, and access to a lot of my writings in a machine-readable form, there's only one person who could have written this time-traveler's diary.

Me.

If the diary was genuine, then so likely were the people named in it. And the person who seemed to be in charge of all this nonsense was one Ching-Mei Huang.

I sat at my battered old desk at the ROM—it dated back to Gordon Edmund's days as curator—and spoke to my desk terminal. "Default search engine," I said. "Boolean: Huang AND Ching-Mei."

"Please spell both search terms," said the computer.

I did so, and my screen instantly filled with references. There were at least three Ching-Mei Huangs in the world: one seemed to be a leading expert on the potato-chip industry. Another was an authority on Sino-American relations. And the third—

The third was clearly my woman: a physicist, judging by the titles of the papers she'd authored, and . . .

Well, I had to read that one: "Professors Arrested in Campus Melee." "Show me number seventeen," I said.

A Canadian Press wire-service story from 18 November 1988 appeared. A Ching-Mei Huang, then a nontenured professor, was one of six faculty members arrested at Dalhousie University in Halifax during a protest over cutbacks in research funding. The article said she'd broken the shin of one of the campus police officers. Feisty woman.

"Back," I said. The hit list returned to my screen. I kept scanning the results—and then I smiled. Apparently, like me, she'd also written a popular book, something called *Time Constraints: The Tau of Physics,* co-authored with one G. C. Mackenzie, published by Simon Fraser University Press in 2003.

The link was to the listing on Chapters.ca, which contained a review taken from *Quill & Quire* (a publication I'd always liked, since it had been very kind to my *Dragons of the North*): "Mackenzie and Huang, both high-energy researchers at Vancouver's TRIUMF, have put together a dry account of current . . ."

That was a decade ago. Still, it was worth a shot. I activated my PicturePhone and asked for directory assistance. "Vancouver, please," I said to the perky computer-generated face that appeared on my screen. "TRIUMF. T-R-I-U-M-F."

The image recited the phone number while simultaneously displaying it on my screen. The museum didn't allow us to use the call-completion feature, since it cost an extra seventy-five cents, so I jotted the number down on a Post-it note, then dictated it back into the phone. After two rings, a man with what might have been a Pakistani accent answered. "Good morning; *bonjour.* TRIUMF."

"Hello," I said, surprising myself at how nervous I sounded. "Ching-Mei Huang, please."

"Dr. Huang is unavailable right now," he said. "Would you like to leave a message?"

"Yes," I said. "Yes, indeed."

Ching-Mei Huang failed to return the three messages I left for her at TRIUMF, but I finally weaseled her unlisted home number out of somebody who answered the phone late one evening. My palms were sweating as I spoke the string of digits to my phone. Christ, I hadn't been this nervous since the first time I'd called Tess and asked for a date.

Toronto was 3,300 kilometers from Vancouver; it was a little after ten in the evening my time, which meant it would be just after seven on the west coast. The phone rang three times before the round Bell Canada logo did its usual self-indulgent backflip off the screen. But instead of Dr. Huang's face, all I got was this graphic:

Audio Only Available

Then, thinned by what sounded like fear—the distance shouldn't have affected the quality at all, of course—a voice made its way across the continent to me. "Hello?"

"Hello," I replied. "May I please speak to Ching-Mei Huang?"

A pause. Finally: "Who's calling?"

"My name is Brandon Thackeray. I'm with the Royal Ontario Museum in Toronto."

"I'm not interested in becoming a member. Good-bye."

"Wait. I'm not from the membership department. I'm a vertebrate paleontologist."

"A vert—? How did you get this number?"

"Then you are Dr. Huang?"

"Yes, I am she. How did you get my number?"

I tried to sound jaunty. "It wasn't easy, believe me."

"This number is unlisted for a purpose. Please leave me alone."

I put as much reassuring warmth as I could into my voice. "You certainly keep a low profile," I said with a laugh.

"That's no concern of yours." A pause, while we both tried to assess who should speak next. Finally, quietly, she said, "My phone says you're calling from area code 905. That's not Toronto."

"No, it's Mississauga, where I live. Just outside of Toronto."

I heard a sharp exhalation of breath. "And you're not on a mobile phone, right? So you're not here in Vancouver?" Her voice brightened slightly, but she still seemed shaken, nervous —hardly the kind of speech I would have thought anyone would have characterized as "precise." What was it the diary had said? *Measured, monotonal, clicking over the consonants like a series of circuit breakers.* That description seemed to belong to a completely different person.

"Do you have a PicturePhone, Dr. Huang? Could we switch to visual?"

"No."

Did that mean, *No, I don't have a PicPhone,* or *No, I won't turn on its camera*? "Uh, fine," I said at last. "That's fine." Suddenly I didn't know how to continue. What I wanted to ask her about seemed so incredible, so inconceivable. If this was a practical joke, there's only one person who could have done it: Klicks, now living in Toronto for his sabbatical. I'd kill him if this wasn't for real. "I've been trying to track you down for some time, Dr. Huang. There's a matter I'd like to discuss with you."

She still sounded edgy. "Oh, very well. But please be brief."

"Of course. Do you happen to know Miles Jordan?"

"I knew a Susan Jordan once."

"No, that wouldn't be any relation of his. Miles is another paleontologist. He's with the Royal Tyrrell Museum in Drumheller, Alberta."

"A great museum," she said absently. "But what has this got to do with me?"

"Does the word 'stasis' mean anything to you?"

"It's Greek for standstill. What do I win?"

"And that's all it means to you?"

"Mr. Thackeray, I value my privacy greatly. I don't wish to seem rude, but I am uncomfortable on the phone."

I mustered my courage. "All right, Dr. Huang. I put it to you: are you, or were you, doing experiments involving the cessation of the passage of time—a process you referred to as stasis?"

"Where did you get that notion?"

"Please, it's very important that I know."

She was silent for several seconds. "Well, yes," she said at last, "I guess 'stasis' would have been a good name for it, although I never called it that. Experiments? Hardly. I came up with a few interesting equations, but that was before—that was a long time ago."

"So stasis is possible. Tell me: did your research give any indication that—that time travel would be a practical consequence of your equations?"

For the first time, the voice at the other end of the line had real strength. "I see now, Mr.—Thackeray, did you say?"

"Yes."

"Mr. Thackeray, you are a crackpot. Good-bye."

"No, please. I'm dead seri—"

Dial tone. I told the phone to redial, but the number in Vancouver just rang and rang and rang.

Countdown: 15

The hottest places in hell are reserved for those who in times of moral crisis remain neutral.

—Dante Alighieri, Italian poet (1265–1321)

Martians.

I'd had a hard enough time typing the words "time travel." But tapping out M-A-R-T-I-A-N-S seemed like asking for a trip to the funny farm. I guess there really are more things in heaven and earth, Brandio, than are dreamt of in my philosophy.

It was close to noon, the hot Mesozoic sun beating down from a silvery-blue sky intermittently visible through gaps in the thick foliage above us. Insects buzzed everywhere, and I kept batting my arms to disperse them.

The three troödons were close enough that I could smell the stench of raw meat on their breath. Their pebbly green skin was almost iridescent in the bright sunlight and their giant yellow eyes reflected back so much light they almost seemed to glow.

"Martians," I said softly—the word came easier to the tongue than it does to the fingertips. "Incredible."

The lead troödon, Diamond-snout, did its patented one-two blink. "Thank you," it rasped, speaking for the Martian jelly creature within its skull.

"But what are you doing here?" I asked.

The elongated green head tilted to one side. "Talking to you."

"No—I mean, what are you doing here, in general? Why did you come to Earth?"

"Come to? Pass out of unconsciousness? No link."

I shook my head. "What was the purpose of your trip to Earth?"

"Purpose not changed," said Diamond-snout pointedly. "Still is."

"Okay, okay. What *is* the purpose of your trip to Earth?"

"Me first," said the troödon. "What your purpose?"

I sighed. There seemed to be little point in telling the thing that it was violating Miss Manners's rules of etiquette. Klicks, standing about a meter away from me, and not taking his eyes off the silent troödon closest to him, answered. "We're scientists. Does that—link? Scientists. Ones whose profession is the quest for knowledge. We came here to discover what we could about the ancient past. We're particularly interested in the event at the boundary between—"

"—in studying the lifeforms of this time," I said, cutting him off, a sudden wave of caution overtaking me. It seemed a good idea not to mention right off that most of the life on this world was about to be destroyed.

"Ah!" crowed Diamond-snout, evidently unperturbed by my having interrupted Klicks. "We are colleges." It looked down, then did that strange one-two blink again. "No, *colleagues*. We, too, came to this place because of the life here."

"One small slither for Martian," said Klicks, "one giant leap for Martiankind."

"No link," said the Martian through the troödon's mouth.

Klicks looked at the ground. "Me neither," he said.

"'Martian' means of or pertaining to Mars?" asked Diamond-snout, turning its attention back to me. When finished speaking, it left its narrow jaws hanging open, showing serrated teeth.

"Yes," I said.

"There are things of or pertaining to Mars that we do not wish to be lumped together with." Given the plastic nature of the Martians, I wondered if "lumped together" meant the same thing to them as it did to me.

"What should we call you, then?"

"When we occupy creatures with versatile speaking orifices, the term we use for what we are is *Hhhet*." It sounded more like a throat-clearing than an English word.

"Het it is," I said.

Klicks threw up his hands. "Martian, Het, what difference does it make? Brandy, we have to talk."

"Talk?" said the Het.

"Confer," I said.

"What have pine trees to do with this?" said the Het.

"*Confer*," I said. "Not conifer."

"Oh," the Het said. "A chitchat."

"Exactly."

"But is that not what we are now having?" it said. "A tit-to-tit?"

"A *tête-à-tête*," I corrected. "Professor Jordan means he'd like to talk to me alone."

"Alone?"

"In private."

The troödon blinked. "No link."

I pointed back the way we'd come. "Our time machine is back that way. May we return to it?"

"Ah," said Diamond-snout. "Yes, we wish to see it."

The three troödons stepped slightly away from us, and we started walking south. Klicks bent over to scoop up his elephant rifle. The one troödon that had been doing all the talking tipped its head at the rifle. "A weapon?" it hissed.

"Kind of," said Klicks.

"Not very efficient."

"Best we could afford," he said.

We came out of the forest and onto the mud plain. Ahead of us was the soft dirt crater made by the *Sternberger*'s impact and, high on the west side of the crater wall, the *Sternberger* itself, indeed looking like a hamburger or a TV flying saucer. Sticking up from the center of its roof was the small instrumentation dome.

"If this is a time vessel," rasped Diamond-snout, "then assume do I that it will return to where it came from. Conservative?"

"Conservative?" I said, completely lost.

Klicks grinned. "He means 'right,' I think."

The troödon's head bobbed. "Right. You will return to origin, right?"

"That's right," said Klicks. "The time-displacement effect will hold us back here for"—he consulted his watch—"almost exactly three more days, then, like reeling in a fish, we'll be hauled back to our launch point."

"It happens aut-o-mat-ic-al-ly?" asked the troödon.

"Yes," I said. "The actual Huang Effect apparatus is located in the future. There aren't any moving parts or controls within our timeship related to time travel, except for the stasis-field unit. Does that mean anything to you?"

"Enough," said the troödon, but exactly how I was supposed to take that, I couldn't say. "And where is launch point?"

"Oh, it's right here," Klicks said. "We call this area the Red Deer River valley in our time. It's pretty rough territory."

"And all your time-travel missions are launched from there?"

"Actually," Klicks said, "time travel is quite new to us. Ours is the first crewed mission back to here."

"Is Earth muchly different in your time?" asked the troödon.

"It is," Klicks said. "Mammals, not reptiles, dominate. The climate is cooler, the continents are more dispersed, the land is drier, and the seasons are more pronounced. And, perhaps most interesting of all, the gravity is maybe two and half times what it is now."

The troödon's neck weaved in an odd swooping motion. "What did you say?"

"Crazy, isn't it?" I said. "The gravity on Earth seems to double or triple over the next sixty-five million years."

"That is most peculiar, Dr. Brandon Thackeray whose friends call him Brandy."

"It is indeed. We can't account for it."

There was no way to read the troödon's expressionless face. Indeed, it seemed to go limp, its muscles relaxing as if the Het within was distracted, lost in its own thoughts. "Higher gravity, say you. Intriguing. Tell me: what is Mars like in your time?"

Klicks was about to answer the creature's question, but I jumped in quickly: "I've never been there."

We'd reached the crumbling crater wall. I noted with astonishment that tiny green shoots had already appeared in the freshly turned soil. Another irrelevant thought hit me. I felt like I was out on a date and that we'd arrived back at the woman's home. It was that awkward moment where you find out if you're going to get invited in. Except that the *Sternberger* was my home, and the Hets were the too-tenacious escorts who didn't seem to be getting the hint that it was time for them to say their good-byes.

Finally the Het said, quite bluntly, "Show us the inside."

Klicks was about to roll out the goddamned red carpet for them, but I cut him off. "Certainly. And we'd like to see inside your spaceships. But not just now, please. Professor Jordan and I have some matters of personal hygiene to attend to, and humans require privacy to do that."

"Privacy," it said again. "Being . . . alone?"

"That's right."

"A strange concept."

I shrugged. "It's important to us."

Diamond-snout looked at me, its head tilted in that gesture I associated with puzzlement. "Oh," it said at last—or maybe it was just a reptilian throat-clearing. "Well, we will speak again." A pause. "*Soon.*" The three dinosaurs strode away, back into the forest.

Klicks and I scrambled up the crater wall. It had been a heck of a lot easier getting down than it was going back up, even in the lighter gravity. I practically filled my boots with soft dirt in the process.

Once we were alone inside the cramped confines of the *Sternberger*'s semicircular habitat, Klicks sprawled out on his crash couch, fingers interlaced behind his head, and said, "Well, what do you make of that?"

I hated the man's infinite calmness. He had to be as excited as I was. Why didn't he show it? Why did I have to show it so transparently? "This is incredible," I said, and instantly regretted my hyperbole.

"Incredible," said Klicks, savoring the word, or, more precisely, savoring my use of it. "Yes, that it is. This changes everything, of course."

"How do you mean?"

He gave me one of *those* looks, the ones he saved for times when he thought the person he was talking to was a little on the slow side. "I mean about our mission. The discovery of the Hets is more important than any paleontological research we were going to do."

I felt anger growing within me. *Nothing* was more important than dinosaurs, as far as I was concerned. "We've got a job to do," I said, as evenly as I could.

"Oh, yes indeed," said Klicks, unlacing his fingers. "We have to bring the Hets forward in time, of course."

I stared at him, dumbfounded. *"What?"*

"Think about it, man. By our time, Mars is dead. Completely abiologic. Every probe since *Viking* has confirmed that."

"So?"

"So something wipes out the Hets between now and then. We've got the opportunity to jump the ones that are here forward, past whatever event kills them. We can repopulate Mars."

"We can't do that," I said. My head was pounding.

"Sure we can. You saw how small those Het slimeballs are. We could take back hundreds of them. It's just a question of balance. Once we empty our water tank, we'll have plenty of room and a big mass deficit that we'll have to fill with something before the Huang Effect switches states. It might as well be the Hets."

"We were going to bring forward some biological specimens. Maybe even a small dinosaur. They've got a habitat all set at the Calgary Zoo—"

"We can do that, too. They're not mutually exclusive propositions."

"I don't know," I said slowly, trying to buy time to think. This was all happening much too quickly. "Maybe it's not our place to do something like that. I mean, we'd be playing God—"

Klicks rolled his eyes as though I'd said something incalculably stupid. "Jesus, man, what do you think bringing home a baby *Ornithomimus* would be? After all, they're extinct, too."

"But this is intelligent life. It just seems—"

"Seems that we should ignore it? Brandy, how would you feel if the shoe was on the other—the other pseudopod? Some natural disaster wipes out all of good old *H. sap.* Wouldn't you want some guy to play Noah for us? We can prevent the extinction of a—what's that word the science-fiction writers use?—a *sentient* lifeform."

He mispronounced it, saying it as three distinct syllables. "That's *sen-shent*," I said. "It rhymes with *quotient*."

"What the hell difference does that make? I'm talking about a bold, sweeping move and you're going all picayune on me."

"Details matter. Besides, we don't have to decide this thing ourselves; we're just the test mission. When they send the big multinational mission next year, they can haul the Hets forward, if it seems the right thing to do."

"Point-five-oh," said Klicks.

This time I failed his little test. I looked at him blankly. "What?"

"The Huang Effect has a .50 percent uncertainty, thanks to the parts of the Throwback calculations that are quantum mechanical. The chances of the big timeship hitting even this same century are minuscule." Klicks shook his head. "No, my friend. No one else can make the decision. This is it, the one and only opportunity to save the Hets from extinction."

My throat felt dry. "But doubtless eventually another mission will hit this particular time. Maybe not one from the twenty-first century, or even the twenty-second. But eventually."

Klicks scowled, his one continuous eyebrow bunching like a knotted shoelace. "Haven't you been reading the papers? Ever since Derzhavin was assassinated by those resurgent hardliners, things have gotten a lot worse between the Americans and the Russians. And even if they do work their differences out, if the global warming trend continues, we're not going to have enough food to feed ourselves. I wouldn't count on there being anyone left by the twenty-second century."

"Oh, things aren't that bad," I said weakly.

"Perhaps not. But it's unfair to the Hets for us to assume that humanity will eventually get around to dealing with their plight sometime in the distant future. We've got to help them right now, while we're sure we can."

"It's a moral decision," I said, shaking my head.

Klicks frowned. "And you hate making moral decisions."

" 'Hate' is a strong word—"

"You don't have a stand on abortion or capital punishment. Hell, you haven't voted in, what, twenty years?"

I despised the sound of his voice. I'd never had any trouble refuting Klicks's claims in print, taking hours to mold letters of response for the journals, but face-to-face he could always run circles around me. "But this isn't a decision we're competent to make."

"I feel up to it." Klicks grinned broadly, but it quickly slipped into a patronizing smile. "Brandy, failing to act is a decision in and of itself."

He's been reading my diary, I thought briefly, but immediately rejected the idea. It was password-protected on my palmtop, and I'm twenty times the programmer Klicks is. Although he's doubtless seen me tapping away at the keyboard, there's no way he could have accessed the file. Still, those words, those cruel words—

Failing to act is a decision in and of itself.

Dr. Schroeder had said that to me when I talked to him about my father.

Failing to act . . .

"It's not a decision I'm comfortable making," I said at last, my head swimming.

Klicks shrugged, then settled back into the contours of his crash couch. "Life isn't always comfortable." He looked me straight in the eye. "I'm sorry, Brandy, but the great moral decision is up to you and me."

"But—"

"No buts, my friend. It's up to us."

I was about to object again, when suddenly, 65 million years before the invention of Jehovah's Witnesses, of Avon Ladies, of nosy neighbors, there was a knock at the door.

Countdown: 14

We know accurately only when we know little; with knowledge doubt increases.
—Johann Wolfgang von Goethe, German dramatist (1749–1832)

Klicks got up off his crash couch and made his way across the semicircular floor of the *Sternberger*'s habitat to door number one. He pulled it open, walked down the short access ramp, and peered out the little glassteel insert in the main hatchway. I followed him down and looked over his shoulder. It was a big drop to the crater wall, but there, standing on it, was a dancing green troödon, hopping like a Mexican jumping bean to keep balanced on the ragged slope.

Klicks opened the outer door and looked down at the thing. "What do you want?"

The reptile was silent for half a minute. At last, it made a series of low roars like corrugated cardboard being ripped apart. Klicks turned to look at me. "I don't think this one talks."

I scratched my beard. "What's it doing here, then?"

The cardboard ripping noises were growing softer, less harsh. Finally, English came from the reptile's mouth. "Nothing, man," it said, except it sounded more like "Nuttin', mon."

I had to smile. "No wonder he's a bit slow, Klicks," I said. "This must be the one who learned to speak from you." I faced the troödon. "Hey, man! *Day O!*"

The reptile looked at the ground as if thinking. "Daylight come and me want go home," it said at last.

I laughed.

"Your wastes are eliminated?" it said. "Your bodies cleansed?"

"Yes," I said warily.

"Then now we shall talk."

"All right," I said.

"I come in?" said the troödon.

"No," I said. "We'll come down."

The troödon held up a scaly hand. "Later." In a flash, it was gone, skittering down the crater wall. I stepped to the threshold myself and looked out. It was shortly after noon. The sun, brilliantly bright against a cloudless sky, had begun to slip down toward the western horizon. Overhead I could see a trio of gorgeous copper-colored pterosaurs lazily rising and falling on columns of heated air. I took the giant first step out the door and skidded down the crater wall and onto the mud flat. Klicks, holding an elephant gun, followed behind me.

The three troödons were standing about thirty meters from the crater wall. As soon as we were both down, they moved toward us with surprising speed, long legs eating up distance rapidly. Their curved necks worked back and forth as they walked, just like pigeons, but because the dinosaurs had much longer necks, the effect was elegant instead of comical. Their stiff tails, sticking straight out from lean rumps, bounced up and down as they moved. At once, the troödons came to an instantaneous halt: no slowing down, the last stride no different from any of the previous ones. They simply stopped, cold, about three meters away from us.

The one with the diamond-shaped patch of yellow skin on its muzzle—the one that spoke like me—once again did most of the talking. "We have questions for you," it said.

"What about?" I asked.

"Mars," said Diamond-snout. I looked into its huge yellow eyes with their rippling irises, almost hypnotically beautiful. "I ask you again about Mars of the future."

I shook my head, breaking away from the gaze. "And I tell you again: I've never been there."

Diamond-snout seemed unconvinced. "But if you ply time, doubtless you also ply space. And even if you donut"—a one-two blink—*do not*, you must have magnifying optical devices that allow you to tell much about our home."

I looked at Klicks. He shrugged. "What you say is true, of course," I offered. "But without knowing what Mars is like currently here in the Mesozoic, we can't very well describe how it differs, if at all, in our time. Surely you can understand that."

"Stop calling me Shirley," said Diamond-snout. It used my voice; it used my jokes. "Doubtless you can give us a thumb-claw sketch of Mars without us wasting time describing its current state. Do so."

"All right, dammit," I said. "You might as well know, any-way." I looked at Klicks once again, giving him a final chance to stop me if he thought I was making a huge mistake. His face was impassive. "I was telling the truth," I said, looking back into Diamond-snout's golden orbs. "No human being has yet been to Mars—but we've sent some robot explorers there. They found a lot of weird chemistry in the soil, but no life." I looked at Diamond-snout. Its head had dipped low, the golden orbs with their vertical, cat-like pupils staring at the cracked mud. It was madness to try to interpret its expressions, to try to apply human emotions to a glob of jelly and its dinosaur mar-ionette, and yet, to me, the thing looked shaken. "I'm terribly sorry," I said.

"Mars dead," said the troödon, looking up again, the reflec-tions of the afternoon sun like little novas in its glistening eyes. "Confirm that that is your meaning."

"I'm afraid it's true," I said, surprised at the emotion in my own voice. "Mars is indeed dead." The beast's muscles went limp as the Het within presumably tried to digest this infor-mation. My heart went out to the being. And yet, on the other hand, if a time traveler were to arrive in 2013 from 65 million years in the future, I'd fully expect him to say that my kind had passed from the face of the Earth, too. "Look," I said softly.

"It's not so bad. We're talking about an inconceivably long time from now."

The troödon fixed me with a steady gaze. It reminded me of Klicks's how-dense-can-you-be look. "As said we before, our history goes back almost double that length of time. For us, it is *not* inconceivably distant." Again it dipped its long face, looking at the dried mud's pattern of cracks and curled edges. "You speak of our extinction."

Klicks smiled reassuringly. "All lifeforms die out eventually," he said. "It's the nature of things. Take the dinosaurs—"

"*Klicks* . . ."

"They've also been around for over a hundred million years and sometime very soon they're going to be wiped out."

Diamond-snout's head snapped up. The golden eyes locked on Klicks. "What?"

It was too late to stop him. "It's true, I'm afraid," Klicks continued. "Earth's ecosystem is about to change and the dinosaurs won't be able to hack it."

"Soon," said Diamond-snout, the single word sounding like a hiss. "You say soon. How soon?"

"Very soon," Klicks said. "I don't mean any day now, of course." He grinned. "But we were aiming for the point in geologic history at which the last dinosaur fossils were found. Our time-travel technology has a fundamental, unavoidable uncertainty about it. The end of the dinosaurs could be as much as three hundred thousand years in the future. Or it could be much, much sooner."

"What is planet five like?" Diamond-snout asked suddenly.

"Planet five?" I said, lost.

The yellow orbs swung on me. "Yess, yess," the thing hissed. "Fifth planet from sun."

"Oh, Jupiter," I said. "In our time, it's pretty much the same as we think it always has been: a gas giant, a failed star." I scratched my ear. "It's got a nice little ring now, though, which might not have existed in this time. Nothing like Saturn's, of course, but still pretty neat."

"Jupiter . . . oh, see I do," said the Het. "And between Mars and Jupiter?"

"The asteroid belt, of course."

"Of course," said Diamond-snout quickly. The three troödons looked at each other, then turned, their stiff tails swishing through the air; Klicks and I had to step back to avoid being whipped by them. In unison they began to march away.

"Wait a minute," called Klicks. "Where are you going?"

Diamond-snout swiveled its pointed head back at us for a moment, but the troödons didn't stop striding away. Giant yellow eyes closed and opened in turns as it rasped, "To attend to our hygiene."

Countdown: 13

I was soon to discover the differences between Canada and the United States. My American peers, starting out as assistant professors like me, could expect their first grants in the $30,000 to $40,000 range. I was told that National Research Council of Canada grants begin at about $2,500.

—David Suzuki, Canadian geneticist (1936–)

I was born the year *Apollo 11* landed on the moon. I was forty-one when the National Research Council of Canada approached me about a time-travel mission. I'd expected our expedition to be along the lines of that moon shot: no expense spared in putting together cutting-edge technology. But there was no big money for pure science anymore—not even in the States, where most of the remaining technological efforts were concentrated on fighting the growing drought in the Midwest. It turned out that big-bucks science had been a purely mid-twentieth-century phenomenon, starting with the Manhattan Project and ending with the fall of the Soviet Union.

The scientific community hadn't been prepared for this end of an era. But in rapid succession in the early 1990s, the planned Super-Colliding Super Conductor was scrapped, leaving a big hole in the ground where it was supposed to go. About the same time, SETI—the search for extraterrestrial intelligence with radio telescopes—was killed. The International Space Station, originally to be called *Freedom*, was downsized so much that people quipped it would have to be renamed Space Station *Fred*, since there wouldn't be room for the full name on its side—and then, as the various national partners (including Canada) backed out, pleading empty pockets, the few modules that had been assembled in orbit were shut down. The proposed trip to Mars—originally planned for just six years from now, the fiftieth anniversary of Armstrong's one small step—was likewise chopped. Beg, borrow, and steal became the order of the day in labs throughout the world; big government grants were a fondly remembered thing of the past.

Oh, some military money had trickled in Ching-Mei's direction for a while. The hawks had seen time travel as strategic, making possible the ultimate in preemptive strikes. They'd provided sufficient funds for Ching-Mei to build a working Huang Effect generator, along with a good-sized power plant to run it. Why, they'd almost finished building *Gallifrey*—that was the code name for the prototype habitat module that ended up being the *Sternberger*—when the implications of Ching-Mei's equations became clear. She'd been quite honest, telling the Department of National Defence from the outset that the amount of energy required for time travel depended on how far back you were going. What she didn't tell them was that it was, in fact, *inversely* proportional to the length of time you wanted to travel.

To go back 104 million years, which seemed to be the maximum that the Huang Effect allowed (one of the equations produced a negative number after that point) required virtually no energy at all. To go back 103 million years required a little energy, 102 a little more, and so on. To cast back 67 million years, as we had done, took a huge amount of power. Any attempt to travel back into historical times, a thousand years or so, would take the entire energy output of the Earth for the better part of a century, and to venture back into the last few decades would require the harnessed energy of a small nova.

Time travel, it turned out, was of little good to anyone *except* paleontologists.

Unfortunately, paleontology has never been a big-money affair. A dig, not a moon shot, became the model for what we were doing. We scraped together what equipment we could, struck sponsorship deals with the private sector, and, slashing expenses as much as possible, came up with just enough to get the two-person test mission going.

Even so, we had to watch every dollar. That's why we did the Throwback in February, a month in which no sane person would normally visit the Red Deer River valley. Since the air temperature was already thirty degrees below zero Celsius, we saved a bundle cooling the superconducting batteries that were a key part of the Huang Effect generator.

Now that Klicks and I were ready to leave the vicinity of the *Sternberger,* I would have loved to have some high-tech vehicle with giant springy wheels and dish antennas and nuclear engines. Instead, we had a plain ordinary Jeep, donated because the chairperson of Chrysler Canada had fond memories of his boyhood membership in the ROM's Saturday Morning Club. There was nothing special about this vehicle; it was just the latest 2013 model from Detroit. It even came with the optional AM/FM stereo and rear-window defogger, both of which had seemed pointless to me.

Getting the Jeep out of its tiny garage was going to be tricky. With the *Sternberger* high on the crater wall, the vehicle would have to be brought down a very steep incline. We were fortunate that the garage door had ended up facing northwest, pretty much over the outer edge of the crater wall, instead of back toward the bowl of the crater. The Jeep never would have been able to climb out of *there,* but at least we had a chance of getting it down to ground level in one piece this way.

From inside the *Sternberger's* habitat, I swung open the middle of the three doors along the five-meter-long rear wall. Four steps led down to the tiny garage's floor, and I squeezed past the left side of the Jeep and slipped into its cab.

Strapping myself in, I looked at the dashboard. I felt like Snoopy in his Sopwith Camel: *I check the instruments. They are all there.* I'd been practicing in this Jeep for weeks before the Throwback, but it really was true that if you learned to drive with automatic transmission, it was hard to become comfortable with manual later on. I hit the button mounted on the dash, and the garage-door opener—a standard model from Sears—slid the articulate strips of glassteel up.

From my vantage point in the cab, I couldn't see any ground in front of me. The crater wall fell away so steeply that the Jeep's hood blocked it from my vision. Instead, I saw the mud plain up ahead and far below. Maybe we could just walk while we're here . . .

I turned the ignition key. In this heat, the engine caught immediately. If I moved slowly forward, the front wheels would roll off the edge of the hull and end up spinning freely. That would mean the rear wheels would have to scrape the chassis over the edge. The whole thing might tip forward on its nose and drop facedown onto the crater wall.

I looked up and saw the tiny figure of Klicks standing far out on the dried mud. He was holding up his walkie-talkie. I picked mine off the passenger seat and thumbed it on.

"It looks like you're going to have to gun it," he said.

Unfortunately, that's what it looked like to me, too. I took off the parking brake, revved the engine, and popped the clutch.

"A breathtaking sight" is how Klicks, who recorded the whole thing in slow motion, later described it. Certainly it took my breath away while I was doing it. The low gravity helped no doubt in carrying me further under my initial acceleration, but the ground came rushing up far too soon anyway, and when I hit the crater wall and began bouncing down I felt like a basketball being dribbled. My heart was racing almost as fast as the car's engine as I rushed toward the mud flat.

The moment I was off the slope of the crater wall, I hit the brakes. Too soon! I began to skid. The Jeep's rear end fishtailed and I saw Klicks running his ass off to get out of the way. I pulled hard on the wheel and the vehicle swung around, heading for the lake. I slammed the brakes once more, and the Jeep spun again, coming to a rest with its rear wheels in the water. I drove it fully onto the mud plain and Klicks came jogging up to me. I rolled down the window. "Going my way?" I said with a grin.

Klicks stood there, shaking his head, hands on hips. "I think I better do the driving," he said.

Well, that was fine by me: this is one trip for which I wanted the luxury of looking at the scenery. I clambered over to the passenger's seat, he got in, and we headed off into the Mesozoic.

Countdown: 12

"My name is Ozymandias, king of kings:
Look on my works, ye Mighty, and despair!"
Nothing beside remains. Round the decay
Of that colossal wreck, boundless and bare,
The lone and level sands stretch far away.
　　　　　　　—Percy Bysshe Shelley, English poet (1792–1822)

Given the dense foliage, we had been afraid that we'd be confined to the mud flats around the lake. But about twenty kilometers from the *Sternberger* we found a broad trail that had been trampled through the forest—by a herd of ceratopsians, judging by the footprints. Klicks turned onto that path, and we made our way into the highlands. We realized that the sound of the Jeep might frighten off some of the wildlife, but, then again, never having heard an internal-combustion engine before, the dinosaurs might also be attracted to the rumbling noise, wondering what strange beast had come into their territory.

We had a tape recorder going and we kept up a running commentary about what we were seeing, describing everything from the texture of the soil (firmly packed, but free of the pebbles so common in post-glacial tills), to the plants (hardwoods, lots of flowers, and a rich ground covering of ferns), to the sky (the clear bowl of earlier had given way to great towering mounds of cumulonimbus, like models of the Grand Canyon done in cotton). A Stedicam on the roof fed images into a VCR installed where the glove compartment would normally be, supplementing the images from our clip-on Micro-Cams. Also on the roof, various instruments recorded atmospheric information and strained the air for pollens that we could bring back to the twenty-first century.

After an hour, we had the most extraordinary bit of luck. There was a bend in the path where the ceratopsian herd had changed the course of its stampede to avoid a dense stand of conifers. We sailed around the curve and almost collided with what could only have been a *Tyrannosaurus rex*. It was easily double the size of the tyrannosaurs we'd seen the first night; a female of late years, a giant truly worthy of the name *king*—or queen—*of the tyrant lizards.*

Klicks hit the brakes. The beast, a dozen meters long, was flopped on its belly, torpid. It was apparently resting after having gorged itself on meat, for its muzzle was caked with drying blood. The giant warty head lifted from the soil and turned to face us. Rex had broad cheeks and fair binocular vision, its eyes gray and wet like pools of mercury. It let out a halfhearted roar, but it didn't seem to feel any need either to run from us or, thankfully, to attack us. Klicks cut the Jeep's engine and we sat there, about twenty meters away, drinking in the sight of this, the greatest hunter ever to stalk the Earth.

Some had suggested that tyrannosaurus was a scavenger, but I'd always rejected that idea. There are no purely terrestrial scavengers in the time of humans, since only birds and fish have the ability to search enough real estate to profitably find dead animals. Besides, Rex's dagger-like teeth and bunching jaw muscles would have been unnecessary just to pick at carrion. Still, there was no carcass anywhere that we could see. I wondered why the beast wouldn't have just taken a snooze at the site of the kill, but, after watching for a few minutes, the answer became obvious.

First one, then another, then finally a small flock of tiny yellow-and-green winged reptiles descended from the sky. They may well have been there earlier, but had been scared off by the arrival of our Jeep. The tyrannosaur opened its jaw, peeling back its thin scaly lips. Its teeth ranged from about seven centimeters long to maybe sixteen. Gobbets of flesh were crammed around the gums and fibrous pieces of meat were caught between adjacent teeth. Several of the bantam pterosaurs, wings half-folded, waddled into the great mouth and proceeded to peck at the remains of the carnosaur's meal, cleaning its teeth and gums. One of the yellow-and-green flyers plucked out a particularly large hunk of meat and two of his friends began trying to grab it away from him. Rex snoozed on, indifferent to the squabble going on inside its gaping mouth. Other pterosaurs landed on its short back and thick tail, their beaks nipping in and out of the leathery skin like surgeon's lances, rooting out worms and beetles that infested the predator's hide.

This was clearly a familiar symbiosis for the tyrannosaur: we could hear a contented rumbling coming from deep in its chest. Heavy with its latest meal, Rex must have marched quite some distance from where it had killed its prey, since the pterosaurs would have had much richer pickings going over such a carcass.

We watched for over an hour, the heat mounting in the cab. Although the roof camera and our MicroCams were getting it all anyway, Klicks and I each brought still cameras to our faces and snapped off roll after roll of slides.

Suddenly I had an idea. I reached into my pack, on the floor behind my seat, and pulled out the loaf of bread we'd brought along to make sandwiches. Tearing a hunk off the crusty end slice, I rolled down the window and tossed the piece halfway between the Jeep and Rex. A couple of the pterosaurs took to the air, then fluttered back to the ground. One of them waddled over to the hunk of bread and eyed it suspiciously. After a moment, satisfied I guess that the bread wasn't going to spit at it or something, it gobbled it up in its long beak.

I threw another piece, this one only about half as far away. The pterosaur hopped over to it and pecked it up immediately. Klicks motioned that he wanted to try. He took a slice from the bag and began shredding it. Other pterosaurs came over to see what was happening. Soon we were throwing pieces as fast we could shred them and perhaps a quarter of the flock had decided it preferred Wonder Enriched to maggots off a tyrannosaur's back. We threw each piece just a little shy of the last, drawing the pigeon-sized reptiles closer. Klicks tossed a few pieces on the Jeep's hood, but the pterosaurs seemed to find the metal too hot to land on, and those went uneaten. Soon we were down to the last slice. Instead of tossing it, I broke off three choice chunks, placed them in my right palm, and stretched my arm out the window. After several minutes of me sitting motionless, one brave little pterosaur did hop up onto my arm, its talons sharp through the fabric of my sleeve. Its body was covered with down of emerald and gold. The loosely folded bat-like wings, with their tiny claws, fluttered in the breeze. With three quick darts, the toothless beak, like needlenose pliers, snapped up the bread. A moment later the creature was gone.

We had exhausted the loaf about the same time as Rex's teeth and back had been picked clean. As one, the pterosaurs rose into the sky, a cloud of shimmering gold and green. Klicks revved the engine and drove slowly past the resting hunter, continuing on our way.

Countdown: 11

The hunter of live game is always bringing live animals nearer to death and extinction, whereas the fossil hunter is always seeking to bring extinct animals to life.

—Henry Fairfield Osborn, American paleontologist (1857–1935)

Crrack!

"What the hell was that?" Klicks brought the Jeep to a halt. We were on a steep slope, having broken out of the forest halfway up the side of a mountain. The cumulonimbus overhead now covered two-thirds of the sky.

Crrack!

"There it is again!" I said.

"Shhh."

We listened intently. Suddenly I caught a blur of orange motion out of the corner of my eye. "My God!" I shouted. "They're going to kill each other!"

Crrack! Crrack!

Off to our right, two individuals of the genus *Pachycephalosaurus* were butting heads. These two-legged giants were the big-horned sheep of this time. Holding their backs and necks parallel to the ground, they charged at each other, smashing the tops of their skulls together.

At first glance, pachycephalosaurs looked like the intellectuals of the dinosaurian era. They had high domed heads and a fringe of knobby horns around the back of the skull that gave the impression of being a balding professor's remaining hair. But the erudite appearance was misleading. The domed skull was almost solid bone, more than twenty centimeters thick.

Crrack!

These must be males, for nearby a larger bonehead, darker rust in color, was using the bumpy knobs on its snout to dig up roots. This one seemed indifferent to the head-bashing going on nearby, but I was sure that it was the female prize the males were fighting for. At six meters in length, the male on the left was a good meter longer than the one on the right—and with reptiles, bigger meant older. The old guy was probably the female's mate and here was being challenged by a young buck, ready to test his prowess in the way prescribed by his genes. I brought my binoculars to bear on the contest. The challenger was losing ground. Since we'd started watching, he had been forced to back away almost fifty meters.

Klicks pointed to the sky. A large pterosaur was circling above the fight, looking like a vulture waiting for the kill. I doubted that the boneheads routinely fought to the death, but this battle had gone on much longer than I would have anticipated a normal territorial challenge to last.

Time for both pachycephalosaurs to catch their breaths. They straightened, rising to their full heights, tilting their heads up and down in a ritualized display of their skullcaps. Although the tops of both their heads were now partially obscured by blood, I could see that there were bright display markings in yellow and blue on each pate.

The head-bobbing continued for a few minutes. Finally, the one who had been losing ground backed off a bit more, then charged forward at full speed, its three-toed feet throwing up divots each time they kicked off the soil. There was no roar to go with the charge, though. Each beast had its jaw locked shut, presumably to minimize the damage done by the impacts.

Old Guy stood his ground, his horizontally held back ramrod-straight, five-fingered hands at the sides of his head to steady it even more. When the impact came, the glass in our windshield rattled. I saw three chunks of the keratin veneer that sat atop the beasts' skullcaps go flying. Old Guy had been knocked on his behind, his thick tail bending at an awkward angle. But he rose quickly, while the challenger staggered back and forth, dazed.

In the distance, we could hear more cracking sounds. Somewhere another pair of pachycephalosaurs were jousting. But the contest we'd been watching seemed to at last be over, the most recent impact finally proving too much for the challenger. He raised his head and looked at his foe. Old Guy looked up, too, and bobbed once, showing his display colors. Then he lowered his head again, ready for another charge. The challenger didn't return the display. Instead, he turned tail and staggered away. Overhead, the frustrated pterosaur flapped its wings and headed off in search of something else to eat.

Old Guy made his way over to the foraging female and began rubbing his neck against hers, the bony nodes on the rears of their skulls making a sound like a washboard as they clicked together. The female seemed indifferent to the male's attentions, but I suspected she was in heat and probably her scent had prompted the unattached younger male to make his challenge. Old Guy continued to rub necks with her, but she simply went about her feeding. After a while, though, she dug up a few more choice roots and, instead of eating them, left them on the ground for the male. He tipped his snout down and gobbled them quickly, obviously famished after his fight. This leaving of the roots was apparently a signal that the female was now ready. Old Guy moved in behind her and she went to her knees. The coupling only lasted a few minutes.

I guess they'd been mated a long time.

As a boy, I'd read a short story by Ray Bradbury called "The Sound of Thunder." It told of a time-traveler who had stepped on a butterfly in the Mesozoic, and that one event—the loss of that butterfly—had cascaded down the eons to result in a different future.

Well, we knew now that small events like that do have big consequences. Chaos theory tells us that the flapping of a butterfly's wing in China really does determine whether it later rains in New York. This sensitivity to initial conditions is even called the Butterfly Effect. I got a kick out of the fact that Bradbury had beat the physicists to the punch. He had known how important butterflies were long before they did. In a way, he was the real father of chaos theory.

But Ching-Mei said we didn't have to worry about any of that. The *Sternberger* was anchored to its launch point back in the sky over the Red Deer River. Her equations said that it would return there, regardless of what we did back here. She'd talked in terms I only half understood about the many-worlds interpretation of quantum physics, saying that our future would be safe.

And so we got to hunt dinosaurs with impunity . . .

"That's the one," said Klicks, pointing.

"Pardon me?"

"That pachycephalosaur, the challenger. That's the one we should kill. It's exhausted by that head-butting contest, so it should be easy to take down. Besides, it obviously doesn't have a mate depending on it."

I thought for a moment, then nodded. Klicks throttled the engine and we drove off in the direction the challenger had headed. It didn't take us long to catch up with him. He was indeed looking bedraggled, but still, at about the same length as our Jeep, I doubted that he would be quite as easy to fell as Klicks hoped.

Klicks stopped the Jeep long enough to fire a shot from his elephant gun out his window. It hit the dinosaur in the shoulder. The beast yelped and turned on us. It apparently had no preprogrammed response for dealing with an attack by humans in a Jeep Iroquois. It bobbed its head at us, showing the blue and yellow display colors on its pate. Klicks swung the car around and fired again. This time the creature broke from instinct. It lowered its head and ran straight for us, a biological battering ram.

Klicks pulled hard on the wheel, but that just succeeded in bringing us broadside to the beast. It hit the passenger door, little shards of safety glass showering me, the metal bending as if we'd been in a high-speed automobile collision. We were sent spinning across the clearing and rammed into a tree. The air bags on the dash inflated. Klicks shifted to reverse and pulled us back a distance.

The air bags should have deflated automatically, but they hadn't—so much for Chrysler's quality control. Feeling like Patrick McGoohan in *The Prisoner*, I pushed against the white sheeting until I managed to find my dissection kit, sitting on the hump supporting the stick shift, and dug out a scalpel. I slit my bag first, then Klicks's, the hot wind that spewed out as they deflated blowing things around the cab.

Klicks shifted back to first gear, and we jerked toward the reptile. The mechanism for rolling down my window had been wrecked by the impact. I found my rifle and used its butt to clear the remaining glass, then fired both rounds at the beast.

It had incredible stamina. Klicks ended up driving in circles around the hapless creature while I kept reloading and pumping round after round into its torso. Finally it staggered forward and slumped to the ground. We brought the Jeep to a halt, and Klicks opened the hood to help it cool off. I took my dissection kit and headed over to the carcass, as big as the biggest bear I'd ever seen at the zoo.

I'd never been good at it, but I did know how to butcher animals. During the Gobi dig that had been part of the Second Canada-China Dinosaur Project, we'd had no way to refrigerate meat, so we'd brought sheep and goats with us and slaughtered them as required. I slit the pachycephalosaur's throat to drain the blood. Gallons of it—the wimpy metric liter was utterly inadequate to describe the flow—poured out onto the soil, steaming.

Severing the head was an arduous task even with my freshly sharpened bone saw. The vertebrae were stiffened and reinforced to help withstand the head-buttings, and the nuchal ligaments running from the back of the head to the neck were exceptionally thick and strong. Being almost solid bone, the head was incredibly heavy even in the reduced gravity. Once I'd gotten it free, I held the head up with both hands and turned it so that its bumpy snout faced me. *Alas, Prehistoric! I knew him well . . .*

We didn't have a drill long enough to cut through the brain-case. However, the back of our Jeep was packed with Huang stasis boxes for keeping specimens in. Klicks had gotten several of them out and had brought them over to me. They came in a variety of different sizes and were one of the few really expensive pieces of equipment we had on this mission. Their walls were made of polished metal, inlaid with the hairline black strands of the stasis grid. Klicks opened the lid on one, and I placed the entire head into the flat-black interior.

We didn't have much time in which to perform the autopsy before the animal's remains would start to turn in the heat. Klicks was of minimal assistance—this wasn't his line of work. But he displayed a commendable lack of squeamishness as he recorded everything with his clip-on MicroCam.

It didn't take long looking at these sophisticated innards to convince me beyond a shadow of a doubt that pachycephalosaurs were warm-blooded, controlling their own body temperature through metabolism instead of relying on basking to heat up. The heart was a sight to behold, even with a bullet lodged in it. The size of a basketball, it was a lovely four-chambered mammal-like affair, with completely separate arterial and venous pathways.

There was an unusual organ behind the heart, yellowish in color, very fibrous in construction, and heavily serviced by blood vessels. It corresponded to nothing in modern birds or reptiles. I did my best to remove it intact and placed it in the ebony interior of another stasis box.

I decided to examine only one of the lungs, assuming the other would be similar. It had massive capacity, further evidence of high metabolism. I'd dissected and studied all kinds of animals over the years, but none matched the sophistication—the utter perfection—of the dinosaurian anatomy. I'd enjoy doing a proper job on that head once we got back to the twenty-first century . . .

"Uh-oh."

I looked up to see what Klicks was referring to. Coming toward us was a small bipedal dinosaur, about the size of a chicken. It had a snaking neck, small pointed head, and a little round body looking a lot like a bowling ball. Its metatarsals were elongated, giving it three functional leg segments and a long stride, a common adaptation for high-speed running. It probably felt that its fleet-footedness meant we didn't pose any threat to it, and certainly it was too small to be a serious threat to us. As it got closer, I saw that it was covered with short feathers and had a crest of red and yellow plumes coming off the back of its head. I guess it figured there was plenty of dead dinosaur meat to go around, and it made a beeline for the pachycephalosaur's open chest cavity. I tried to shoo it away, but it just squawked at me and helped itself to a prize chunk of gizzard.

Klicks was nonchalantly making his way back to the Jeep. I didn't understand what he was up to at first, but a moment later he was coming back with our largest stasis box, a silver cube a meter on each side. He waited until the thief had nipped into the carcass for another piece of meat, then charged. The feathered dinosaur must have felt the ground vibrate as Klicks ran toward it. It swung its head right around to look at him, blinked twice, then scrambled forward, up onto the back of the dead animal. Klicks wasn't to be deterred so easily. He climbed right up on top of the corpse, too, and proceeded to chase the little saurischian along the length of the pachycephalosaur's spine. His prey hopped off and began to hightail it for the safety of a distant stand of trees, but Klicks had the advantage of muscles used to much greater gravity. His legs swung in giant strides, each one sending him sailing ahead three meters. He finally caught up with the tiny meat-eater. Pouncing, he brought the stasis box down upon it. The dinosaur let out a loud yelp, but it was cut off in mid-note as Klicks flipped the box around and slammed the lid, locking the interior into stasis. At least we'd have one live specimen to bring forward with us.

Turning back to my dissection, I slit through the stomach's wall, taking care not to let the gastric acid spill on me. I wasn't surprised to find it mostly empty; I wouldn't want to start a head-butting contest on a full stomach either. What was within seemed to be soft vegetation, including well-chewed gunnera leaves. I wondered if—

"*Christ, Brandy, watch out!*"

There were tons of flesh spread out before me and it took me a second to see what Klicks was pointing at. There, down near the middle of the back, over the hips, a mound of blue Het jelly was percolating to the surface.

Countdown: 10

Unbidden guests
Are often welcomest when they are gone.

—*Henry VI*, Part I, Act II, Scene 2

⟨▲⟩ I jumped back, the thought of touching one of those alien slimeballs again being enough to send my heart racing. The blue jelly had finished exiting the pachycephalosaur and sat there, a pulsing mound, on its hip.

"What do we do with it?" asked Klicks, standing about five meters from the dinosaur corpse.

Set fire to it was my first thought. What I said was, "What do you mean?"

"I mean, we can't just leave it here," he said. "You've carved up its vehicle."

"Serves it right. It almost wrecked our Jeep."

Klicks shook his head. "I don't think so."

"Huh?"

"Well, you saw the way the pachycephalosaur behaved. A territorial challenge, a ritual head-butting. I think the Het was a passenger within it, not a pilot. It was observing the way the dinosaur behaved, rather than controlling its actions."

I thought about that, then looked at the butchered mounds of flesh in front of me. External observation followed by dissection seemed inadequate study tools compared with climbing inside the animal's skin, living its life, feeling its sensations. Klicks was probably right; the pachycephalosaur had been behaving of its own volition, not under Het control. And it had attacked the Jeep with considerable justification, after all.

I nodded. "Okay, then. What do we do?"

"We could take it back to the *Sternberger* with us. I'm sure our Het friends will be visiting us again there."

It seemed a sensible course of action, except for one thing. "But, Klicks, if this one's been up here in the mountains for the last few days, it may not know about us. As far as it's concerned, we're strange creatures it's never seen before."

"Good point." Klicks cleared his throat and spoke to the blue mound. "Hello," he said. "Do you understand me? Do you understand English?"

The thing pulsed more quickly. It was obviously reacting to the sound of Klicks's voice, but whether with an attempt to respond or with sheer terror I couldn't say.

"I'm sure it can't talk without a vehicle with vocal cords," I said.

"Maybe not," said Klicks. "But it should be able to listen."

"It has no ears," I pointed out.

"But it surely can feel the air vibrating as I speak." He turned to the creature again. "We come in peace," he said. Funny, I thought, that our language should already have a cliché for greeting aliens. The jelly's rapid pulsing continued; evidently those words hadn't calmed the creature. Klicks pointed at the Het, then straight up, apparently trying to convey that he knew that the creature came from the sky. He hoped, I guess, that if the Het realized that we understood that, it would assume that we'd already made friends with others of its kind. There was no response at first, so he tried the gesture three more times. Perhaps the Het finally did catch his meaning, for it soon seemed less agitated.

"Well, I don't know if I got through to the thing or not," said Klicks with a shrug. Then an evil smile overtook his features. "Hey, man, perhaps you could lie down next to it and let it crawl into your head. That would be a good sign of friendship."

"The hell I will! Why don't *you* do that?"

"You're the one whose English they seemed to like best."

"No, thank you. Once was more than enough."

"Well, then, what are we going to do?"

"Let's leave it up to the Het." I walked back to the Jeep and got a stasis box out of the rear compartment. I put it on its side near the grapefruit-sized mound of jelly. The Het was still for a while, then began to flow toward it, undulating its way along the pachycephalosaur's haunch. It hesitated at the lip of the box, then pulsed its way into the dark interior. I went to close the lid.

"Don't!"

I looked at Klicks. "Why not?"

"Once you close the lid, the stasis field will turn on. We can't shut the field off without a Huang Invertor, and the nearest one of those is sixty-five million years in the future."

"Oh, hell, right. Okay." I picked up the box by its handles and looked inside. This was the first chance I'd had to examine a Het with any detachment. I felt a wave of revulsion as I looked at the thing, quivering and blue. It wasn't uniformly transparent. Rather, there were cloudier parts within, representing places where the jelly was thicker or perhaps of a different constitution. And the faint phosphorescence I'd observed earlier came from thousands of tiny pinpoints of light. They swirled within the plasma, like fireflies moving through molasses. The pulsing of the body wasn't a contraction and expansion, like a lung. Rather it was an arching motion, the Het pushing itself up from beneath, alternately forming then destroying a concave hollow under its body.

It was completely different from all the lifeforms I had ever studied. Of course, its macro structure probably no more reflected its constituent parts than the body of a man resembles the cells he's made of, or the dunes in a desert reveal the crystalline nature of the quartz grains of which they're composed. I'd love to get the Het under a microscope, to find out what made it tick.

I placed the box on its side in the back of the Jeep, but left the rear door open so that the creature wouldn't cook in the heat and so it could get out if it wanted to. Then I went back to my dissection of the pachycephalosaurus. When we returned to our vehicle two hours later, the Het was still there.

As we drove back to the *Sternberger*, Klicks had evidently decided that the Het in the back either really didn't understand English or, if it did, couldn't hear us talking over the roar of the Jeep's engine. "Made any progress on the great moral decision?" he said, his voice edged with just enough sarcasm to make clear that he thought I was weak for not having his knack for decisive action.

"It's not that easy," I said softly. Nonetheless, I was surprised to find that I was getting closer to coming to a conclusion. "I guess I'm leaning toward agreeing with you."

"You realize the world will have our hides if we *don't* bring the Hets forward. Humanity has been waiting decades to meet extraterrestrials. People aren't going to be happy if we deprive them of the chance to do just that."

I was silent for several seconds. Then: "Did I ever tell you what my father asked me to do?"

"How is Leon?" asked Klicks. "Responding to the treatments?"

"Not really, no. He's in a lot of pain."

"I'm sorry."

"He wants me to give him some poison so that he can end his life."

Klicks's foot eased up on the accelerator. "My God. Really?"

"Yes."

He shook his head, but more in despair than negation. "It's a shame. He was such a vital man. Still, they should have euthanasia laws in place shortly."

"Shortly?" I looked out at the wild landscape. "I suppose that a couple of years is a short length of time—except when every moment you live is torturing you."

"What are you going to do?"

"I don't know."

"Give him the poison."

"That one's easy for you, too, eh?"

"What's to think about? He's your *father*, for Christ's sake."

"Yes. Yes, he is."

"Do it, Brandy. I'd do it for my dad."

"It's easy to say that now. George is strong as an ox. Hell, he'll probably outlive you. It's completely different when it stops being a theoretical question. You can't answer it truthfully until you *really* have to answer it."

Klicks was quiet for a long moment as our Jeep bounced over the uneven ground. "Well," he said at last, "you *really* have to answer the question about the Hets in the next—what?—sixty-four hours. Sooner, in fact, because I'm sure they'll need time to prepare."

"I know that," I said, my voice weary.

We drove the rest of the way back to the *Sternberger* in silence.

Countdown: 9

Monster one minute, food the next.

—Kiakshuk, Inuit hunter (fl. 1950s)

Paleontology has a long history of famous meals. On New Year's Eve, 1853, Sir Richard Owen hosted a dinner for twenty fossil experts inside a life-size reconstruction of *Iguanodon* made under his direction by Benjamin Waterhouse Hawkins.

Almost a century later, Russian paleontologists enjoyed a meal of mammoth steaks and the finest vodka after one of the hairy elephants was found frozen in Siberia.

Klicks and I weren't to be outdone. Late that afternoon we built a fire near the base of the crater upon which the *Sternberger* was perched and set two choice pachycephalosaurus steaks to cooking.

While the meat was grilling, I went over to check on our Martian hitchhiker. I found some shady ground and set the stasis box down on its side, and, in case the Het wanted something to drink, I placed a bowl of water next to it. Evidently it wasn't thirsty, since after pulsing its way over to the bowl to see what it contained, it ignored it.

I normally like my meat medium-rare, but we grilled the steaks for a long time, flipping them repeatedly. We wanted to be sure that any parasites and germs had been killed. When it finally came time to eat the meat, I felt a certain reluctance. For one thing, although all modern bird, reptile, and mammal meat is edible by humans, there was always the small chance that dinosaur flesh would prove poisonous. For another, well, it somehow *seemed* wrong.

As usual, Klicks had no such misgivings. He immediately sliced a piece off and brought it to his mouth.

"How is it?" I asked.

"Different."

This from the gourmet of Drumheller. Oh, well. Making sure my cup of water was handy, in case I had to wash down some foul taste, I took a tenuous nibble. I'd never eaten reptile before, but I expected it to resemble chicken. It tasted more like roasted almonds. I don't think I'd ever want to have it again, but it wasn't bad—just a bit too stringy to be a comfortable chew.

I didn't know if the Het needed to eat—really, we didn't know much about them at all—but I took a plate over to it with both some cooked and uncooked pachycephalosaur and a mound of fronds. It ignored these, too, and seemed content just to throb quietly. I couldn't understand a lifeform that neither drank water nor ate. Although I wasn't looking forward to seeing other Hets again, I hoped some would come soon and take our reluctant guest off our hands.

It was getting too dark to do any serious exploring, so we just sat around on some bald cypress trunks, letting the meal digest.

"Hey, Brandy," Klicks said at last.

"Yeah?"

"How do you define gross ignorance?"

"Beats me."

"One hundred and forty-four Brits." He flashed a grin.

"Oh, yeah?" I said, rising to the challenge. "What do sugarcane and unwanted pregnancies have in common?"

"Dunno."

"They both pop up all over Jamaica."

He laughed out loud. "Good one. Why does King Charles want to abdicate?"

"Too easy. So he can go on welfare like everybody else in England. What has six legs and goes 'ho-de-do, ho-de-do, ho-de-do'?"

"What?"

"Three Jamaicans running for the elevator."

Klicks roared. "Well, fuck me," he said.

I sipped my coffee. "Not while there are still dogs in the street."

I sighed contentedly. It was like old times. We'd whiled away many an evening in the twenty-odd years we'd known each other telling jokes, slagging each other's ancestors, and just shooting the bull. We'd shared a lot in that time, and I'd always enjoyed his company. We'd even said, back in the simpler days at university, that we'd never let marriages destroy our friendship. We'd seen too many people drop off the face of the Earth once they'd gotten hitched. No way we were going to let that happen to us. We'd keep in touch, do things together, stay a team. But then reality got in the way. There were precisely three really good jobs for dinosaur specialists in Canada: Chief of the Paleobiology Division at the Canadian Museum of Nature in Ottawa, Curator of Paleobiology at the Royal Ontario Museum in Toronto, and Curator of Dinosaurs at the Royal Tyrrell Museum of Palæontology in Drumheller, Alberta. I ended up at the ROM; Klicks at the Tyrrell—with 2,500 kilometers between us. And we each did get married, although Klicks's union with Carla had lasted less than a year.

Still, we did a better job than most of keeping in touch, of remaining friends. We got together at the annual meetings of the SVP and Klicks always came back to Toronto for his vacations. We were the best of friends until . . . until . . . until . . .

I threw my plate down onto the mud plain, the uneaten portion of my pachycephalosaur steak bouncing onto the dirt.

Klicks looked up. "Brandy?"

But at that moment our campsite exploded in light, then, just as quickly, everything was darkness again. My head snapped up at the sky. Off in the west, a huge spherical object was moving above the trees, its shape visible only as a black nothingness that blocked the stars. Another eye-jabbing flash of brilliance, followed by the black of night, afterimages burning in my retinas. Searching beams, like those from light-houses, were probing the landscape. Suddenly all the beams converged on the *Sternberger*, perched high up on the crater wall. Then, as one, they scanned down the mound of earth, past our parked Jeep, and over to Klicks and me and our splut-tering fire.

I shielded my eyes from the glare and tried to make out the source of the searchlights. The giant spherical object must have been sixty meters in diameter, floating silently above our heads. As it descended from the sky, the sphere's color—an un-even mixture of tawny and beige—became visible as the light from its beams reflected back at it from the cracked surface of the mud plain. Dead leaves and loose pieces of dirt swirled up-ward in a small cyclone directly beneath the lowering sphere.

As it descended, something thick and gray began to ooze from its bottom, a glistening amorphous lump. The lump touched the ground and spread out like a slug's body as it took the weight of the sphere. There was a brief period while the sphere settled in, the gray foot expanding to form a Poli-Grip seal with the mud plain.

The sphere's surface seemed to be plated with meter-wide hexagonal scales that had a rough, natural appearance. The whole thing pulsed gently, exposing fibrous pink tissue in the cracks between the scales as it did so. I'd at first assumed that this was one of the Het spaceships we'd seen flying high over-head early this morning, but the sphere seemed to be *breathing*. A living spaceship? Well, why not?

Suddenly there was a sound from the sphere, a whispering sigh as an opening appeared above its landing foot. A slit was widening, the scales bunching up on either side, as thick verti-cal lips stretched wide. The interior glowed softly. More of the amorphous gray material pulsed within, but it seemed to be expanding, growing larger. It extruded through the opening, a great wet tongue sticking its way out into the night. Slowly the extension reached the ground. It continued to grow, to lengthen, until it had formed a gently sloping ramp leading from the thick-lipped mouth of the spaceship out onto the mud plain. The tongue stiffened and flattened, then the moisture on its surface seemed to dry as though it had been sucked back into pores.

Nothing happened for several seconds, then a shape appeared at the top of the ramp silhouetted against the glowing mouth. I knew in an instant that what I was seeing was a truly alien form of life. It had two arms and two legs, but they were reversed from the human norm. The legs—the limbs used for locomotion—were attached at the shoulders of the broad torso. They stretched a meter and a half to the ground, ending not in feet but in round pads. The arms—the limbs used for manipulation—were attached at the bottom of the torso, where human hips would be. It was as if this creature's four-footed ancestors had gained bipedalism by rising up on their knuckles, freeing the rear limbs to dangle freely. No form of life on Earth had ever made that evolutionary choice; this was a true brachiator, a creature that propelled itself using its upper limbs—something that had formed in a different ecosystem.

The brachiator came down the ramp, its giant stride bringing it close to us far more quickly than human steps could have managed. I looked it up and down. The head, if you could call it that, was a broad dome rising directly from the shoulders. There was no neck. Long sausage-shaped eyes seemed to completely encircle the edge of the dome. Each eye had two pupils in it, again, a decidedly nonterrestrial solution to the problem of stereoscopic vision.

The body seemed at first glance to be covered with copper fur, but on closer inspection it was something different: thick spiraling cables of tissue. They overlapped and intertwined in complex patterns, providing not only thermal insulation but also what looked like very sensitive touch sensors.

I focused on the manipulatory appendages, and immediately realized the benefit of having them below and inside the walking limbs, instead of above and exposed as human arms are. These appendages were much more complex than ours. Each seemed to be jointed in four places instead of two and ended in a ring of delicate tentacles surrounding a trio of pincers, each of a different size. One pincer looked like needlenose pliers, another like a parrot's beak, the third an open circle like the letter C. Protected, closer in to the body, these manipulators had been able to evolve much more exquisite and widely differentiated structures than had the forelimbs of terrestrial animals. Behind these arms I was shocked to see that there were two smaller, less sophisticated manipulators as well—this beast's ancestors had had *six* limbs, not four.

There was a vertical mouth slit about halfway down the brachiator's broad chest. It fluttered open, but I saw no sign of dentition. Perhaps these beings didn't play the risky game that so many of Earth's lifeforms did, trying to use a single orifice for breathing, speaking, and eating. "Where is our brethren?" it asked. The warbling voice, high-pitched, like an adolescent boy's, was clear and easily understood, although it still had those small gaps between each word that characterized Het speech.

I stood dumbfounded for a moment, then, gathering my wits, said, "This way." I walked over to where I'd set down the stasis box. My heart skipped a few beats. The mound of Het jelly was gone. We'd be in deep trouble if anything had happened to it. I looked around frantically, but the brachiator had already come over to stand next to me. Fortunately, its many eyes were apparently better suited than my myopic peepers for crepuscular searching. "Ah," it said. It bent its ambulatory appendages at what would correspond to the knee, lowering its torso to the ground. I saw that there was a smooth area on its back that was free from the coiling body covering, showing a rough gray skin with a pebbly texture. The jelly throbbed quickly over to that spot and began to percolate into the brachiator's body.

In the short time it took for the jelly to enter, I came to a conclusion about the brachiator. It wasn't an intelligent form of life. Rather, it must be a domesticated Martian animal. It made sense, of course, that there were creatures on their native world that the jelly beings used for locomotion, for hands, and for eyes. This must have been one of those. Since it had spoken, it must already be occupied by a Het. The Hets had said earlier that they weren't individuals. I wondered if the two mounds of jelly, the one that had just entered and the one already within the brachiator, would unite into a single entity. I hoped they weren't mad at us for killing its pachycephalosaur.

"You killed our pachycephalosaur," said the brachiator at once.

"I'm sorry," I said. "We didn't know it was occupied. We just wanted to study its physiology. Please forgive us."

"Forgive?" The brachiator's speaking orifice twisted in what must have been a facial expression of some sort. "It was only an animal."

I'm the one who had slaughtered that unfortunate dinosaur, but somehow the alien's words struck me as harsher than my actions. "I didn't want to kill it," I said. "But we learned much by studying its interior."

"Of course," said the Het in that alto voice.

"You came to retrieve your friend?" I said.

"Friend?" echoed the brachiator's mouth.

"The Het who had been in the pachycephalosaur."

"Yes, we came to retrieve that one. When it did not return from its mission, we went looking for it. We found the butchered dinosaur and markings in the dirt that we eventually realized must have been made by some sort of vehicle belonging to you. We see now that you did no harm to the Het, but we believe our response was a prudish—a prudent—one." It had said all that without a pause for breathing. I hadn't yet found the thing's respiratory orifices, but I was sure now that they were completely separate from the mouth. The brachiator headed back to the fireside, and I had to jog to keep up with its Goliath strides.

Klicks was on his feet, staring at the brachiator, mouth agape. "My God," he said slowly. "You really are from somewhere else, aren't you?"

"Yes," said the Het—the first time I'd heard it manage that word without it trailing off in a reptilian hiss.

Klicks pointed at the brachiator's wide torso. "And that thing you're in?"

"A vehicle. Not particularly well suited for this ecosystem— it has trouble extracting nourishment from the plant life here, and finds the sunlight too bright—but, for some application forms, a much more useful creature to inhabit."

Klicks gestured at the massive sphere behind him. "And that's one of your spaceships?"

"Yes."

"It's alive."

"Of course."

"Remarkable." He shook his head. "I'd give anything to take a spin in one of those."

The brachiator's sausage eyes blinked all at once, single lids lifting up from below. "Spin," it said. "The action of a gaming wheel, no? Or to give events a desired interpretation?"

"No. *Spin*. A journey, a trip, a ride."

"Ah," said the brachiator. "This we can do."

"Really?" Klicks was practically jumping up and down.

"Now hold on a minute," I said.

"Seize time? No link."

"Klicks, we can't go up in that thing."

"Why the hell not?"

"Well, look at it. It's alive, for God's sake. We'd have to go *inside* it."

"Hey, man, if Jonah could hack it in the whale, I'm all set to try my luck in a breathing spaceship. This is a once-in-a-lifetime opportunity."

I shook my head. "Have you ever noticed how many once-in-a-lifetime opportunities come at the end of a person's life? Count me out."

Klicks shrugged. "Fine. But I'm going." He turned to the brachiator. "Can we do it now?"

"Our business here is concluded. Now is fine."

Klicks jogged alongside the brachiator, over to the gray tongue entrance-ramp. I cringed as he stepped on it, but, although it yielded slightly, he didn't seem to stick to it as I was afraid he might. The ship continued to breathe, expanding and contracting slowly. Klicks made it to the top of the ramp before I shouted out, "I'm coming! *Wait up!*"

I ran up the tongue and into the mouth.

Boundary Layer

The mind is its own place, and in itself
Can make a heaven of hell, a hell of heaven.

—John Milton, English poet (1608–1674)

I came in the front door of our house, pulled off my Totes, and placed them on the Rubbermaid mat. When I was a child in the 1970s, February in Toronto had been a month full of snow. But recent Februarys had been quite mild, with the spring rains starting before Valentine's Day. I hung my trench coat and umbrella in the closet and made my way through the front hall and up the five steps to the living room. Tess was sitting on the couch, reading a magazine on her datapad.

"Hi, honey." I sat down next to her, brushed aside her red hair, and gave her a kiss on the cheek.

"Howdy, stranger." Her husky voice, so unlikely given her tiny frame, carried no hint of sarcasm, so I ignored the little dig about the long hours I'd been keeping.

"How was work?" I said.

"Okay." Tess was a pension and benefits counselor for Deloitte & Touche. She made more money than I did. "I think we're going to get that contract with the provincial government."

"Good," I said. "That's good."

The left window on her datapad was showing an article about mergers amongst American advertising firms. The other window was filled with an ad from the Franklin Mint for a collectible chess set, with pieces shaped like classic sitcom stars from the twentieth century. I read the ad.

"Tess," I said at last, "I'm going out of town for a few days."

"Again?" She pouted slightly, her full lips curving downward, her green eyes studying the carpet. It was an expression I always loved. "I thought you were through traveling for a while, now that the Chinese thing is over." The Second Canada-China Dinosaur Project had taken me away from her—something neither of us enjoyed—for four months last year.

"I'm sorry, Lambchop. This is important."

Sarcasm did tinge the throaty tones this time. "It always is. Where are you going?"

"To Vancouver."

"What's happening out there?"

"Nothing, really. I—I just have to do some research at one of the university libraries."

"Can't they E-mail you what you need?" She indicated her datapad, the ubiquitous window on the world.

"Nobody seems to be able to find the information I want," I said. "I'm afraid I'm going to have to do some digging for it." I paused for a moment. "Say, do you want to come along?"

Tess laughed her throaty laugh. "Vancouver in February? No, thank you. I can get all the freezing rain I want right here." She touched the bookmark button on her datapad. Her freckled arm reached out to slip around my neck. "Can't you do your research in Orlando? Or Freeport?" Her eyes danced, twin emerald flames. "It's been years since we had a proper vacation."

"I wish I could."

She ran her fingers through what was left of my hair. "Maybe I shouldn't let you go. There are a lot of lovely Japanese ladies out in British Columbia. I've seen the way you glue your eyes to *Canada A.M.* every morning. You've got the hots for Kelly Hamasaki."

Was it that obvious? Kelly, queen of the radiant smile, was the most gorgeous newscaster North American television had ever seen. "Very funny."

"Seriously," she said, with a tone that made clear that her intention was anything but, "how do I know I can trust you with all those west-coast beauties?"

I felt something snap deep in my chest. "Christ, Tess, I'm the one who's leaving you here alone. How do *I* know I can trust you? How do I know you won't jump in the sack with—with God knows who while I'm gone?"

She pulled away from me. "What's gotten into you?"

"Nothing." I looked at her, her narrow face, the high cheekbones, the mane of orange hair. God, I didn't want to lose her. She was my whole life. But if what the diary said was true, I was *nothing* to her. I knew I should apologize, recant before it was too late, before the words became part of the immutable past, the foundation for a wall between us, but I couldn't bring myself to take them back. I was hurt by—by what? By what she might do? By what she might have done if things had been different? Finally I looked away from her astonished green eyes and got up from the couch. "I'm going upstairs to pack for my trip," I said.

I arrived in Vancouver on a Tuesday. Dr. Huang ignored my calls until late Wednesday afternoon, when I managed to get her to answer at her office. She was all set to hang up on me again, when I broke into Chinese. That shocked the hell out of her, but I'd learned more than enough to get by while participating in the Canada-China Dinosaur Project. She finally agreed to see me but insisted it be during the day, not the evening, and at her office, not her home. That meant running up an extra night's stay at the Holiday Inn, but given that I didn't have much of a bargaining position, I agreed.

Driving up to TRIUMF, at the edge of a beautiful pine forest on the outskirts of the University of British Columbia campus, I was greeted by two signs. The one on the right, made of seven three-meter-long boards of prime B.C. lumber, told me in both English and French that I'd arrived at Canada's national meson center, operated by four universities under a contribution from the National Research Council. The one on the left, in government-issue red and white, reminded me that my tax dollars were hard at work here.

There were dozens of buildings spread around the grounds, including a bunch of temporary structures, and it took me a while to find the main entrance. None of the brochures I picked up at the desk wanted to tell me what TRIUMF stood for, but I had a vague memory from a trivia game I'd played once that it was "Tri-University Meson Facility." That meant, I guessed, that one of the four institutions sponsoring it had been a Johnny-come-lately, and the acronym had been deemed too clever to change. I knew next to nothing about physics, but apparently this place boasted the world's largest cyclotron. Although I wasn't exactly sure what a cyclotron did, it certainly sounded like the kind of thing one might find quite handy while trying to invent a time machine.

Besides the brochures, the ancient man at the desk also gave me a clip-on dosimeter which looked like an old-fashioned car fuse. I told him I was there to see Dr. Huang but before he got around to phoning to ask her to come and get me, a nerdy-looking fellow in a navy-blue lab coat said, "I'll take him back, Sam." He led me through a warren of corridors to an unmarked door. I took a moment to gather my thoughts, then knocked.

I was glad to see that physicists enjoyed no more glamour than did paleontologists. Ching-Mei Huang's office wasn't much more than an oversized closet. Still, it provided plenty of room for its diminutive occupant. Huang looked to be about sixty, with a small amount of gray streaking her close-cropped black hair. Her clothes were plain, almost frumpy. She wore no makeup or jewelry. Her eyes were darting, haunted; her movements quick and nervous.

"Dr. Huang, I presume."

"Mr. Thackeray."

"It's 'Doctor,' Doctor, but please call me Brandy."

She made no move to invite me into her office. Indeed, she seemed to be blocking the doorway as best she could with her small body. "We can't talk in here," she said. "Come with me to the cafeteria."

"What I have to say is private, Dr. Huang. Can't we use your office?"

"No." She looked up at me and, for a brief moment, her eyes stopped darting long enough to hold mine. "Please."

I shrugged. Hell, I'm never going to see any of the potential eavesdroppers again. So what if they think I'm a loon?

It was early enough in the morning that the cafeteria was mostly empty. I caught snatches of conversation as we moved to a table at the far end of the room: a knot of people discussing something to do with Higgs bosons, whatever they were; two guys arguing about the Thunderbirds, which I gathered were the campus football team; and three women discussing in locker-room detail the physique of a new male coworker.

We found a table and sat down. I looked at the person seated opposite me, nervous and small. "Did you ever teach at Dalhousie?" I asked.

"Yes," she said, looking surprised at the question, "but I lost my job there—what?—sixteen years ago." She smiled for the first time, one academic to another sharing the universal lament. "Budget cuts."

She'd broken a police officer's shin there, the Canadian Press story had said. She looked too timid to do anything like that now. I wondered what had happened in the interim to take the fight out of her. "I'm sorry," I said.

Her voice was wistful. "So was I, Dr. Thackeray. Now, what can I do for you?"

Well, if she was uncomfortable with the intimacy of first names, I wasn't going to push it. "I've got a manuscript I'd like you to read. It's—it's my diary. Except I didn't write it. I—I don't know where it came from. I found it in my computer." I swallowed hard, then said it all in one breath. "It describes a journey back to the end of the Mesozoic Era, made possible by a device called a Huang temporal phase-shift habitat module." I saw her eyes widen, just for an instant. "The creator of that device is specifically referred to as Ching-Mei Huang." I pulled a sheaf of papers out of my briefcase. For a moment, I hesitated about handing the printout to her. There was so much in there that was personal to me—things about Tess, about Klicks, about myself. It was my *diary*, for Christ's sake! This was the first time I'd ever made a printout of anything from that memory wafer. I placed the papers on the tablecloth, laser-printed sheets in eleven-point Optima, the Royal Ontario Museum's official correspondence font. "Please keep this confidential."

She began reading. *"Fred, who lives down the street from me, has a cottage on Georgian Bay. One weekend he went up there alone and left his tabby cat back home with his wife and kids. The damned tabby—"*

"Not out loud, please."

"Sorry." She read in silence for a few minutes, then looked up, her face puzzled. "How did you know I'm an atheist?"

I thought back to what the diary said. *I was sure that little reference to God was for the sake of the network cameras. Ching-Mei was an atheist. She only had faith in empirical data, in experimental results.*

"I didn't know it, until I read it there."

She went back to reading, her brow furrowed. I occasionally looked over, reading upside down to see what part she was at. How I wished I had a technical document from—from whatever place this came from—instead of something that, almost incidentally, laid my soul bare.

I got up, crossed the room, and fed a five-dollar coin into a vending machine, which in return dispensed a couple of prepackaged donuts. When I returned, Ching-Mei was still reading, engrossed. At last, when she got to the end of the part about the twilight visit by the goose-stepping tyrannosaurs, she looked up, scanned the cafeteria, and saw that we were now alone in it, all the others having trickled out while she was reading. "I can't stay here any longer," she said, her voice nervous again.

"What about the diary?"

"I'll finish reading it tonight."

"Can I come by your house, then?"

"No. Meet me here tomorrow." And, before I knew what was happening, she had scurried out of the cafeteria like a frightened animal.

Countdown: 8

Oh, wad some power the giftie gie us
To see oursels as others see us!
                        —Robert Burns, Scottish poet (1759–1796)

The interior of the spherical Het spaceship was dimly lit by what appeared to be strips of bioluminescent dots along the walls. Once Klicks and I were inside the thing, it seemed less like a lifeform. However, it didn't seem like a spaceship, either. There were no right angles anywhere. Instead, floors gently curved into walls, which in turn melded smoothly into ceilings. Nor were there any corridors. Rather, rooms were honeycombed together, each with passageways to the adjacent ones not just on the same level but also above and below.

Most of the passages were permanently open—I supposed that beings without individuality had no need for privacy. A few chambers did have valve-like coverings; apparently those rooms were used for storage.

We saw dozens of brachiators, some walking, others swinging from stiff hoops that seemed to grow out of the roofs. There were also a couple of troödons on board, and countless Het jelly mounds pulsing about freely. The ship was cooler than anywhere we'd been since we'd arrived in the Mesozoic, and it was filled with a faint odor like wet newsprint.

"It's tremendous," Klicks said, gesturing about him. "When do we take off?"

The brachiator, its coppery coils of fur looking almost black in the faint light, made a facial gesture. "We did take off a short time ago," it said in its thin voice.

"Incredible," said Klicks. "I didn't feel a thing."

"Why would you want to feel anything during flight?"

Klicks looked at the creature's sausage-shaped eyes with their disquieting double pupils. "That's a very good question," he said with a grin. "Where are the windows?"

"Windows?"

"Portholes. Glassed-in areas. Places where you can see outside."

"We have nothing like that."

"You mean we don't get to feel anything and we don't get to see anything?" Klicks sounded sad. "And I thought Virtual Reality World was a rip-off . . ."

"We can let you look out if you desire so," said the brachiator.

"How?"

"There are eyes on the surface of the sphere. You merely have to meld with one."

"Meld?"

"Join minds with the ship. Share what it sees."

"Hold on," I said. "Does that mean more jelly in the head?"

"Yes," said the brachiator, "but not much."

I shuddered.

"We can enter you much less uncomfortably now," continued the Het. "We have a rough map of how your brains work. The area for processing visual information is located here." The brachiator arched its back so that one of its manipulatory appendages could reach me. A pink tentacle tapped the rear of my head near the base of my skull. I jumped at the touch.

"Uh, no thanks," I said.

"Oh, come on, Brandy," said Klicks. "It's not going to kill you." He turned to the brachiator. "What do I do?"

"Just sit down here. Put your back to the wall. Yes, like that." Behind Klicks's head, I saw some blue jelly seeping out of the wall. There must have been Hets throbbing their way throughout the structure of the ship. The jelly touched his nape just below the hairline. That was lower down than the visual cortex—oh, I see. It was going to enter the braincase through the foramen magnum. Clever.

"Are you okay?" I said to Klicks.

"Fine. It feels weird, but it's not painful. It's like—my God! That's beautiful! Brandy, you *have* to see this!"

"What?"

"We're kilometers high! It's breathtaking."

Against my better judgment, I sat down next to him, my back against the wall. I felt something warm and wet on my neck, but Klicks was right. It wasn't painful. Then I experienced a strange pressure along my cervical vertebrae. The brain itself has no internal sensors, and I could feel nothing as the tendril passed into it. Everything went black and for a panicky moment I thought that the Het had accidentally wrecked my visual cortex, rendering me blind. But before my panic grew too severe, something else was in my brain, another's thoughts, feelings, aspirations. They were dim shapes at first, shadowy forms, ghosts from somebody else's past. Slowly they took on substance. A black man, his face, although contorted by rage, strangely familiar. It was like Klicks's face, only different. Narrower, the eyes closer together, a scar on the forehead, a sparse beard. It hit me then: George Jordan, Klicks's father, looking thirty years younger than I'd ever seen him. He had liquor on his breath and he was towering over me, a leather belt in his hand. Oh, God, no! *Stop it! Stop it! Please, Daddy* . . .

Blackness again, the connection broken, the Het linking us perhaps realizing that it had made an error. Had Klicks seen into my mind as deeply as I had seen into his? What did he now know about me?

Suddenly I was falling through space, ground over my head, my body plummeting toward the stars. Faster and faster, falling, falling, falling . . .

The image flipped, the Het, I guess, realizing that the human mind normally inverts what it sees, since images focus upside down in our eyes. I was rising now, the ground receding beneath me, thin clouds rushing by, the sky growing nearer, blacker, clearer, colder.

Space. Christ, the things were taking us right up into orbit. Stars wheeled overhead, the Milky Way a thick band spinning like a bejeweled windmill's blade across my field of vision. It was magnificent: uncountable points of brightness piercing the dark, red and yellow and white and blue, strings of Christmas-tree lights across the firmament.

Rising over the limb of the Earth was the moon, gloriously gibbous, almost too bright to look at. It was still showing us a large part of what would someday be its backside. As we raced ahead, tiny Trick swept into view, too, here, above the atmosphere, cratering clearly visible on its face.

Soon the panorama was cut off from left to right, unbroken blackness swallowing the stars. We were swinging around to look down on Earth's nightside. But it wasn't completely dark—flickering lights were visible here and there. Forest fires, probably sparked by lightning storms.

We rushed toward the dawn, a glow clearly defining the sharp curve of the Earth's surface. Within minutes the sun was up again, a hot fire illuminating the globe.

Broadly speaking, Earth looked much as it did from modern space photos: a blue ball covered with twists of cottony whiteness. My eyes finally got used to the scale of the planet and began to make sense of the partially obscured continents. Their shapes had changed over the millennia, but I knew enough about tectonic drift to easily figure out which was which. There was Antarctica, a tiny white splotch much smaller than it is in the twenty-first century. Just splitting from it was Australia, turned at an odd angle. India was moving freely across the Tethys Ocean on its way toward its inevitable impact with Asia, the event that would push up the Himalayas. South America had only just begun to pull away from Africa, the perfect jigsaw-puzzle fit of their coastlines obscured slightly by a seaway that ran from where the Sahara Desert would one day be to the Gulf of Guinea. Another giant seaway, broken only by a long north-south archipelago, separated Europe from Asia. Between South America and North America was open ocean, thousands of times wider than the Panama Canal would one day be. Still, the Gulf of Mexico was clearly visible, and—

Christ.

Jesus Christ.

"Klicks!" I shouted.

"What?" said his voice.

"Look at the Gulf of Mexico!"

"Yeah?"

"Look at it!"

"I don't—"

"It's all on dry land," I said, "not half-submerged as it will be in our time, but, look—*it's already there."*

"What are you ta—oh. Oh, my God . . ." Klicks's voice was full of astonishment.

"Het!" I called out, wishing I had a name to use. "Het! Any Het!"

"Yes?" came the emaciated voice of a brachiator.

"How long has that crater been there?"

"Which crater?"

"The one on the rim of that large gulf at the southern end of the landmass we took off from. See it? It's about a hundred and fifty kilometers in diameter . . ." I wasn't that good at estimating distances from this high up, but I knew how big it *had* to be.

"Oh, that crater," said the voice, each word a distinct, separate sound. "It formed about ninety of our years ago—two hundred or so of yours."

"You're sure?" asked Klicks's voice.

"We had tracked the asteroid that made that crater. For a brief time we thought it might pass near Mars; as you may know, our two moons were once asteroids, captured by our gravity. But it did not come particularly close to us; instead, it struck your planet. The explosion was visually spectacular."

"But . . . but . . ." Klicks was trying to make sense of it. "But the impact that made that crater is what we'd thought had killed off the dinosaurs."

"An incorrect assumption," said the Martian, simply. "After all, the dinosaurs live on."

The best resolution in the geologic record this far back was maybe ten thousand years, and that only under extraordinary circumstances; a hundred thousand was much more common. Events that had occurred centuries or even millennia apart could easily seem simultaneous.

"The impact must have had a big effect on the biosphere, though," said Klicks, a note of desperation in his voice. I felt myself grinning from ear to ear.

"Not really," said the Het. "Those plants and animals at the crater site were destroyed, of course, but the worldwide effect was negligible." It paused. "Your people and mine inhabit the same messy solar system. Impacts happen—surely you know that. But life goes on."

I wished I could see the look on Klicks's face—but all I could see was the glorious planet below. We were whisking back toward the night, the terminator hurrying toward us. Our view swung back up to look at the stars. There were so many that discerning any pattern, anything that one might call a constellation, seemed impossible. I enjoyed the spectacle; Klicks had been in line to possibly go to Mars, but I'd never dreamed that I would see the stars from space. The sight was magnificent, breathtaking, truly the most beautiful thing I'd ever seen, and—

"What's that?" Klicks's voice intruded again from the outside world.

I scanned the heavens, trying to find whatever had caught his eye. There, far down in the southern sky: a tight rosette of brilliant blue points. I watched it as we swung around. The points didn't shift at all in relation to the background stars as we continued in our orbit, meaning they weren't nearby.

"What is that?" Klicks said again.

"What" "is" "what?" The reedy voice of the brachiator.

"That cluster of lights," said Klicks. "What is it?"

"We do not speak of it."

"You must know what it is."

"We do not."

"Is it in this solar system?"

"No. It is some three-to-the-fifth light-years away. Clarification: Martian light-years, and two hundred forty-three of them in your counting. About double that in Earth light-years."

"Then what is it?"

"It's a beacon, isn't it?" I said, surprising myself. "A visual signal to the rest of the galaxy that there's intelligent life there." The rosette was beautiful, with mathematically precise construction. "Look at it: the points are arranged in a geodesic. It'd look like a sphere from any angle. It has to be artificial."

I'd read about a similar idea years before, but on a much smaller scale. Some astronomer had suggested planting crops in giant geometric patterns across the face of Africa in hopes of signaling the presence of intelligence to anyone looking at Earth through a telescope. But this was so much more! A civilization that could arrange suns into patterns—it was mind-boggling. The rosette of lights would have been clearly visible from anywhere in Earth's southern hemisphere, or Mars's for that matter.

"It must have been wonderful having your society grow up with that in the sky," I said to the brachiator. "Incontrovertible proof that you weren't alone, that there are other, more advanced civilizations out there." I shook my head, the jelly connection with the wall making a squishy sound as I did so. "God, when I think of all the soul-searching that humans go through wondering if we're alone in the universe, if there's anyone else out there, if it's possible to survive technological adolescence. It must give you great comfort."

"*It galls us.*"

"But—"

Everything went black again. The Het oozed out of my neck. We returned to the ground in silence. I thought about the rosette of lights; about the Hets; about troödons, dinosaurs that might be on the way to developing intelligence of their own. It seemed that humanity had missed the heyday of sapient life in the galaxy by 60 or so million years. It was only because the Cretaceous-Tertiary extinctions wiped out the great reptiles that the second-string team, the mammals, had an opportunity to rise to the level of conscious thought, but by the time we did, the Milky Way was a much less crowded place. How could the Hets not be thrilled by the mere knowledge of the rosette-makers being out there somewhere?

I guess I'd offended them. Without a further word, they dumped us back at our campsite, now almost completely dark, our campfire having decayed to a few glowing coals. We watched from the ground as their pulsing sphere silently made its way off to the west, then we clambered in the darkness up the crater wall and went back into the *Sternberger*.

The sky was completely covered with clouds. Probably just as well. Now that we'd seen the heavens from above the obscuring cloak of Earth's atmosphere, the view from the ground—breathtaking though it had seemed last night—would pale in comparison. My only regret, though, was that the rosette would never be visible in this hemisphere. I'd love to have gotten a picture of it.

"Brandy," said Klicks, unbuttoning his shirt, "what do you know about how the Huang Effect works?"

I was gathering up my pajamas; I'd wanted to gloat a bit about the discovery that the Chicxulub crater predated the end of the dinosaurs, and wasn't surprised that Klicks was avoiding the topic, but, now that he mentioned it . . .

"So you've been thinking about that, too?" I said. "Christ, it's like a stupid commercial jingle. I can't get it out of my mind either. I keep running over what little I comprehend."

"Which is?"

"Diddly, really. I'm no physicist. Something to do with the tunnel-diode effect and, uh, tachyons. I think."

"Hmm," said Klicks. "That's more than I knew. Why do you suppose—?"

"Oh, good Christ! I knew those Martians weren't just being friendly neighbors. Klicks, they took us up, showed us some views of space to keep us preoccupied, then went sorting through our minds, looking for the secret of time travel."

"I bet they were disappointed when they didn't find it."

"I'm not sure anyone besides Ching-Mei understands it completely."

"Well," said Klicks, "you can't blame them, really. Besides, they'll have plenty of chances to ask her face-to-face once we bring them forward."

I looked at him, standing there across the room, arms folded across his chest. "Bring them forward?" I said, disbelief in my tone. "Klicks, they tried to steal the secret of time travel from us. And you still want to bring them forward?"

"Well, you seem incapable of making a decision one way or the other. Yes, I still want to bring them forward. Hell, we've *got* to bring them forward. It's the only reasonable thing to do."

"But they just tried to steal time travel from us! How can you trust them?"

"They also voluntarily exited our bodies. In fact, they've done that twice now. If they really were evil, they would have stayed in us tonight, and simply forced us to take them back to the future."

"Maybe. Maybe not. They know the Huang Effect won't reverse states for"—I glanced at my watch—"another, ah, sixty-three hours. Maybe they couldn't stay that long inside us even if they wanted to."

"You don't know that that's true," said Klicks.

"You don't know that that's *not* true."

He harrumphed.

"I wish we didn't have to make this decision," I said quietly.

"But we do," said Klicks.

My gaze shifted out the window. "Yes," I said at last. "I suppose we do."

Countdown: 7

O tempora! O mores!
Oh, what times! Oh, what morals!
> —Marcus Tullius Cicero, Roman orator (106–43 B.C.)

Klicks was driving me crazy with his cocksure attitude. Things were always so simple for him. For every political debate, for every moral question, he had a glib, pat answer. Should we legalize devices that directly stimulate the pleasure centers of the brain? What rights do genetically tinkered apes with the power of speech have? Should female priests be allowed to be surrogate mothers? Ask Klicks. He'll tell you.

Of course, his opinions on mindbenders are similar to those of the editorial writer for *The Calgary Herald.* His stance on simps bears a startling resemblance to that of Mike Bullard. And his viewpoint on celibate surrogates comes right out of that article in *Playboy.*

A deep thinker? Not Klicks. But he's smooth, oh so smooth. Microsoft mouse. "Miles is so articulate," Tess had said after the last New Year's Eve bash we'd given together, the same week that Klicks and I had been named as the crew for this mission. "He could charm the pants right off you."

And so he did.

I'd known him for years. I was even the one who gave him his nickname. How could he, he of all people, steal Tess from me? We had been friends. Friendship is supposed to mean something.

I found out that Klicks and Tess were together less than a month after I'd moved out of our house. Just when I needed my friends most, my best friend—practically my only friend— was off boffing my ex-wife. A man who would steal another man's wife doesn't worry about morality, doesn't weigh the principles, doesn't consider the repercussions, doesn't mull over the larger consequences. Doesn't give a bloody fuck at all.

And yet here he is, all set to grant a reprieve, to—I will say it again, dammit—to *play God* for an entire race.

We'd spent a lot of time in mission planning debating whether Klicks and I should always stay together. But since there was so little time and so much to do, it had been agreed that we'd have separate lists of tasks to perform. Each of us was armed and carried a radio, so the risk in separating seemed acceptable. Klicks had gone off after breakfast in our Jeep to find a good spot to take core samples. Now that we knew the asteroid had hit two centuries before the end of the Cretaceous, he wanted to collect some samples to see if the iridium, shocked quartz, and microdiamonds thought to be associated with the impact were indeed already present in Earth's rocks.

Klicks had set out toward the east. I headed west, ostensibly to examine some hills in that direction, but really just to put as much distance between him and me as possible.

The sun had reached its highest point in the sky, a hot orb that looked perhaps a tad whiter than it did in the twenty-first century. Insects buzzed around me in tiny black swarms. I wore a pith helmet with a cheesecloth rim that kept them away from my face, but their constant droning was giving me a headache.

The air was tormentingly hot; the vegetation lush, with vines hanging between stands of dawn redwood. I must have walked at least five kilometers from the *Sternberger*, but hadn't felt the distance in this light gravity. I looked over my shoulder, but trees obscured my view. No matter. I had a Radio Shack homing device to find my way back.

My head was still swimming from Klicks's insistence that we bring the Hets forward. I hated having to make big decisions. If you avoid them long enough, they go away.

Just like Dad will go away eventually.

Dr. Schroeder's voice echoed in my head, his Bavarian accent making the words harsher, colder: *Failing to act is a decision in and of itself.* Then the same words again, but in a lilting Jamaican accent: *Failing to act is a decision in and of itself.*

Screw Schroeder. Screw Klicks. There's nothing wrong with not liking to make hasty decisions.

Of course, I always end up buying whatever car the dealer has left on the lot from the previous model year so that I won't have to make all those choices about color and features. And it's true that I haven't voted in years. I've never been able to decide between the parties—but hell, who *can* tell them apart? There's nothing wrong with any of that, damn it all. One shouldn't make decisions until one is sure.

Besides, it's not as simple as Klicks made it out to be. Mars of our time is almost airless. Oh, we'd known for half a century that water had once run freely there, carving great valleys. The planet's atmosphere had been thicker, too, and had probably contained much oxygen. Perhaps Mars was quite pleasant during the Mesozoic. Indeed, it might—I thought of the emerald star I had seen the first night as I'd scanned along the ecliptic. Could it have been Mars, a younger, vibrant world alive with growing things? A planet of life, green with chlorophyll, blue with oceans? A sister to Earth, fully as glorious as this planet?

Perhaps.

But I was a prophet, able to foretell the future with absolute certainty. Mars was doomed, destined to become a stunted, barren dust bowl, cold and desolate, a realm of alien ghosts, a haunt for the memories of things long dead. Granted, no one had been there yet; the joint U.S.–Russia mission had been canceled when neither of them could come up with its share of the money. So it looked like no human being would make it farther than the moon in—well, in my lifetime, I guess. And more than half of Earth's population had been born after the last person had set foot there, back in 1972. Still, in a weird way, the moon was more inviting than Mars. Luna was sterile and pristine, but Mars was dead, decaying, an oppressive crypt, with the attenuated screams of chill winds raging across the landscape.

The two visions of Mars—one green, one red—could not be more different, and yet sometime in the next 60-odd million years one would give way to the other, that planet being laid waste. Mars would fall prey to some catastrophe even greater than the one that would wipe out the dinosaurs. Or perhaps it had been the same catastrophe. Maybe a great belch of radiation had been expelled from the sun on the side that happened to be facing Mars. If Earth had been on the opposite side of the sun, it might have felt comparatively minor effects by the time it passed through the dissipating cloud of charged particles six months later.

Still, dramatic though the mechanism of the Hets' demise might be, it didn't really matter what it was. The fact remained that Mars of my time was uninhabitable, what free oxygen there had once been now locked up in the rocks and ice. I still knew next to nothing about Het biology, but if they were comfortable on Earth now, they could probably no more live in the open on the Mars of the future than I could.

That meant that they'd have to stay on Earth. I could just see them being interviewed on *Good Morning America* and *Canada A.M.*, or being signed up as spokesthings for some headache pill. *Does your head feel like you've got one of us crawling around in your brain? Take Excedrin Plus and relax!*

But wait a minute. That wouldn't work, either. The gravity would be more than twice what they are used to, since sometime between this present and that present Earth's gravity increases to what I consider normal. Would it be enough to flatten out their jelly bodies, pinning them to the ground? Probably. And even if we did bring forward some of their dinosaur vehicles for them, they would be no good either, not having the musculature to hack a full *g*. What could the Hets use instead? Dogs? No manipulatory appendages. Apes? Watch the simian-rights lobby after it gets wind of that idea!

The kilometers added up as I continued my hike. The sky overhead was blue and cloudless, like that of a Toronto summer. The vegetation, though, was decidedly un-Canadian. It was lusher than anything I'd ever seen north of the thirty-fifth parallel: green shot through with a rainbow of flowers. When the insects relented enough for me to hear anything besides their buzzing, I occasionally detected a rustling among the plants. There were small animals about and I saw a great flock of a thousand or more violet pterosaurs at one point, but, as for dinosaurs, no luck.

God, it was hot out. But no, that couldn't be the problem. I reminded myself that Torontonians are supposed to be impervious to shifts in temperature. We always blame our discomfort on something else. In winter we say, "It's not the cold, it's the wind." In summer our lament becomes, "It's not the heat, it's the humidity."

Well, whether it was temperature or moisture that was at fault I didn't know, but I was sweating like the proverbial pig. And, indeed, there was a third potential culprit—exertion. I suddenly realized that the ground tilted up at a sharp angle. I must have gained more than thirty meters in elevation already. Although we'd been able to make only rough guesses about what the landscape would be like here in the late Cretaceous, we'd expected a uniformly flat terrain at this particular site. Certainly there was no trace in the geological record of a steep hill.

I decided to rest upon a boulder. Like everything in this landscape, even this rock teemed with life: it was covered with a blanket of moss so dark green as to be almost black.

It seemed peaceful here, what with all this unspoiled nature, and yet I knew the peace was illusory, that the wild world was a violent place, a gridiron of mindless brutes fighting a game of kill or be killed in which there were no time-outs, no substitutions, and, in the long run, no way for you or even your species to win.

But still I felt a strange calmness. There was a simplicity here, a sense of great burdens lifted from my shoulders, a feeling that a yoke that I—and all humankind—had worn throughout our lives was somehow gone. Here, in the innocence of Earth's youth, there was no unending famine in Ethiopia, with children, in one of anatomy's cruel jokes, looking potbellied as their guts distended with hunger. There were no race wars in Africa, no burning of synagogues in Winnipeg, no Ku Klux Klan in Atlanta. No poverty in New York City, growing worse year by year, gangs no longer content just to kill their victims, now actually eating them, too. No knife-wielding thugs slashing the throats of cabdrivers in Toronto. No mindbenders starving to death while juice trickled into their brains. No blood washing down the streets of the Holy Land. No threat of nuclear terrorism hanging over all our heads like a glowing sword of Damocles. No murderers. No molesters robbing sons and daughters of their very childhood. No rapists taking with force what should only be given with love.

No people.

Not a soul in the world.

Not a soul . . .

An inner voice came to me, rising tenuously from that part of my mind that knew that it normally had to keep such ideas hidden, buried, lest it reveal itself to those who ran the world, those who saw such notions as signs of weakness.

What about God? said the voice. What role did he play in all this? Was there even a God? Klicks said no, of course. An easy enough decision, logically arrived at, based on science and reason. But I could never be so sure. I'd never allowed myself to truly believe, and yet I'd never been able to close my mind to the possibility, to the hope, that in fact the lives of us little people did, in reality, amount to more than a hill of beans in this crazy world.

I'd never prayed in my life—not seriously anyway. With six billion other souls to worry about, why should God care about the concerns of one Brandon Thackeray, a fellow who had a roof over his head, plenty to eat, and a good job? But now, in this world devoid of people, perhaps, just perhaps, it was a good time to bend God's ear. Who knows? I might even get his full and undivided attention.

But ... but ... but ... this was silly. Besides, I really didn't know how to pray. No one had ever taught me. My father is a Presbyterian. He'd had an antique prayer rug by his bed, but I never knew whether he used it. When I was little I sometimes heard mumbling coming from his room as he got ready for bed. But my father often mumbled under his breath. Or else, he would grumble, and my world would shake.

My mother had been a Unitarian. I had gone to their Sunday school for five years as a child, if you can call a series of field trips that started from the North York YMCA a Sunday school. They used to take us for walks by the Don River, and I got soakers. All that I learned about God was that if you wanted to get closer to him, you'd probably end up with wet socks. Once, when I was an adult, an acquaintance had asked me what Unitarians believed in. I didn't have a clue; I had to look it up in an encyclopedia.

Well, perhaps the form of the prayer didn't matter. Did I have to speak out loud? Or was God a telepath, plucking thoughts from our heads? Upon reflection, I hoped the latter was not the case.

I reached up to my lapel, thumbed the MicroCam off, then cleared my throat. "God," I said quietly, feeling sure that although perhaps the words had to be spoken, there was no reason to think the Good Lord was hard of hearing. I was silent for several seconds, listening to the word echo in my head. I couldn't believe I was doing this. But then again, I knew I'd never forgive myself for not trying if I didn't take advantage of this unique opportunity. "God," I said again. And then, at a loss for what should come next, "It's me, Brandy Thackeray."

I was quiet for a few seconds more, but this time it was because I was listening intently, both within and without, for any acknowledgment that my words were being heard. Nothing. Of course.

And yet I felt as if a gate within me had burst open. "I'm so confused," I said into the wind. "I—I've tried to live a good life. I really have. I've made mistakes, but—"

I paused, embarrassed by this babbling start, then began again. "I can't fathom why my life is falling apart. My father is dying the kind of death we all hope to be spared. He was a good man. Oh, I know he cheated on his taxes and maybe even on his wife, and he hit her once, but only just that once, but now you're punishing him in a way that seems cruel."

Insects buzzed; foliage rustled in the breeze.

"I'm suffering right along with him. He wants me to release him from all that, to let him die peacefully, quietly, with a modicum of dignity. I don't know what's right and what's wrong here. Can't you take him? Can't you let him die quickly instead of robbing him of his strength but leaving his mind to feel pain, to suffer? Can't you—won't you—relieve me of having to make this decision? And will you forgive me if I can't find the strength within myself to choose?"

I was suddenly aware that my face was wet, but it felt good, oh so good, to get this off my chest. "And, as if that wasn't enough to put me through, now you've taken Tess from me, too. I love her. She was my life, my whole existence. I can't seem to find the energy to go on by myself anymore. I want her back so very much. Is Klicks a better son to you than I? He seems so . . . so shallow, so unthinking. Is that what you want from your children?"

The word "children" triggered a thought in my mind. God's putative son, Jesus, wouldn't be born for almost 65 million years. Did God know how the future would go? Or did the Huang Effect supersede even his omniscience? Should I tell him what would happen to his beloved Jesus? Or was he aware already? Was it inevitable that humans would reject his son? I opened my mouth to speak, but then closed it and said nothing.

A twig cracked and my heart jumped. For one horrible instant I thought that Klicks had followed me, had overheard me, had seen me making a bloody fool of myself. I looked into the forest but couldn't see anything unusual. Clearing my mind, I quickly rose to my feet, brushed pieces of moss off my bum, and headed forward.

Countdown: 6

The present contains nothing more than the past, and what is found in the effect was already in the cause.
—Henri Bergson, French philosopher (1859–1941)

The sun was sliding slowly down the bowl of the sky. My watch still showed modern Alberta time, but it looked to be about 3:30 P.M. My nose was a bit stuffed, perhaps from crying but just as likely from the pollens. Little golden motes and things like dandelion seeds danced in the air all about me. I saw a small tortoise at one point, pushing itself with splayed, wrinkly limbs across my path. It seemed ironic that such a humble creature would survive the coming changes that would kill every last one of the magnificent dinosaurs. Like Aesop's fable: slow and steady wins the race.

Suddenly the ground dropped away. I was at the lip of a sheer precipice of crumbling reddish-brown earth, a sawtoothed row of various hardwood stumps lining its edge. Without any warning, I'd come across a valley, perhaps a kilometer long and half that in width. It looked like an open-pit mine, gouged out of the Earth, an incongruous landscape wound amidst the unspoiled wilderness.

And it was full of dinosaurs.

It was a paleontologist's dream, or most other people's nightmare. Two—no, three *Triceratopses*. An equal number of small tyrannosaurs, and one monster even bigger than the T. rex Klicks and I had seen yesterday afternoon. A herd of ostrich-like ornithomimids. Four duck-billed hadrosaurs.

Two of the hadrosaurs looked to be the genus *Edmontosaurus*, the quintessential duckbill, with the keratin sheaths at the fronts on their shovel-like prows looking like black lipstick. The other pair of duckbills had head crests, a rare occurrence this late in the Cretaceous. These crests were unlike any I had seen before: one tubular projection going straight up, another, longer one, parallel to the animal's back. Three of the four hadrosaurs were walking away from me on splayed feet and mitten-like hands, their thick, flattened tails held stiffly above the ground, great bellies swinging back and forth like pendulums. The fourth, one of the edmontosaurs, had risen on its hind legs and was dully surveying its surroundings.

Dancing around the valley were several dozen troödons. About two-thirds of them were the same bright green as the ones we'd met earlier, but the rest were smaller and more brown in color. Males, probably. A group of them—three males and two females—galloped toward the valley's far wall, their clawed bird-feet kicking up small clouds of dust. They covered the five hundred meters in a time short enough to make even an Olympic gold medalist seem like a slowpoke. Their goal was a cluster of stationary objects that I hadn't noticed before: three giant tawny spheres, a trio of those strange breathing Martian spaceships resting on their amorphous slug feet.

Where my wits had been for the last few minutes I didn't know, but they finally came home to roost. I realized that I was inadvertently spying on an encampment of the Hets. If I was going to do that, I figured I'd better not be seen. I dropped to my belly, the buzz of insects abating for a moment as the confused creatures were left in a cloud around where my head had been.

Christ, my MicroCam! The thing was still off. I fumbled for the switch, then lifted the cheesecloth to wipe sweat from my brow. It was as hot as hell out here. I propped my binoculars in front of my face, resting their weight on my elbows, and twiddled with the knob to bring one of the Het ships into focus. It was indeed the same type of vehicle Klicks and I had ridden in last night: sixty meters across, covered with hexagonal scales, pulsing with respiration.

A plaintive cry split the air, a throaty dirge that seemed to tremble with an equal mixture of pain and sadness. I scanned the valley. A huge, blood-red tyrannosaur was squatting in the sand. A thick yellowish-white sausage dropped from between its legs and I realized that it—*she*—was laying eggs. No sooner had the soft-shelled package rolled onto the earth than a wiry troödon darted between her massive thighs and scooped it up, running with it up the broad tongue and into the vertical mouth slit of one of the spherical ships.

The hapless tyrannosaur was probably under Het control— I doubted any beast would otherwise lay eggs out in the open like that. But despite the Martian within, it let out another heart-wrenching yell, the cry of a mother who had just lost her child—a stronger display of maternal love than I ever thought I'd see from a Mesozoic carnivore. A few minutes later, with visible effort, it squeezed out another egg. This one was also promptly seized in the opposable digits of a troödon and whisked into the spaceship. I commiserated with the giant reptile. To have something you loved snatched away hurt, I knew, more than any physical injury . . .

I shook my head, trying to fling the tormenting thoughts out of my skull. The movement startled the insects that had landed on the cheesecloth around my pith helmet into buzzing flight.

I forced my attention onto one of the triceratopses. Charles R. Knight, the father of scientific dinosaur illustration, always painted triceratops so that it resembled a tank. Like many paleontologists, I first became interested in dinosaurs as a child, seeing Knight's century-old paintings in a book. It was uncanny how much three-horned-face looked like Knight's renditions of him: quadrupedal, that great bony frill with a fluted rim around the thick neck, two massive white horns sticking straight out above the beady eyes, a third, shorter horn projecting from above the parrot-like beak. But the beast had adornments that had been unknown in Knight's time, since all he'd had to go by were heavily eroded specimens. Tiny horns pointed downward from the corners of the skull over the jaw hinges, more tiny horns aimed backward from where the eye horns met the bony frill. The perimeter of the frill was lined with squat triangular spikes, giving it a chainsaw edge. The beast measured a good six meters in length from the tips of its eye horns to the end of its stubby tail. But whereas Knight's triceratopses had plain dun-colored skin, this one's leather hide was greenish blue dappled with large orange splotches. The design reminded me of—what? Camouflage? Not in that garish color scheme, but the pattern was right.

Suddenly the triceratops I was looking at moved out of my binoculars' field of vision. By the time I had refocused on it, it had turned around so that it was facing the other way, its left side to me instead of its right. I put the binoculars down and saw that the two other horned-faces were falling in beside this one, their array of facial armament pointing forward like jousters' lances. One of the beasts was pawing the ground with its stubby foreleg, looking for all the world like a bull about to charge.

I glanced toward the far end of the valley and my jaw dropped. Three mechanical tanks, each one just a tad smaller than the horned dinosaurs, had appeared near the Het ships. Flat, beetle-shaped, they were painted in a cool aquamarine shot through with veins of red, a color scheme very close to that worn by the triceratopses. On a tank, this *surely* was camouflage, meaning—meaning what?

Each tank sported a tapering crystal tube, presumably a gun, mounted on a hemispherical turret. The tanks must have come from within the ships, for all three of the pulsing spheres now had their thick-lipped mouths open and their gray access tongues stretched out to the ground.

These tanks were the first machines I'd seen with the Hets, and they seemed incongruous with the living spaceships and dinosaur vehicles, almost as if they belonged to some other alien technology. That impression was reinforced as I noticed that one of the tanks had an open door on its curving side. Although the door measured about two meters by one, the right proportions to comfortably allow a Het riding inside its trusty troödon or brachiator to enter, it was oriented the wrong way, with the long axis parallel to the ground. There was another door just inside the first, forming an airlock-like chamber.

The triceratopses now stood one hundred meters from the tanks, as if waiting for some signal. Many of the other dinosaurs had walked to the near end of the valley, except for poor old mother tyrannosaur. She was flopped on her belly near the spaceships, apparently too tired to move.

It soon became apparent which of the beasts were currently Het-ridden. The trio of small tyrannosaurs stood in rapt attention, as did the giant female T. rex. Perhaps these great theropods were too dangerous to ever let run free. By contrast, the placid hadrosaurs seemed to be unoccupied. One was defecating. Another had ambled off and was using its shovel-like bill to sift through the dirt of the valley floor, apparently looking for roots. About half of the ornithomimids, looking like plucked ostriches, were likely hosting Hets, for they were looking intently at the tableau of tanks and triceratopses. The other half were busy grooming themselves or each other. As for the troödons, most had their bright eyes riveted to the scene in front of them.

Everyone was clearly waiting for somebody to make the first move. The anticipation—of what, I still did not know—was palpable, and I found myself holding my breath. Seconds passed, the buzz of insects in my ears like the drone of an electric motor.

Suddenly the middle tank squeezed off a crystalline projectile. It was hard to see, just a glint of light as it arced through the air. As soon as they heard the gun's report—a reverberating metallic sound like sheet metal being warped—the trio of horned dinosaurs burst into action. They moved with surprising speed for animals of their bulk, musculature rippling under their gaudy hides. Magnificent, energetic beasts! Even this far away, I felt a rumbling in the soil beneath my belly as they ran. One veered to the right, its body snapping to the side like a sprung mousetrap. The second continued its forward charge, but weaving in a complex pattern as it did so, a mad dance to which only it could predict the next step. The third triceratops, much to my surprise, reared on its hind legs, like a horse whinnying, and let out a multi-note roar. It dropped back to all fours and deked left. The projectile hit where this one would have been if it hadn't changed course, sending up a cloud of dirt.

The one who'd almost been killed charged even faster, its legs pumping beneath its body. It escaped a second impact by once again rising up on its hind legs, the crystal shell exploding in front of it. Red slice marks appeared on its lean belly as shards carved into the beast's hide. With its one-ton frilled head lowered and eye horns pointing dead ahead, it rammed into the beetle-like tank. The horns pierced the tank's plating and there was a sound like a pop can opening as pressure equalized.

The triceratops dug in its forelegs, dropped to its rear knees, and arched its powerful neck, tendons distending, muscles bulging. With massive grunts, it lifted the tank impaled on its horns a meter off the ground and then quickly smashed it down. It did this twice more in rapid succession, and the tank's hull cracked like an eggshell. Through the broken casing I could see the interior. It was made of an iridescent, amber-colored metal.

Meanwhile, the remaining two tanks were pumping off rounds of glassy ammunition, the *whoomp-whoomp-whoomp* of their report echoing off the valley walls. The vehicles apparently could move in any direction, sliding left and right, forward and backward with ease. The other two ceratopsians danced to avoid the shells.

One triceratops saw an opening as the transparent gun tube that had been trained on it swung away to take a bead on another horned-face. It charged, head low, bringing its eye horns underneath the tank's lens-shaped body. With a quick movement, it flipped the vehicle onto its back. The tank's underbelly, made of that same amber metal, was tightly packed with glistening meter-wide ball bearings, explaining its agility.

I glanced at the watching gallery. Even the unoccupied hadrosaurs had become intrigued by the battle, for they had risen on their hind legs, their tails bending stiffly against the ground. The Het-ridden beasts stood quietly, though, nothing giving away the thoughts of the aliens within them.

Evidently one of the triceratopses had let its attention wander from the fight for a second as well, for I swung my binoculars back just in time to see a crystal projectile explode in a flash of green light against its face. The detonation smashed its neck frill, snapping off its nasal and right-eye horns. They flew into the air like white missiles. Slick with blood, half its skull gone, the thing still managed to charge. How could it move with its brain—? Of course. A Het rode within the animal. It must be farther back, perhaps stretched out along the spinal cord to better control the creature's body. I imagined it would be under a lot of pressure now, having to take over the hornedface's autonomic functions, which must have been about all the beast's fist-sized brain had been good for anyway. A lumbering corpse, the injured horned-face slammed into the side of the tank, which spun away under the force of the impact.

The triceratops that had earlier impaled a tank had managed to disentangle its face from the twisted wreckage and it, too, charged the remaining armored vehicle. Rearing up on its hind legs, it made a quick, sheering bite with its parrot-like beak, snipping off the crystal gun tube. The two uninjured triceratopses shouldered against the tank, pushing it toward the far valley wall.

The half-headless beast, apparently blind, had collapsed onto its belly, its forelimbs twisted at an angle that would have been excruciating had the animal still possessed a mind with which to register pain. I zoomed in on its shattered skull and saw a phosphorescent blue lump the size of a beach ball— much larger than any of the Hets I had yet seen—oozing out of the splintered bone onto the blood-saturated soil.

I turned back to the remaining tank. The two triceratopses were still butting it with their shoulders, the lens-shaped body denting slightly each time they hit it. Within minutes the dinosaurs had rammed the beetle-like vehicle against the sheer wall of the valley. I lowered my binoculars and surveyed the scene: one tank smashed, another flipped on its back, and a third taken prisoner. Incredible.

I snapped off rolls of still pictures—I'd left our electronic camera back at the *Sternberger*—but I knew nonetheless that I'd have a hard time convincing Klicks of what I'd seen.

Triceratops fossils represented three-quarters of all dinosaurian finds from Alberta and Wyoming during the last million years of the Cretaceous. I tried to imagine what kind of destruction a herd—an assault force—of these great beasts could inflict. That rasping voice of the Martian Het, spoken around bloody spit through the troödon's mouth, came back to me. "We, too, came to this place because of the life here."

I'll say.

Boundary Layer

I claim not to have controlled events, but confess plainly that
events have controlled me.
　　　—Abraham Lincoln, 16th American President (1809–1865)

I sat alone in the TRIUMF staff cafeteria for a while, nib-
bling at one of my stale vending-machine donuts, trying
to understand why Dr. Huang had run off. It didn't make any
sense.

I threw out the second donut and made my way out of the
room. I had a whole day to kill waiting for Ching-Mei to finish
reading the diary, so I decided to take a tour of the research facility. I identified myself to the old man at the front desk as a
curator from the Royal Ontario Museum and suddenly found
the red carpet being rolled out for "a distinguished visiting scientist." That was great because it meant that I got to see areas
normally closed to the public.

My guide, an enthusiastic young Native Canadian named
Dan Pitawanakwat, wanted to be sure I understood everything I saw, but most of it still went over my head. He showed
me giant 30,000-kilogram magnets that looked like yellow Pac-
Man characters, a room full of bright blue consoles with models
of famous movie starships, including the *Enterprise-F, Starplex,*
and the *Millennium Falcon* hanging by fishing line from the
ceiling, and a Positron Emission Tomography scanner, used to
take pictures of the insides of people's brains. But the most interesting thing to me was the Batho Biomedical Facility, where
cancer patients received concentrated beams of pions. According to Dan, this method caused less general damage than con-
ventional radiation therapy. I watched, riveted, as a man lay
under the pion beam for treatment of a brain tumor. His face
was held steady by a transparent mask. The plastic obscured

his features and my mind kept superimposing my father's own craggy visage onto the head. It brought back the suffering and the torture and the loss of human dignity that Dad was going through. When they finally did remove the mask, I saw that the hairless head beneath belonged to a boy perhaps sixteen years old. I had to look away from the effusive Dan to wipe my eyes.

Later on, I said, "Dan, do they do any studies here about the nature of time?"

"Well, the thrust these days is always toward practical applications," he said. "That's the only way we can get the grant money to keep coming in." But then he nodded. "However, we've typically got four hundred researchers here at once, so some of them are bound to be doing work in that area. But it was really Ching-Mei's—Dr. Huang's—forte. She even wrote a book on it with Dr. Mackenzie."

"Time Constraints: The Tau of Physics." I nodded knowingly and was pleased to see that the young man was impressed. "But that was ten years ago. What's happened since?"

"Well, when I came here in 2005, everybody thought Ching-Mei was going to make some kind of breakthrough. I mean, there was talk of a trip to Stockholm, if you catch my drift." He winked.

"You mean her work was important enough to win her a Nobel Prize?"

"That's what some people were saying. 'Course, she probably would have shared it with Almi at the Weizmann Institute in Israel—he was doing similar work. But he was killed in that freak earthquake, and nobody there was able to pick up where he left off."

"That's a shame."

"It's a friggin' crime is what it is. Almi was the new Einstein, as far as a lot of us were concerned. We may never recover what he knew."

"And what happened here? Why did Ching-Mei give up her research? Wasn't it going anywhere?"

"Oh, it was going places, all right. There was a rumor that she was close to demonstrating a stopped-time condition. But, well, then she . . ."

"She what?"

"You're a good friend of hers, aren't you, sir?"

"I came all the way from Toronto just to see her."

"So you know about her troubles."

"Troubles?"

Dan looked uncomfortable, as if he'd put his foot in something distasteful. I held him in my gaze.

"Well," he said at last, "don't tell anybody, because I'll get into a lot of trouble if you do, but, well, something bad happened to Ching-Mei about five years ago." Dan looked over his shoulder to see if anybody was listening. "I mean, she never talked about it to me, but the gossip got around." He shook his head. "She was attacked, Dr. Thackeray. Raped. Absolutely brutalized. She was in the hospital for a week afterward, and away on—you know what they call it—on 'rest leave' for the better part of a year. They say he attacked her for three hours solid and, well, he used a knife. She was all torn up, you know, *down there*. She's lucky to be alive." He paused for a long moment. "Except, she doesn't really seem to think that."

I winced. "Where did it happen?"

"In her house." Dan sounded sad. "She's never been the same since. Frankly, she doesn't do much of anything anymore. Her job is mostly scheduling other people's access to the cyclotron, instead of doing any original work of her own. They keep her on here, hoping that one day the old Ching-Mei will come back, but it's been five years now." He shook his head again. "It's tragic. Who knows what she would have come up with if that hadn't happened?"

I shook my head, too, trying to clear the mental picture of that defenseless woman being violated. "Who knows, indeed?" I said at last.

I went to TRIUMF again first thing the next morning. This time, strangely, Dr. Huang did invite me into her little office. There were awards and diplomas on the walls, but none with recent dates. Books and papers were piled everywhere. As soon as I'd entered, we realized there was a problem: the office only had one chair in it.

"I'm sorry, Dr. Thackeray. It's been a long time since I've had a visitor here." She disappeared out the door and returned a few minutes later wheeling a stenographer's chair in front of her. "I hope this will do."

I sat down and looked at her expectantly.

"I'm sorry about you and your wife," she said abruptly.

"We're still together."

"Oh. I'm glad. You obviously love her immensely."

"That I do." There was silence for a time. "You've read the entire diary?"

"I have," she said. "Twice."

"And?"

"And," she said slowly, "based on dozens of little details that you couldn't have possibly known, I believe it is genuine. I believe it really does describe what my studies would have made possible."

I sat up straight. "Then you could go back to your research! You could make stasis and then time travel possible. Hell, Ching-Mei, you could win your Nobel Prize!"

"No." Her face had lost all color. "That's over. Dead."

I looked at her, still not comprehending. She seemed so delicate, so fragile. Finally, softly, I said, "Why?"

She looked away and I could see that she was rallying some inner strength. I waited as patiently as I could and, after a minute, she went on. "Physicists and paleontologists," she said. "In a way, we're both time travelers. We both hunt backward for the very beginnings."

I nodded.

"As a physicist, I try to understand how the universe came into being. As a paleontologist, you're interested in how life began." She spread her arms. "But the fact is, both fields of endeavor come up short when you go right back. The origin of matter has never been satisfactorily explained. Oh, we talk vaguely about random quantum-mechanical fluctuations in a vacuum somehow spontaneously having given rise to the first matter, but we really don't know."

"Uh-huh."

"And," she continued, "you can read the fossil record back to almost the beginning of life, but as to how life actually arose, again, no one is really sure. We speak nebulously about self-replicating macromolecules supposedly arising spontaneously through some random series of events."

"What are you talking about?" I said, baffled by where all this was going.

"I'm talking about time travel, Dr. Thackeray. I'm talking about why time travel is *inevitable*."

She'd lost me completely. "Inevitable?"

"It *had* to come into existence. The future must be able, with hindsight, to rewrite the past." She leaned forward slightly in her chair. "Someday we'll be able to create life in the laboratory. *But* we will only be able to do it by reverse-engineering existing life. Something as complex as the universe, as complex as life, *has* to be reverse-engineered. It has to be built from a known model."

"Not the first time, obviously."

"Yes," she said, "*especially* the first time. That's the whole point. Without time travel, life is impossible."

"You mean someone from the future went back into the past and created life?"

"Yes."

"And he knew how to do it because he had the lifeforms from his time as models to study?"

"Yes."

I shook my head. "That doesn't make sense."

"Yes, it does. For years, physicists have bandied about something called the strong anthropic principle. It says the universe must—*must*—be constructed in such a way so as to give rise to intelligent life. The purpose of the anthropic principle was to explain the existence of our unlikely universe, which has a number of remarkable coincidences about it, all of which were required for us to be possible."

"For instance?"

Ching-Mei waved her hand. "Oh, just as one of a great many examples, if the strong nuclear force were even five percent weaker than it is in this universe, protons and neutrons couldn't bind together and the stars wouldn't shine. On the other hand, if the strong force were just a little more powerful than it is in this universe, then it could overcome the electrical repulsion between protons, allowing them to bind directly together. That would make the kind of slow hydrogen burning that stars do impossible; instead, hydrogen clouds would explode long before they could coalesce into stars."

"I think I'm getting a headache."

She smiled ever so slightly. "That goes with the territory."

"You're saying someone from the future went back in time four billion years and created the first life on Earth."

"That's right."

"But I thought the Huang Effect could only go back—what did the diary say?—a hundred and four million years."

"The Huang Effect was a first-generation time machine, created for a very specific purpose. It might not be the only or the best solution to the problem of time travel."

"Hmm. Okay. But it's not just the creation of life you're talking about."

"No."

"You're also saying that someone from the future—the very far future, I'd guess—went right back to the beginning, back some fifteen billion years, and *created* matter."

"That's right."

"Created it, with exactly the properties needed to give rise to us, having learned how to do so by studying the matter from his or her own time."

"Yes."

I felt slightly dazed. "That's mind-boggling. It's like— like . . ."

"It's like we're our own God," said Dr. Huang. "We created ourselves in our own image."

"Then what about the *Sternberger*?"

"You've read the diary. You know what that other version of you does in the end."

"Yes, but—"

"Don't you see?" she said. "The *Sternberger* mission was only one of many instances in which time travel was used to set things right. The flow of events requires periodic adjustment. That's chaos theory for you: you can't accurately predict the development of any complex system. Therefore, you can't just create life and leave it to evolve on its own. Every once in a while you have to give it a push in the direction you want it to go."

"So—so you're saying that someone determined that the timeline had to be altered in order to give rise to us?"

"That's right," she said.

"But the time-traveling Brandy wrote that he could hunt dinosaurs, or do anything else, with impunity—that any changes he made wouldn't matter."

"I'm sure he believed that—he had to, of course, or he never would have done the things that needed doing. It was crucial that he believe that lie. But he was wrong. There was a mathematical string between the *Sternberger* in the past and the launch point in the present. The changes he made did indeed work their way up that string, altering the timeline as they did so, rewriting the last sixty-five million years of Earth's history, making our world possible. By the time the string had been hauled all the way back to 2013, the conditions that had given rise to the *Sternberger* had been eliminated, and our version of the timeline existed instead."

I sagged against the padded back of the steno chair. "Wow."

"Wow, indeed."

"And the other you who invented the time machine?"

She looked down. "I'm clever, but not that clever. I think it was more likely that its birth was induced."

"Induced?"

"Made to happen. The technique must have somehow been given to me from the future, perhaps by little clues or experiments that went a seemingly serendipitous way."

"But why you? Why now?"

"Well, here near the beginning of the twenty-first century we're probably at the very earliest point in human history at which a time machine could be built, the very earliest that the technology existed to put the parts together, even if we couldn't really understand the theory behind those parts. In fact, it was necessary that we *not* fully understand it, that the time-traveling Brandy believe that he'd spin off a new time-line, which he would then abandon, rather than actually change the one and only real timeline."

"So you don't know how to make a time machine anymore."

"No. But there was one. It did exist. The *Sternberger* did go back into the past, did change the course of prehistory in such a way as to make our present existence possible."

"But then what happened to that other Brandy? That other you?"

"They existed long enough to make a midstream correction, to steer the timeline in the way it was meant to go."

"Meant to go? Meant to go by—by the powers that be?"

She nodded. "By what we will become. By God. Call it what you will."

My head was swimming. "I still don't get it."

"Don't you? The trip by the *Sternberger* was necessary to adjust things, but it also means that there's no way another time-travel mission from this present to that part of the past could ever be made to happen again. Once the correction had been made, once the temporal surgery had been performed, the—the incision, shall we call it?—the incision would be sutured up, to prevent any further tampering, lest the correction be undone." She sounded wistful. "I can't ever build another time machine, and you can't ever travel in time again. The universe would conspire to prevent it."

"Conspire? How?" And then it hit me. "Oh my God. Oh, Ching-Mei, I'm sorry. I'm so terribly, terribly sorry."

She looked up, a tightly controlled expression on her face. "So am I." She shook her head slowly, and we both pretended not to notice the single teardrop that fell onto the desk. "At least Dr. Almi was killed quickly in that earthquake." We sat in silence for a long, long moment. "I wish," she said very softly, "that that had been what had happened to me."

Countdown: 5

Being entirely honest with oneself is a good exercise.
  —Sigmund Freud, Austrian psychoanalyst (1856–1939)

My Radio Shack homing device guided me through the Mesozoic heat back toward the *Sternberger,* an arrowhead on the unit's LCD showing the direction from which it was receiving radio beeps. It wasn't taking me along the same route I'd used going out, meaning, I guess, that I hadn't ambled in a straight line. No matter. I didn't mind cutting through the forest, since the shade shielded me from the inferno of the late-afternoon sun.

Klicks and I both carried portable radios, of course, but what I had to discuss with him required a face-to-face meeting. Even then, it would be hard to convince him of the incredible spectacle I'd just witnessed.

And yet, exactly what had I seen? A fight involving animals? They still allow bullfights in Spain, and just the week before we'd left, I'd read about a dog-fighting club in Oakville being charged by the local police. If the Hets had stumbled onto humans involved in those cruel sports, what would they have made of us?

But no. What I'd observed was clearly something more, something on a grander, sicker scale.

War games.

But who could they be fighting? What kind of squat, low foe had those mechanical-tank doorways originally been designed to accommodate? That the beetle-like vehicles weren't of Martian manufacture I felt sure. Captured war machines, then— spoils of some previous skirmish, now used to train living armored vehicles. The triceratopses were clearly expendable.

Het slimeballs rode within them, jerking the dinosaurs' strings like dragon marionettes.

Was there another civilization on Earth at this time? Had the Hets come here to invade this planet? My sympathies immediately went to the beleaguered Earth beings, a knee-jerk reaction. But it all seemed so incredible, and so unlikely. In China, in Russia, in Australia, in Italy, in England, in the United States, and in Canada paleontologists had examined rocks from the end of the Mesozoic, painstakingly sifting for even the smallest bone chip. It was inconceivable that the remnants of a large-scale technological civilization could pass unnoticed through such scrutiny. But, then, who were the Hets fighting?

I was having trouble thinking clearly—my head pounded with an ache brought on by the heat. The backs of my hands were tingling and I realized too late that they, the only exposed skin on my body, had been sunburned. The presence of all these deciduous trees seemed clear evidence that seasons were well established by this point in Earth's history, but we must have arrived in high summer. To make matters worse, somehow an insect had gotten under my cheesecloth face mask and bitten my neck, the puncture swelling and itching.

As I made my way back, I came across a couple of wild hadrosaurs, spatulate bills nipping in and out of clusters of pine needles, the horny sheaths impervious to the sharp jabs. Their up-and-down chewing, so unlike a cow's, made sounds similar to wood rasps as the batteries of thousands of flat molars ground the foliage and small cones. This was the closest I'd come to any large living dinosaurs outside of the protection of the Jeep. I could hear their stomachs rumbling and was made woozy by the pungent methane wind they gave off.

I also ran into my first mammal, a chocolate-colored furball with long limbs, a naked rat-like tail, and an inquisitive chipmunk face, complete with little triangular ears on top. Mammalian paleontology wasn't my field, but I fancied that this little beast might even have been *Purgatorius*, the first primate,

known from a lot of Paleocene material from nearby Montana
and from one admittedly contested tooth from the very end of
the Cretaceous.

We regarded each other for thirty seconds or so, the mammal's quick black eyes locked with mine. For me, it was a special moment, meeting my great-to-the-nth grandfather, and I
kidded myself that the little proto-monkey sensed our kinship,
too, for he didn't scamper away until one of the hadrosaurs let
out a multi-toned bleat. I watched him scurry off into the undergrowth, feeling both sad and proud that soon he would no
longer have to peep around the legs of the mighty colossuses
that now strode the land. The meek shall inherit the Earth. . . .

The little arrow on my homing device told me that I should
go straight ahead, but the forest looked dense that way, with
thick vines and foliage like cooked spinach draped from the
branches. If I veered to the east, perhaps that would—

Claws dug into my right shoulder.

My heart skipped several beats. I jumped forward and
twisted around, fumbling for the rifle in my backpack. A troödon stood there, its drawn-out head tilted to one side, great
unblinking eyes regarding me. Was the beast Het-ridden? Or
was it wild? I rested the butt of the rifle against my shoulder
and the two of us continued to stare at each other. This troödon
was smaller than the ones Klicks and I had encountered earlier,
and its face was freckled with brown spots. Probably a male.

"No."

The word, as before, sounded raw, torn from the animal's
throat. That the reptile was a vehicle for a Het made me no less
nervous. In fact, I thought I'd better take some precautions.
"Back off," I said. "I want you to stay at least five meters away
from me."

"Why?"

"So you won't try to enter me."

"Why?"

"I don't trust you."

"What is trust?" said the thing.

"Back off! Now!" I gestured with the rifle.

The troödon hesitated for a moment, then took a couple of steps back.

"Farther," I said.

It took two more long steps.

I set the rifle on the ground in such a way that I could scoop it up in an instant. I then swung my backpack off my shoulders. Inside I had a bunch of things, including two cans of Diet Coke and our only can amongst all our provisions of diet A&W root beer. I grabbed the root beer with my left hand and fumbled for my walkie-talkie with my right. I thumbed the unit on. "Klicks?"

Static for several seconds. Then: "Hey, Brandy—good to hear from you. Listen, I'm finding a dusting of iridium in a recent sedimentation layer, all right—as you'd expect given the impact crater we saw in Mexico—and there's some shocked quartz, too. But neither are present in the quantities I'd have anticipated based on terminal-Cretaceous samples collected in our time, and—"

"Not now," I said.

"What?"

"I've been approached by another troödon occupied by a Het."

"Where are you?"

"About ten kilometers west of the *Sternberger*, I think."

"I'm at least twenty-five kilometers east," said Klicks. Probably a couple of hours' drive for him, given the rough terrain.

"Klicks, I'm holding in my hand a can of A&W diet root beer."

The troödon tilted its head at me oddly.

"Good for you," said Klicks.

"*Shut up and listen*," I snapped. "I'm holding the only can we've got of A&W diet root beer. I've got my finger on the pull-tab. If the troödon gets too close to me, or if I'm attacked in any way, or any attempt is made to enter me, I'll pull the tab."

"I don't—"

"When you next see me, make me show you the can. Make sure it's unopened."

"Brandy, you're paranoid."

The troödon's head bobbed. "Un-nec-esss-ary," it hissed.

"Klicks, I want you to get some object that you can use the same way," I said into the walkie-talkie. "I want you to have a signal for me."

"Brandy—"

"Do it!"

Static again. Then: "I've got a pen here. I could click it open if I'm entered."

"No. It's got to be something that's not undoable. Something you can do fast. And something that we only have one of."

More static. "Okay. I've got a cellophane-wrapped package with two Twinkies in it."

"You've got Twinkies?"

"Uh, yes."

"All right. What are you going to do with them?"

"Umm, okay. They're in the breast pocket of my jacket now."

"You're wearing that loose-fitting khaki jacket, right?"

"That's right. If I'm approached too closely, I'll squish them."

"Okay. One more thing, Klicks. How much do you weigh?"

"About ninety kilos."

"Exactly how much? You had a final physical just before we left. Exactly how much do you weigh?"

"Umm, eighty-nine point five, I think."

"All right. I'm one-oh-four point nothing."

"That much? Goodness!"

"Just remember the damn figure."

"One hundred and four. The number of weeks in two years. Got it. But Brandy—"

He was about to point out that we didn't have any scales with us, except for a tiny mineralogical one that only went up to two kilograms. "That's fine," I said, cutting him off. "I'm heading back to the ship now."

"I want to finish these core samples," Klicks said. "I'll still be several hours."

"Okay. Just don't eat the Twinkies. Talk to you later."

"Bye."

I returned the walkie-talkie to my backpack and picked up the rifle again.

"About what was all that?" hissed the Het.

I held up the pop can. "Just keep your distance. See this metal tab? If I pull it, it will break the seal on this container in such a way that it can't be reclosed. It'll only take me half a second to do that. I doubt you can enter me that quickly."

"I do not intend to enter you now."

"*And,*" I said, "if you do enter me, Klicks knows how much I weigh. The discrepancy caused by your mass within me would be a dead giveaway." Actually it wouldn't. Even if we'd had a big enough scale, Klicks's and my weight would normally fluctuate by more than the weight of a Het glob, depending on how much food and waste we were carrying around. Still, it was a credible-sounding threat.

"You seem concerned about us," said the Het. "All we want to do is talk."

I lowered the gun barrel, but made no move to return the rifle to my backpack. "Very well. What do you want to talk about?"

"Cabbages and kings," said the beast. That was my taste in literature, not Klicks's, and this troödon also spoke with what Klicks would call a Canadian accent. Although this wasn't old

Diamond-snout from yesterday morning, evidently its rider was the same Het I had encountered then. Or maybe—it was hard to wrap my mind around these concepts—maybe, as the Het had tried to explain before, individuality meant nothing to them. Did they all know what any one of them knew? How did they communicate?

"Cabbages and kings?" I repeated, then shrugged. "Charles III is king. And I only eat cabbage in coleslaw."

The dinosaur, still many meters away, cocked its head at me and then digested the information with a measured one-two blink. "Thank you for sharing that," it said, a vacuous little phrase that I'd picked up from Dr. Schroeder. "You are some considerable distance from your timeship."

"Humans have to walk for exercise. It—aids our digestion."

"Ah."

I regarded the beast. "This isn't one of the troödons that we encountered before," I said.

"True."

"But you are the same Het?"

"More or less."

"Why did you change dinosaur bodies?"

The troödon blinked. "It's medium-rare for us to occupy the same vehicle for more than a day or two. We find it . . ." The rasping voice trailed off as the Het searched for the appropriate term. "Claustrophobic." It shuffled its feet. "Also, we need to leave our vehicles so that we can interact directly to share memories."

If that was true, then the Hets vacating Klicks's and my bodies of their own volition didn't necessarily mean they weren't evil. I wondered . . .

"Tell me," the thing said casually, "where exactly is asshole Klicks?"

"*What?*"

"Klicks the bastard asshole. Where is he?"

"Why are you calling him that?"

"Klicks? Ah, is pun. Pun links now. His unique identifying word is Miles, but you call him Klicks, short form for kilometers." The beast tossed back its long face. "Ho ho."

"No, why are you calling him names? Asshole, bastard. Why those names?"

"Names you call him. I just—Is usage wrong?" The troödon tipped its head a little. "Your language difficult, imprecise for us."

"You've never heard me call him those things. He'd knock my teeth out."

"Interesting. But you call him by such words constantly. We absorb that from you."

Oh, shit. "You mean, that's what you found in my head?"

"Yess, strong connections. Syllogism, no? All Klickses are assholes, but not all assholes are Klickses. Asshole, bastard, home-wrecker, wife-stealer, shithead, coon—"

"Coon? My God, do I really think that?" I felt my cheeks growing red. "The others are all subjective, at least. But a racial slur . . . I didn't, I mean—"

"Coon not good? No, it is—ah, a reference to his skin color. It is darker than yours. That is significant?"

"No. It's a meaningless difference—an adaptation to more equatorial sunlight, that's all. Listen, don't call him that, please."

"'That'? Why would I call him 'that'?"

"No, I mean, please don't call him coon. Or asshole. Or any of those other names."

"Inappropriate terms? What should I call him?"

"Klicks. Just Klicks."

"Klicks-just-klicks. Links."

Racial slurs. I felt ashamed. You think something is dead and buried, but it's there, all along, waiting for a chance to come back to life.

Still . . . I was fascinated by what the reptile had said. I knew I should let the matter drop, but I couldn't resist. "Tess," I said after a moment. "What words do you—link—to Tess?"

"Tess." The reptile shifted its weight between its two feet and a nictitating membrane passed over each of its iridescent eyes in turn. "Dear. Honey. Bunny. Sweetheart. Lambchop." I cringed at the litany of pet names. "Lover. Only-one-for-me. Lost. Stolen. Gone."

"Okay," I said quickly. "I get the idea. What about 'Dad.'"

"Dad?" A moment of silence. "Burden."

"That's all?"

"That's all."

I looked away. I'm sure the alien couldn't detect or even comprehend my embarrassment, but a wave of guilt washed over me. "What did you really want to talk about?" I said at last.

"Where have you been?"

"Out. Just walking around."

"Ah, good. Did you see anything interesting?"

"No. Nothing. Nothing at all."

"Shall I walk you back to the *Sternberger*?"

I sighed. "If you must. It's this way."

"No. Go this way. Cutshort."

As in, *his life was cut short,* no doubt. "You mean shortcut, I hope."

"Yess."

We headed off into the woods.

Countdown: 4

A good tree cannot bring forth evil fruit, neither can a corrupt tree bring forth good fruit.

—Matthew 7:18

I didn't like being alone with the Het. Although its drawn-out skull was less than thirty centimeters long, and its teeth were tiny, it could still kill me easily enough with a bite to the neck.

The beast's natural walking speed seemed to be about three times what mine was, but after a few minutes of it getting ahead then hopping back to join me, it matched my pace and we continued on, side by side. It was quite a hike back to the *Sternberger,* and I downed both Diet Cokes along the way, but all the time kept a finger on the pull-tab of my aspartame grenade.

The Het asked me an endless barrage of questions, most of which seemed innocuous. But when they'd picked me for this time-travel mission, I'd gone back and read all of H. G. Wells. A line of his kept echoing in my head: "I was mad to let the Grand Lunar know." I did my best to keep my answers neutral and nonthreatening. After a while, I figured the Het had accrued enough of an information debt that it would feel obligated to answer some of my questions, so at last I broached the subject that had been foremost on my mind. "I'm curious about your biology," I said.

Rather than look at me as I spoke, the thing kept its head facing forward, one of its two-centimeter-long vertical ear slits toward me. "I do not have the words to explain," it said at last.

"Come now. I'm a trained biologist and you have my vocabulary. Let's take a stab at it, shall we? You're obviously not based on cells like those that make up life on Earth. You must consist of much smaller units, or you wouldn't be able to slip through our skin."

The thing bobbed its head. "A reasonable assumption."

"Well, then, what are you? I know a fair bit about Mars. Chemically, it's similar enough to Earth that I can't believe you are completely different from us. And besides, you survive unprotected under terrestrial conditions."

"True."

The creature infuriated me. "Damn it, then. What are you? Tell me what makes you tick."

"Tick? We are not bombs."

I wasn't so sure about that, but what I said was, "I know what you aren't. I want to know what you *are*."

The creature looked down at the ground, as if searching for the right words to express the concept. Finally it turned to face me and said, "We are very small and yet very large."

I stared into those giant yellow eyes, even though I knew that they were the poetic windows to the troödon's reptilian soul, not the Het's. It was a Delphic proclamation, and yet, somehow, I saw what the Het was getting at, perhaps because I'd already started to suspect as much based on what I'd felt during my two brief mind contacts with Martians. "You're made of microscopic units but in fact you are one big creature," I said. I thought about the beach-ball–sized Het I'd seen ooze out of the half-headless triceratops. "You can lump together into large groupings, or form smaller concentrations. But you're a colonial creature, like coral without the reefs, able to break apart into your tiny constituents—each smaller than a cell—to percolate through other living matter." I'd never have submitted such wild speculation to a scientific journal, but I felt I was on the correct path. "I'm right, aren't I?"

"Yess. Rightish, anyway."

I decided to start with basics. "Life on Earth is based on self-replicating macromolecules called nucleic acids."

"This we know."

"Are you based on a nucleic acid?"

"Yess, we are nucleic acids."

A funny way to phrase it. "Which one? DNA?"

"That is the one in the nuclei of your cells? The double helix? Yess, some of our individual components are DNA."

"And the rest of your components?"

"Nondeoxy."

I had to replay the beast's response in my head a few times before it made sense to me. "Oh. RNA, you mean. Ribonucleic acid."

The reptilian mouth hung open, showing dagger-like teeth, then the jaws drew together and, more simple hiss than English word, the thing said, "Yess."

"Anything else?"

"Protein."

I was silent for a time, digesting this. *We are nucleic acids*, it had said. I thought about that, and I thought about RNA. A nucleotide chain found in the cytoplasm of cells, it's also associated with the storage of long-term memory and—*of course!*—with viruses. "You're a virus," I said.

"Virus?" It seemed to be trying the word on for size. "Yess, virus."

It all made sense. Viruses are orders of magnitude smaller than cells, only one hundred to two thousand angstroms wide. A viral lifeform could easily slip through the cracks between cells, percolating through skin, muscle, and organs. But . . . but . . . "But viruses aren't really alive," I said.

The troödon looked at me, golden eyes catching the sunlight. "What mean you?"

"I mean, a virus isn't complete until it enters a host."

"Host?"

"A true lifeform. Viruses consist of stored instructions in DNA and RNA, and coats of protein, and that's it. They can't grow and don't have any way to reproduce on their own; that's why we say they're not alive. They have to . . ."

The troödon blinked innocently. "Yess?"

I fell silent. Viruses have to take over, to seize, to *invade* the cellular machinery of an animal or plant. Then they force the cell to reproduce the virus's own nucleic acids and make copies of its protein coat. I tried and tried to think of an example of a beneficial virus, but there are none. Viruses are, by definition, pathogenic, dangerous to cellular life, causing everything from influenza and poliomyelitis through measles and the common cold to the AIDS epidemic of the 1990s and early 2000s. Indeed, because of AIDS, virus research had become quite the hot topic in Western science, the way Star Wars weapons technology had been earlier. At least this time the money had been well spent: a cure for AIDS had been approved for human use in 2010. In fact, this new drug—Deliverance, as it was aptly called—was able to neutralize just about any virus, using a process called adaptive fractal bonding; it was now used to cure everything from colds and flus to Ebola infections.

But if the Hets were viral, then they had to . . . to *conquer* . . . other forms of life.

There were those who said humanity was inherently violent because of its carnivorous ancestors. How would the need to literally enslave cell-based life affect the psychology of the Hets? Would they be bent on conquest, driven to control living things? That could explain why they don't like retaining the same animal bodies for any length of time. The drive to enslave could only be satiated by constantly taking over different creatures—

Hold on a minute, Brandy. Just hold on. Don't go overboard. But . . . *viruses.*

Come on, Brandy. You're a scientist. Nothing wrong with a wild hypothesis, but you have to test it, prove it.

The Hets are a hive mind; they have no individuality. Maybe they don't know anything about lying or deception.

So why not just ask the thing?

"You take over other lifeforms, don't you?" I said. "So that you can use them."

A double blink. "Of course."

"And even if they're intelligent life?"

And, again, a blink. "We are the only true intelligence."

I shuddered. "I saw dinosaurs fighting mechanical tanks back there."

The troödon tilted its head. "Oh."

"Those were war games, weren't they?"

"What is game?"

I shook my head. "'Game' is the wrong word, anyway. I mean they were practice sessions for a conflict."

"Yess."

"A conflict between your kind and some other intelligent life."

"We are the only true intelligence," the Het said again.

"All right, then: a conflict between your kind and those who made the mechanical tanks."

"Yess."

"Who started the conflict?"

"I don't understand," said the Het.

"What are you fighting over?"

"Over the ground."

"No, I mean, what is the central issue in your conflict?"

"Oh, that." The troödon scratched its lean belly. "They don't want us to invade their bodies. They don't want to be our slaves."

"*Shit.*"

The Het looked at me through the troödon's giant golden eyes. "I thought you required privacy for that activity," it said.

Countdown: 3

And ye shall know the truth, and the truth shall make you free.

—John 8:32

When the Het and I arrived at the mud plain near the *Sternberger,* Klicks was nowhere to be seen. Judging by the position of the sun it was late afternoon, and I didn't expect him to return before dinner. I could call him on the radio and tell him to hightail it back here, but there seemed no point in that. I couldn't talk freely until after the Het left—and it gave no sign of wanting to do so. The troödon hopped from one foot to the other, its long tail held stiffly. After a moment, it tipped its drawn-out head up at the crater wall. Perched high above was our timeship.

"Take me inside," it said suddenly.

It was bad enough being near the troödon, but to be near it inside a confined space . . . "I'd rather not," I said.

The troödon turned its giant eyes on me, fixing me with a steady gaze. "Reciprocate, Brandon/Brandy. We allowed you to come inside our ship. Must now you allow us to come inside yours."

Fancy that, I thought: my manners being corrected by a dinosaur. "But look at where the *Sternberger* is located," I said, pointing up. "See how it juts out over the crater rim? I know you can make it up the crater wall, but that's a big jump up to our hatchway. I doubt you can do it."

The troödon was off like a shot, clambering up the crumbling crater wall, using its long, dangling arms to help it climb. "Is no problem for me," it called once it had reached the top.

From the outside, our main door was painted electric blue, with a bright red trim—the mandrill's mouth, one of the engineers had dubbed it. I had no doubt that the dinosaur could see that, since all living reptiles and birds have color vision. The loss of the ability to see color by dogs and many other mammals was a recent evolutionary occurrence, a trade-off to provide better sight in the dark. The troödon accomplished the same thing simply by having huge eyes. "In I go," it called.

There was a vertical gap of a little less than a meter between the crumbling edge of the crater and the bottom of our main doorway, but the troödon had no trouble hopping up high enough to grab hold of the door handle. It then braced its feet against the blue door panel, lifted the latch, and swung inside with the door. Next, it let go, dropping to the deck inside the accessway. It couldn't turn around in there—there wasn't enough clearance for its stiff tail—but it swung its neck back to look down at me and waved.

Well, I was damned if I was going to let that thing go inside unsupervised. I climbed up the crater wall myself. Although the dirt was dry now, it had apparently rained briefly last night, and all the tyrannosaur tracks from before had been washed away. The troödon had already gone up the ramp that led to interior door number one and had made its way through into the cramped confines of our semicircular habitat. I hurried after it.

It was slowly circumnavigating the small room, looking at the food refrigerator and storage lockers, peering through the window in door number two at the garage, opening the medicine fridge—and quickly closing it when a blast of cold air hit its face—swinging open door number three to have a look at the tiny washroom, then coming along the curving outer wall past the kidney-shaped worktable, the radio console, and, at last, the mini-lab. Despite its protestation earlier, the troödon's sickle claws did indeed sound like the ticks of a bomb on the steel floor.

"This controls your time machine?" it hissed, pointing at one of Klicks's lab instruments.

I wasn't about to move away from the access ramp to the outside door; I wanted to be able to escape in a hurry if the troödon tried anything funny. "No, that's just a mineral analyzer. As I said before, all the working parts for time travel are up the timestream some sixty-five million years."

The troödon stepped in front of the radio console and eyed it suspiciously. "What about this?"

"It's just a fancy radio."

"Radio?"

"Umm, electromagnetic telecommunications."

The troödon tapped the console with a curved claw. It seemed fascinated by the fake plastic woodgrain that ran around the edges of the unit. "Yes, we have such communications. But who can you call? Does your radio operate across time?"

"No, no. It's just regular radio gear. Our timeship was dumped from a helicopter—a flying vehicle. The radio let us communicate with the copter pilot, and with Ching-Mei— that's the person who invented the time machine—at the ground base. The base was many kilometers away, at the Tyrrell Field Station. We also use the radio to relay signals from our walkie-talkies—portable transceivers—and for our homing devices to lock onto. Oh, and the radio used satellite signals to determine our exact position at the time of the drop from the helicopter, crucial for the Throwback to work. It can even send signals to search-and-rescue satellites, in case we return at other than our expected location. Highly unlikely, or so we're told, but it could happen." I gestured at the gleaming panel. "Anyway, it's far more sophisticated than what we needed, but the corporate sponsor—Ward-Beck in this case— wanted to showcase this particular piece of equipment. Our actual needs were pretty irrelevant."

"Very strange culture have you," said the troödon.

I forced a laugh. "That it is."

Klicks drove back into our camp shortly after sunset, parking the Jeep so that it would be in the morning shade of the crater wall. The troödon and I met him down on the mud flat. I held up my A&W can so that Klicks could see the intact pull-tab. He opened his jacket's breast pocket and pulled out the Twinkies. They were slightly squished—hard to avoid that with Twinkies—but certainly showed no sign of having been deliberately flattened.

The troödon hung around for hours, keeping me from talking candidly to Klicks. The little dinosaur did help us gather bald cypress wood and we built a small fire to cook some steaks. Cow steaks, that is—no more pachycephalosaur for me. The idea of cooked food was new to the Het, and it asked if it could feed some to its vehicle. With one gulp about fifty dollars' worth of prime sirloin disappeared down the troödon's throat. It tasted a lot like shrew, according to the Het, insectivores being one of the few mammalian groups well established by this time.

Even with the sun down, it was still warm. As we sat around the campfire, I watched the flames dance in the dinosaur's giant eyes. The troödon paid no attention to our theatrical yawns, and at last Klicks simply said, "It's time for us to go to sleep."

"Oh," said the Het. Without another word, it stalked away into the darkness. Klicks and I doused the flames and scrambled back up into the *Sternberger.* As soon as we'd entered the habitat, I turned to him.

"Klicks," I said, finally able to talk without a Martian eavesdropping, "we can't bring the Hets forward in time."

"Why not?"

"Because they're evil."

Klicks looked at me, his jaw kind of slack, the way you'd look at someone who had just said something completely out of left field.

"I'm serious," I said. "They're at war."

"At war?"

"That's right. The troödon who came back here with me confirmed it."

"Who are they fighting?"

"I don't know. He didn't say."

"What are they fighting about?"

"The Hets want to enslave the other side."

"Enslave?"

"Crawl in their heads; make them do whatever the Hets want."

"The Het said this to you?"

"Yes."

"Why would it tell you that?"

"Why *wouldn't* it tell me? Don't you see, Klicks, they're a single entity, a hive mind. Those globs of jelly come together and share memories. The idea of one individual deceiving another is foreign to them. About the only good thing you can say about them is that they're pathological truth-tellers."

"They seem harmless enough to me."

"They're viruses," I said.

Klicks looked at me blankly.

"Viruses? You mean metaphorically . . ."

"I mean it literally. They're viral-based; they consist of nucleic acids, but they can't grow or breed on their own. They have to infest a living host. Only when they do so are they really alive."

"Viral," said Klicks slowly. "Well, I guess that would explain how they percolate through living tissue. Certainly viruses are small enough to do that."

"But don't you see? Viruses are evil."

Klicks gave me a what-are-*you*-on look. "Viruses are just bits of chemistry," he said.

"Exactly. Bits of programmed instructions, instructions to take over living matter and convert the cells of that matter to producing more viruses. They are always harmful to their hosts."

"I suppose."

"They're harmful to their hosts by definition. What's good for the virus is never good for the cells it has invaded."

"And you're saying that if the Hets are viral, they must have a psychology based on this?"

"I'm not saying it could only have been that way. But in this particular evolutionary case, yes, that's the way it turned out: the Hets are conquest-driven. You heard what they said about the rosette of stars we saw. 'It galls us.' They hate the fact that there's some life out there that they can't reach, can't subjugate."

"I don't know, Brandy. You're going out on a limb."

"It's the truth, damn it. The Het told me so."

"In exactly those words?"

"No, not exactly."

"You know, Brandy, you're picking the wrong guy to tell this to. This viral-nature stuff sounds a lot like you've made up your mind that the Hets are inferior, and are trying to use science to justify that belief. That sort of thinking did my people a lot of harm over the years."

"But, look," I said, "you're alive."

"Thank you."

"I mean you're a living creature. So am I. Black people, white people, all people, all animals, all plants. We're all alive."

"Uh-huh."

"*But viruses aren't.* They're not alive, not in the scientific sense. They have to conquer if they are to exist at all. That's their only purpose. It's not a question of potentials one way or another. It's what they do. The one and only thing they can do. To be a virus is to be bent on conquest—by definition."

"It's an interesting theory, but—"

"It's more than a theory. I saw their war games."

"Whatever you saw, you must be misinterpreting it."

It was frustrating as hell. I'd recorded the whole thing on my MicroCam, but had no way to play the images back until we returned to the twenty-first century. "I tell you it's true," I said. "They're using dinosaurs as armored vehicles and attack machines."

"Dinosaur tanks?"

"Think about it: biological tanks are self-repairing, self-replicating, and the slimeballs can operate them by direct mind control." I swung my crash couch around and sat on it sideways. "You've studied dinosaurian physiology: you know they'd make perfect killing machines. They're incredibly strong—theropod jaws can cut through steel pipe—and their nervous systems are simplistic enough that they wouldn't even know they'd been mortally wounded until after they'd taken down a few dozen of their opponents. These creatures were bred to kill, born to fight."

Klicks shook his head. "Who could they possibly be at war with?"

"I don't know. I don't think it's here on Earth. I saw them loading up dinosaur eggs into their spaceships. I think they transfer the eggs to wherever the battle is raging. Somewhere—somewhere with orange and blue vegetation, I think."

"What?"

"The ceratopsians I saw were patterned in those colors. Camouflage, I suspect."

Klicks shook his head in wonderment. "But you don't know who they're fighting?"

That this was a good question irritated me. "There are lots of possibilities," I said too quickly, my tone betraying that I didn't have a real answer. "Maybe a different type of Martian. Or maybe some lifeform on one of the moons of Jupiter."

"That seems unlikely, Brandy. None of those moons has an environment even remotely like Earth's, and I find it hard to envision a platoon of tyrannosaurs in giant space suits."

"Hmm. Hadn't thought of that."

We were both silent for a few seconds.

"There is one other possibility," said Klicks slowly, a hint of gentle teasing in his tone.

"Eh?"

"Well, there *could* be an Earth-like planet between the orbits of Mars and Jupiter. You know—where the asteroids are in our time. As long as it had a mild greenhouse effect, it could be quite temperate." He filled an Envirofoam cup with water and placed it in our microwave.

"There's not enough rubble in the asteroid belt to have ever made up a decent-sized planet," I said.

"Hey, man, I'm just trying to get into the spirit of your delusion." His fingers drummed on the microwave's membrane keyboard, and it beeped in response. "See, in the final battle, the Hets will use a total-conversion weapon, turning three-quarters of the enemy planet's mass into energy. Or maybe they just pounded the planet until it shattered and the bulk of it fell into Jupiter or the sun, or spiraled out to become Pluto." His one eyebrow arched in the center. "In fact, now that I mention it, that explains something that's been bugging me. We've always assumed that the water-erosion features on Mars are incredibly ancient, created at a time billions of years before the era we're in now. But, really, the only indication of the age of those features is the heavy cratering that overlays them. We made some assumptions about the rate of cratering, and then extrapolated that the water features underneath must be a couple of billion years old. Well, Mars would have been scoured by asteroid impacts after the planet in the belt was pulverized, giving the water-erosion landforms the appearance of being a lot older than they really are. That would explain how Mars could indeed be covered with free-flowing water right now."

Klicks was smiling, but it made sense to me. "Right!" I said. "The bloody Martian asked us about the fifth planet, then seemed surprised when I told it about Jupiter. In this time, Jupiter's the *sixth* planet." My head was spinning. "Good Christ. And that explains why they're here on Earth."

The microwave beeped. "You've lost me, Sherlock," said Klicks.

"Earth would be strategic in such a war," I said. "When Mars is on the opposite side of the sun from the—the belt planet, but Earth is on the same side as it, Earth could be a great platform for launching attacks."

"The 'belt planet,' eh?" Klicks laughed. "It needs a better name than that."

"Okay. How about—"

"Not so fast. You got to name Earth's second moon. It's my turn."

He had a point there. "Okay."

Klicks scratched his head. "How about . . ."

"How about what?"

His grin had slipped away. "Nothing," he said, making a show of sifting decaf coffee crystals into his steaming cup. "I—I want to sleep on it."

He wished to name it Tess, of course. That was fine with me, but I wasn't going to tell him that. Klicks continued: "That would be one hell of a war, Brandy. Mars laid waste. The other side's home world reduced to rubble."

"So you can see that we can't bring the Hets forward."

Klicks shook his head. "I'm not sure about that. I'm still not convinced by your virus theory—"

"It's not my theory, dammit. It's what the Het told me."

"And, besides, if fighting wars was enough to disqualify a species from being otherwise decent, you'd have to kiss humanity good-bye, too. Plus, they've voluntarily left our bodies twice now."

"They have to do that," I said. "They get claustrophobic if they inhabit the same body for too long; they need to constantly conquer new creatures." Klicks rolled his eyes. "It's true," I said. "The Het told me. Look, they knew it would be over three full days until we headed back; sticking around inside our bodies that long would be the viral equivalent of waiting endlessly at the airport. Of course they exited us; they knew they could always reenter just by having a swarm of troödons overpower us, if no other way worked out."

"You're putting the worst possible spin on everything," said Klicks.

My turn to roll eyes. "Look, these creatures can dissociate into components small enough that you'd need an electron microscope to see them. Once they're loose on Earth in the twenty-first century, there would be no putting the genie back in the bottle. Bringing them forward in time would be an irrevocable decision, a real-life Pandora's box."

"You're mixing your metaphors," said Klicks. "Besides, leaving them back here would be an irreversible decision, too. We're the one opportunity the Hets have to be saved."

"We can't risk that." I set my jaw. "I'm convinced—*convinced* —that they're, well, evil."

Klicks sipped his coffee. "Well," he said at last, "we all know how reliable your conclusions are."

I felt a knotting in my stomach. "What's that supposed to mean?"

He took another sip. "Nothing."

My voice had taken on a little shakiness at the edges. "I want to know what you meant by that crack."

"It's nothing, really." He forced a smile. "Forget about it."

"Tell me."

He sighed, then spread his hands. "Well, look—all this non-sense about me and Tess." He met my eyes briefly, then looked away. "You stand there all high-and-mighty, both judge and jury, condemning me for something I didn't do." His voice had gotten small. "I just don't like it, that's all."

I couldn't believe what I was hearing. "Something you didn't do?" I sneered the words. "Are you denying you're having an affair with her?"

His eyes swung back to mine, and this time they held their lock. "Get this through your thick head, Thackeray. Tess is single. Divorced. And so am I." He paused. "Two single people together does not constitute an affair."

I waved my hand. "Semantics. Besides, you were fooling around with her even before Tess and my marriage was over."

Klicks's voice was ripe with indignation. "I never touched her—not even once—until you and she were as extinct as your bloody dinosaurs."

"Bull." I put my hand down on the lab table—really, I'd just intended to gently place it there, but all the instruments clacked together. "Tess got her divorce on July third, 2011. You were boffing her long before that."

"That date was just a formality, and you know it," Klicks said. "Your marriage had been over for months by then."

"Its end hastened no doubt by your constant flirting with her."

"Flirting?" There was now a hint of derision in his lilting tones. "I'm not sixteen, for God's sake."

"Oh, yeah? What did you say to her that night the three of us went out to see the new *Star Wars* film?"

"How the hell should I remember what I said?"—but the slight change in his vocal tone told me that he did indeed remember very well.

"She'd just gotten new glasses that day," I said. "The ones with the purply-pink wire frames. You looked right at her and said, 'You certainly have a lovely pair, Tess.'" I could see that Klicks was fighting not to smile, and that made me even more furious. "That's a hell of a thing to say to another man's wife."

He drained his remaining coffee in a single gulp. "Come on, Bran. It was a joke. Tess and I are old friends; we kid around. It didn't mean anything."

"You stole her right out from under me."

He absently broke a piece of Envirofoam off the cup's rim. "Maybe if she *had* been under you a little more often, it never would have happened."

"Fuck you."

"Why not?" he said, lifting his eyes. "You certainly weren't fucking her."

I was quaking with anger. "You son of a bitch. We did it once a week."

Klicks nodded knowingly. "Sunday mornings, like clockwork. Right after *This Week with Peter Jennings*. Pretty poor excuse for foreplay."

"She told you that?"

"We talk a lot, sure. And about more than just the latest find reported in *The Journal of Vertebrate Paleontology*. Face it, Brandy. You were a lousy husband. You lost her all on your own. You can't blame me for recognizing a good thing when I saw it. Tess deserved better than you."

I tasted bile in my throat. I wanted to lunge at the man, to make him take back every one of those cruel lies. My hands, sitting on the lab table, clenched into fists. Klicks must have noticed that. "Just try it," he said, ever so softly.

"But you didn't even give us a chance to work things out," I said, forcing a semblance of calm back into my voice.

"There wasn't any hope of that."

"But if Tess had only said something to me . . . This—this is the first I've heard of any of this."

Klicks sighed, a long, weary exhalation, then shook his head again. "Tess had been screaming it at you for months—with every glance she made, with the look on her face, with body language that everyone but you could read." He spread his arms. "Christ, she couldn't have been much more obvious about her unhappiness if she'd had the words 'I am miserable' tattooed on her forehead."

I shook my head. "I didn't know. I didn't see any of that."

The long sigh again. "That was apparent."

"But you—you were supposed to be my friend. Why didn't you tell me about this?"

"I tried, Brandy. What do you think I was getting at that night in that bar on Keele Street? I said you were working too hard on the new galleries, that it was crazy not to get home till ten o'clock each night when you've got a lovely wife waiting for you. You told me that Tess understood." He frowned and shook his head. "Well, she didn't. Not at all."

"So you decided to make your move."

"I've got news for you, Brandy. I didn't go after Tess. She came after me."

"What?" I felt my world crumbling around me.

"Ask her, if you don't believe me. You think I'd go after my best friend's wife? Christ, Brandy, I turned her down *three times*. Do you think that was easy for me? The Tyrrell Museum is in a pissant all-white Prairie town, for God's sake. I'm middle-aged and have permanent dirt under my fingernails from years of fieldwork. How many of the women in Drumheller do you think wanted to get down with me? Jesus, man. Tess is gorgeous and I pushed her aside three fucking times for you. I told her to work it out with you, to return to her husband, to not flush nine good years down the toilet. She kept coming back. Can you blame me for finally saying yes?"

I looked away, my eyelids locked shut to prevent tears from escaping. The moment between us stretched to a minute, then two. I didn't know what to say, what to do, what to think. I wiped my eyes, blew my nose, and turned to face Klicks. He held my gaze for only a second, but in that second I saw that he'd been telling the truth and, worst of all, I saw that he pitied me. He got up and put his coffee cup in the trash.

Thirty-eight more hours, I thought. Thirty-eight more hours until we return. I didn't know if I could take it, being here with him, being here with my memories of her—

It was night. Time to go to bed. I'd have to take sleeping medication again, or else I'd toss and turn until dawn, tormented by what Klicks had said.

I began to gather my pajamas.

"You've got a job to do," said Klicks.

I looked at him, but didn't trust myself to speak.

"The night-sky photo."

Oh, right. I would have done it last night, except it was clouded over. I went through door number one, but instead of going down the ramp to the outer hatch, I went up the little ladder, angled at forty-five degrees, into the instrumentation dome on the roof. In training, I'd always found climbing that ladder hurt my palms, given that my full weight was on them, but in this lower gravity, it wasn't uncomfortable at all.

The instrumentation dome was about two meters across and made of glassteel. Several cameras were set up to shoot through its transparent walls, and a vertical slit, very much like that in an observatory dome, let the warm Mesozoic night air flow into the sensors within. The slit closed automatically when rain was detected.

Several automated cameras were taking sky photographs, and one tracked the sun during the days. But there was one astronomical photograph the staff of the Dominion Astrophysical Observatory had asked us to take that couldn't be easily automated, and that was a traditional time-lapse night-sky photo. See, all our automatic cameras were off-the-shelf models, and they had automatic exposure timers, but none of them went past sixty seconds. The photo the DAO wanted required an exposure of four hours, and that demanded manual intervention.

I'd originally volunteered to bring along my Pentax to take this photo, but when I'd asked that jerk from my insurance company if my personal belongings would be covered if I took them 65 million years into the past, he didn't miss a beat: "Sorry, Mr. Thackeray, that would mean that any loss or damage took place before the effective coverage date of your policy." Oh, well. In the end, we'd borrowed a fancy electronic camera from the McLuhan Institute at U of T. It, too, only had a short-term exposure timer, but it also had a manual shutter and so I did what generations of sky photographers had done before me: I set up the camera in the dark, slipped a rubber band around its case to hold the shutter button down, then gingerly removed the lens cap.

The result would be a time-exposure photo—an electronic one, since this was a filmless camera—with arcs representing the paths of stars through the night sky. The common center of all these arcs would indicate Earth's true north pole. Also, such a photo would show the tiny streaks of meteors. A count of those would give some indication of how much debris was floating around local space, and, given we knew how long the exposure had been for, a precise measurement of how many degrees the arcs encompassed would tell us the exact length of a Cretaceous day.

I fiddled with the tiny studs on my wristwatch—I always found the thing frustrating to operate—and set the alarm for four hours from now, which would be at something like 3:00 A.M. local time, so that I would get up and put the lens cap back on the camera.

I headed down the ladder, back through door number one, and into the habitat. Klicks walked over to me. "Here," he said gently, proffering a cup of water and a silver sleeping caplet. I accepted them silently.

There was a long moment between us, a moment when we both thought over the words we had exchanged. "She did love you," Klicks said at last. "For many years, she loved you deeply."

I looked away, nodded, and swallowed the bitter pill.

Countdown: 2

Things are in the saddle,
And ride mankind.

—Ralph Waldo Emerson, American writer (1803–1882)

Like most people, I guess, I only remember my dreams when I wake during them. I was dreaming about Tess, her wild mane of red hair; her intelligent green eyes; her slim, almost girlish figure. It wasn't Tess Thackeray, my wife, though. No, this was the reborn Tess Lund, a name that had been retired years ago but was now pressed back into active service by the liberation of divorce.

Tess was lying naked in bed, the twin light of two moons playing across her heart-shaped face, lofty Luna still accompanied by tiny Trick. Someone was in bed with her, but it wasn't me. Nor was it a stranger, which probably would have been a less disquieting sight. No, the powerful brown arms wrapped around her pale waist belonged to Professor Miles Jordan, *bon vivant*, respected academic, my friend. My best friend in the world.

I was observing them, a disembodied camera, through a window in her bedroom. It had changed since the days when I had shared that room with Tess: the furnishings were richer, more refined. Our old queen-sized bed had been replaced with an elegant Victorian four-poster. Its canopy, a tapestry of pension and benefit contracts, was raised high over their heads by thick brown poles carved from mahogany trunks.

Tess was talking to Klicks in that sexy, deep voice that always seemed so incongruous coming out of her tiny body. She was telling him about me, sharing with him all my deepest, darkest secrets—an endless succession of humiliations, defeats, and shames. She told him about my fascination with my cousin Heather and the horrible public scene Heather had made when I'd drunkenly tried to act on those emotions at her brother Dougal's wedding. She told him about the time I was caught shoplifting at age thirty-four, walking out of a Lichtman's with a stupid porno magazine that I was too embarrassed to take up to the cash counter. And she told him about the night a mugger beat the crap out of me in Philosopher's Walk behind the museum, and, finding that picture of my mother in my wallet, had, cruelly, oh so cruelly, forced me to eat it.

Klicks listened raptly to everything Tess revealed about me, things so hidden, so private, so personal that Doc Schroeder would have given his eyeteeth to hear me divulge them on that sticky vinyl couch of his. Klicks heard secrets that should have been mine alone to carry to my grave. He knew my very soul. The thought of him living and knowing such things, having such power over me, was unbearable—

Beep!

Klicks stroked Tess's mane, his thick fingers passing gently through the orange strands the way mine used to, the way mine still ached to do each time I ran into her. I thought for a moment that he was going to laugh at what she had told him, but what he did was much, much worse, cutting me like troödon teeth. "There, there," he said, his too-smooth baritone the perfect complement to her throaty sexiness. "Don't worry, Lambchop"—*Lambchop!*—"He's gone now."

Beep!

Suddenly my disembodied being coalesced into physical form. I smashed my right hand through the window pane, the glass shredding my knuckles like mozzarella cheese. I was going to kill him—

Beep!

"Huh?" Groggy, I reached down and pressed buttons on my

wristwatch until I found the one that shut off the alarm. "Klicks?" There was no answer. I guess the alarm hadn't awoke him. Perhaps he was still doped up by a sleeping pill. I must have been, too, for I imagined just for a second that yellow billiard-ball eyes were peering at me from out of the darkness. I rolled off my crash couch, felt my way along the back wall until I found door number one, and fumbled up the ladder into the instrumentation dome. I clipped the lens cap back onto the camera and removed the rubber band to release the shutter. Noises echoed in a funny way inside that tiny dome and it sounded like the main timeship door downstairs was swinging shut and the latch clicking closed.

I stumbled back down the ladder and reentered the habitat. "Brandy?"

My heart jumped. "Klicks?"

"Yeah."

"Did my alarm wake you?"

"I don't know. But I can't sleep."

I thought about it for a moment. I probably could fall back to sleep easily enough—that medication was powerful stuff—but . . . "Want some coffee?" I said at last.

"Decaf? Sure."

"Mind if I turn on the lights?"

"No."

I fumbled for the switch and the overheads sputtered into activity. The brightness was stinging. I shielded my eyes and looked over at Klicks. He was alternating between having his left eye closed and his right, squinting.

"What about the Hets?" he said. "They're going to ask us tomorrow if we will take them back to the future. What do we tell them?"

I filled two cups with water and put them in the microwave. "I still say we have to tell them no."

"You're wrong," Klicks said slowly, most of the Jamaican lilt gone from his voice, a brief pause between each of the words. "We must help them get past whatever natural catastrophe caused their extinction."

"Look," I said, trying to summon my strength of will, "the Royal Ontario Museum is in for much more funding for this mission than is the Tyrrell. That makes me *de facto* mission leader, and, if necessary, I'll invoke that right. We leave the Hets behind."

"But we must take them forward."

"*No.*" I turned my back on Klicks, furious.

"Well," said Klicks, his voice growing closer, "if you feel that strongly about it . . ."

"Thank you, Miles." I breathed a sigh of relief, and then, just in time to save me, refilled my lungs. "I appreciate—"

Thick fingers closed around my neck from behind. I tried to cry out, but couldn't force enough air through my constricted windpipe to generate anything beyond a faint grunt. I brought my hands up to pry Klicks's fingers free, but he was too strong, much too strong, his arms like a robot's, crushing the life out of my body. My vision was blurring and my lungs felt like they were going to burst.

I twisted and bent frantically from my waist. In a mad, desperate moment, I tried throwing Klicks—something I knew I'd never be able to do—but damned if he didn't flip right over my shoulder, me tossing his ninety kilos as if they were less than half that amount. Of course—the reduced gravity!

I gulped air, my vision slowly clearing. Adrenaline pumped within me, fighting off the effects of the sleeping pill. Klicks picked himself up and we squared off, hands on knees, facing each other. He swung, a great sweeping movement of his right arm, like a grizzly scooping fish from a stream. I jumped back as far as I could in the tight confines of the habitat. From bear to tiger in an instant, he crouched and leapt, his body colliding with mine, knocking me to the cold steel floor next to his crash couch, a great thundering bang from the partially empty water tank beneath our feet echoing throughout the chamber. Then he smashed me across the face, the stone in a ring Tess had given him slicing open my cheek.

What the hell had gotten into Klicks? *A Martian, that's what.* Of course. The yellow eyes in the dark. If my wrist alarm hadn't woke me while the aliens were inside the *Sternberger,* they would have taken me over, too, then used our timeship to bring themselves forward, neatly cutting us out of the decision-making process. It was only thirty-one hours until the Huang Effect reversed states; I guess the Hets felt they could comfortably remain in our bodies for that long. These creatures played for keeps, that was for damn sure. My only chance of preventing them from seizing the *Sternberger,* it seemed, was to kill Miles Jordan.

That was easier said than done, though. As much as I sometimes disliked the man, as much I had fantasized about splitting his skull with the trusty cold chisel I had used for years to open slabs of rock, I had strong moral compunctions about physically hurting another human being. Even in self-defense, I found it hard to fight. My natural reaction was that a reasonable person would respond better to words than to fisticuffs. But Klicks, or at least the Het riding within him, had none of those same misgivings—as the bit of white froth at the corner of his mouth made clear.

He smashed me again in the face, hard. Although I'd never experienced the sensation before, I was sure *that* was what a breaking nose felt like. Blood soaked my mustache.

Still, I realized, he wasn't trying to kill me. He could have done that just by shooting me in the back with his elephant gun. Vast suspicions would be aroused if both of us didn't return from the Mesozoic. Hell, Tess had joked that she'd expected only one of us to come back alive, given how poorly we'd been getting on of late. Of course, nobody on the project knew what I wrote in this diary, or what I said to Schroeder, and the idea of psychological testing, mainstay of the moon shots (back when the world could afford moon shots), was completely foreign to those putting together paleontological digs. Hell, paleontologists routinely go off into the field for weeks on end without anyone taking steps to see if those particular people could get along.

Whether the Hets knew or understood any of that, I couldn't say. But they obviously wanted me incapacitated so that I could be entered by one of their kind. For that experience, twice had been more than enough. Fear and revulsion at the idea renewed my strength. I reached behind my head for the footrest of Klicks's crash couch and with all my energy spun the chair on its swivel base, slamming its arm into the side of his head. The armrest was padded, but Klicks, in his lackadaisical way, had left his shoulder strap hanging across it. The aluminum buckle split the skin across the top of his ear where it hit. The blow put him off balance long enough for me to knock him over. I scrambled to my feet, putting the bulk of the crash couch between him and me.

He tried to feint left and right but, as he did so, I noticed his movements were awkward, his torso turning by repositioning his legs instead of pivoting from the waist. It was as if the Het within him hadn't yet worked out the finer points of controlling a human body.

We circled the small room several times, me rotating the chair to always keep its long dimension between us. I didn't know whether my fear was valid, but I worried that if he chased me much longer in a counterclockwise direction the damned thing would unscrew from its base.

As we swung by the lab bench, I grabbed our mineralogical scale and threw it at his forehead. If he had been operating under his own volition, Klicks would have easily avoided the impact, but the Het seemed to hesitate about which muscles to move. By the time it pulled Klicks's head aside, it was too late:

the heavy base hit just above Klicks's one continuous eyebrow. He screamed in pain. Blood welled from the wound and I hoped it would obscure his vision.

No such luck. A thin layer of phosphorescent blue jelly seeped out of the cut, stanching the flow. I was running out of ideas, not to mention stamina. My heart pounded and I felt my strength flagging.

Klicks had screamed in pain.

That was my one hope. I gave his crash couch a healthy twist, setting it spinning around, then jumped as far as I could across the room. Klicks wheeled to face me. We danced for position, him swinging his great arms again the way a bear swipes with its paws. Finally he thought he had me trapped in the corner where the flat rear wall met the curving outer wall. He stood spread-eagle, his legs apart, his arms raised, trying to prevent me slipping past. This was the moment. The one chance, the only hope. I ran straight at him and, with all the force I could muster, brought my knee up into his groin, slamming it as brutally as I could, all my inertia and all my strength concentrating on bashing his testicles back up into his body cavity.

Klicks doubled from the waist, his fists moving under human instinct instead of Het command to protect his private parts from further assault. In the brief interval while the Het struggled to regain control of its biological vehicle, I made my final move. I grabbed Klicks's elephant gun from where he'd left it propped up next to the microwave-oven stand and smashed the length of its steel barrel across the back of his neck. He stood as if frozen for several seconds, then slumped to the ground, possibly dead, certainly unconscious. I suspected that if Klicks had survived the blow, and that was indeed in doubt, it would only be a matter of minutes, or even seconds, before the Het would find a way to turn this biological machine back on.

I hurried to the medicine refrigerator, mounted between

doors number two and three. We'd been provided with a complete pharmacopoeia, of course, since no one knew what Mesozoic germs would do to us. I hadn't spent much time inside the thing before, but thankfully all the drugs were categorized by function. Peering through clouds of my own breath condensing in the cold air from the interior, I scanned the labels. Analgesics, antibiotics, antihistamines. Ah! Antiviral agents. There were several vials in that section, but the one I seized upon was para-22-Ribavirin—better known as Deliverance, the miracle AIDS cure.

I plunged a syringe through the rubber cap, drawing forth the milky liquid. I knew how to use needles from my work in the comparative-anatomy lab, but—my father's pain-racked face flashed before me—I'd never injected a human being before. I ran to Klicks, my footfalls echoing in the steel-walled room, and bent over his crumpled form. He was still breathing, but shallowly, slowly, life apparently ebbing from him. I forced the needle through the thick wall of his right carotid artery, pumped the plunger down, and, never taking my eyes off him, slumped back against the door to our garage, the agony from my shattered nose growing, throbbing, multiplying.

It took a while—I'd lost track of the passage of time—but finally small amounts of blue jelly began to seep from Klicks's temple. But something was wrong. It wasn't undulating the way I'd seen the Hets move before, nor was it glowing. I rolled him over so that his bruised face was visible. One of his eyelids was stuck shut by dried blood, but the other fluttered open for a few seconds and he spoke in a rasping whisper. "You *animals—*"

I got an orange garbage bag and a spoon and, taking immense care not to touch it, began scraping away what little of the jelly had escaped. No more than two tablespoonfuls. The rest, dead or dying I hoped, seemed destined to remain inside Klicks's head until his own antibodies and white corpuscles could deal with it as they would any other inert viral material.

I stuffed the bag into a metal box, went down the ramp to our outside door, and heaved the box as far as I could in the reduced gravity. It sailed out onto the cracked mud plain far below; in the moonlight, I saw it bounce twice when it hit.

I made it back to the medicine refrigerator, filled another syringe with Deliverance, and injected myself as a precaution. Then I opened the first-aid kit mounted on the refrigerator's top and found a wad of white gauze. I held it tightly against the center of my face, stumbled back to my crash couch, and lay down on my back, the shift in posture sending daggers of pain through my head. I hoped and prayed with all my might that Klicks would pull through.

Boundary Layer

A man travels the world over in search of what he needs and returns home to find it.

—George Moore, Irish writer (1852–1933)

Tess gave me a big hug and a kiss when I got back to Toronto from Vancouver. I squeezed her, but my mind was elsewhere. We'd had a good marriage, as far as I could tell. We'd enjoyed each other's company. Both of our careers had prospered. And the lack of children? Well, she had always said that it didn't bother her, that she, too, felt they'd be an inconvenience, at odds with our lifestyle. And yet, in that other, original iteration of the timeline, she had left me for Miles Jordan. Klicks had always wanted kids. Was that part of the reason?

I wished to God that I'd never found that alternative diary. Ignorance really can be bliss. To think that my personal life was as tenuous and unstable as Ching-Mei said the universe itself was—it was enough to drive me crazy.

Ching-Mei had tried to explain how that other diary had come to be in my possession, how the memory wafer in my palmtop could have somehow swapped contents with the one the time-traveling Brandy had taken to the past with him. She spoke about shunting and Huang-Effect reversals and chaos theory, but she was guessing, really. It didn't matter. The damage was done.

"How was the flight?" asked Tess, removing her arms from me.

"Typical Air Canada." My tone was cold, dry.

Tess's eyes flicked across my face, looking, I guess, for the emotion underlying the weariness in my voice. "Sorry to hear that," she said at last.

I hung my coat in the hall closet and we made our way up to the living room. We sat together on the L-shaped couch, beneath a framed landscape painting done by Tess's uncle, a not-bad artist who lived in Michigan. "Anything exciting happen while I was away?"

"Not really," she said. "Wednesday, I went to see that new James Bond film—I must say Macaulay Culkin makes a surprisingly good 007. And last night I had Miles over for dinner."

Klicks here? While I was away? "Oh."

"By the way, I balanced our bank account while you were gone. Why'd you charge your plane tickets on your Master-Card? Shouldn't the museum have paid for those?"

Oh, crap. "Uh, well, the research was personal."

Tess blinked. "I beg your pardon?"

"I mean, it's not important."

She looked up at me, searching. "Is everything all right?"

"Everything's fine. Just fine."

Silence for a time, and then, softly: "I think I'm entitled to a better answer than that."

"Look," I said, and instantly regretted it, "I'm not giving you the third degree about what you did while I was away."

Tess smiled with her mouth, but I could see by the corners of her eyes that the smile was forced. "Sorry, honey," she said, false sun in her voice. "It's just that I worry about you." Her eyes flicked over my face again. "I wouldn't want you to have a midlife crisis and go running off with somebody else."

"I'm not the one who's likely to do that, am I?"

She went stiff. "What do you mean by that?"

Christ, I was saying things that I shouldn't. But if what we had wasn't as special to her as it was to me, I had to know. I had to. "How was Klicks?" I said.

She was bristling. "He was fine, thank you very much. Pleasant. Nonargumentative. A damn sight nicer than you've been of late."

"I see. Well, if you prefer his company—"

"I didn't say that." She slapped the arm of the couch, air forcing its way out of the plush armrest with a soft *whoompf.* "Jesus, you're a frustrating man sometimes. You run off on some junket clear to the other side of the country. You've accused me twice now of, of infidelity. What in God's name is wrong with you?"

"There's nothing wrong with me." The same weary tone I'd used to describe the flight from Vancouver.

"The hell there isn't." She looked up at me again and this time her eyes locked on mine. Those lovely green eyes, the same two haunting orbs that had fueled my fantasies before I'd worked up the courage to ask her out; the same two compassionate orbs that had helped me through the death of my mother, through the loss of that job in Ottawa, through so many tragedies; the same two intelligent orbs that had danced as we had held real discussions about things that had seemed oh so very important in our youth—war and peace and love and international relations and great moral controversies, she always quick with a point of view, me ponderously weighing the evidence, trying to decide what was right and what was wrong. Physically the eyes had changed only slightly over the years: their color was bluer now and there were fine wrinkles at their corners. But where once they had been great expansive windows for me, and me alone, to peer into her very soul, they now seemed silvered over, mirrored, reflecting back my own doubts and fears and insecurities, while revealing nothing of the mind that dwelt behind them.

"Do you still love me?" she said at last, a slight quaver to the words.

The question hit me with unexpected force. We didn't speak of love, not openly, not anymore. That was a topic for those who were still young. We lived a peaceful coexistence: old friends who didn't have to say much to each other; old shoes that grew more comfortable each time you put them on. Did I still love her? Had I ever loved her—the real her, the actual

Tess—or had I only loved an image of someone else, someone I'd created in my mind, sculpted in my dreams? I realized, fast enough, fortunately, that this was one of those moments of truth, one of those significant butterflies, one of those decisions that could bend the timeline so severely that I'd never be able to correct its course.

"More than life itself," I said at last, and it was only when I heard the words free in the room that I realized how right and true they were. "I love you with all my heart." I swept her tiny body into my arms and squeezed so hard that it hurt us both. Who said that I had to give her up without a fight? "Come on, Lambchop. Let's go upstairs." And then I thought, screw that, that's what old people do. "No, on second thought, let's stay right here. It's been years since we gave this couch a proper workout."

Countdown: 1

There are only two species that actually go to war: men and ants.
There is no possibility of any change in the ants.
—John G. Diefenbaker, 13th Prime Minister of Canada (1895–1979)

My broken nose throbbed with each beat of my heart. It had taken seemingly forever, but at least for the time being it had stopped bleeding.

I lay back in my crash couch, exhausted. But Ching-Mei's clock was ticking: we had only twenty-seven hours until the Huang Effect switched states. I had to stay within the *Sternberger*, waiting to see if poor Klicks would regain consciousness, but I wondered whether there was any useful work I could do in the meantime.

My night-sky photograph. At least I could check on that, see if it had turned out all right.

I got up from the couch, every joint in my body aching, found my palmtop computer, and slipped it into one of the baggy pockets on my khaki jacket. It was pure agony climbing up the ladder to the instrumentation dome.

I removed the electronic camera from the little tripod, then plugged it into the USB port on my palmtop. The night-sky photo blossomed on the color liquid-crystal display. At first I thought that the picture had been ruined by stray light: two curving bands of solid white passed across the lower right corner of the photograph, one thick, the other thin. Of course: the paths of Luna and Trick as they strolled across the night.

Except for these, it looked like all other time-lapse sky photos: a series of hairline concentric arcs, the paths drawn by stars as the heavens wheeled about Earth's axis. Since I'd left the lens open for about four hours, each arc was approximately one-sixth of a circle (we expected the Mesozoic day to be a little shorter, but not much).

Still, something wasn't quite right about this photo. There were six white dots in a line about halfway between the zenith and the southern horizon. I used the palmtop's touch pad to point at each of the dots in turn, then zoomed in for a closer look. The dots showed no movement arcs at all. One or even two could have been photographic glitches—dust on the lens, single-bit errors in the processing—but six in a row had to represent something real.

The only thing I could think of that would show no movement as the Earth rotates was a geostationary satellite orbiting above the equator. Well, I suppose it isn't surprising that the Hets put satellites up around Earth, although the precisely even spacing seemed strange to me. Perhaps they were for weather forecasting or communications, but there appeared to be more of them than were necessary for either of those jobs. A trio of evenly spaced satellites in the Clarke orbit could provide complete coverage of the entire planet; there were six satellites visible in this photo, meaning there might be twenty or thirty evenly spaced ones in total—

A crash came from downstairs. Rather than taking the time to disengage the camera from my palmtop, I tucked them both into the baggy pocket and hurried down the diagonal ladder. Klicks was standing, supporting himself against the lab bench. He had managed to knock some of his geological instruments to the floor as he'd hauled himself to his feet.

"Brandy," he said, "I'm . . ." He tried again. "Look, man. I didn't mean—" That didn't seem to cut it either. "It's just—" Finally he simply fell silent and shrugged. I sympathized with his predicament. After all, how do you tell someone you're sorry you tried to kill him?

I looked Klicks up and down. One of his ears was caked with dried blood. The gash across his forehead was nasty; it could have used stitches, but at least it had stopped bleeding.

I'd held my own quite well, given how much more muscular he is than me. I felt a smug satisfaction. In retrospect, I guess I'd taken a certain secret pleasure in beating the crap out of him with impunity. "That's okay," I said quietly. "You weren't yourself."

Klicks nodded and, after a time, looked away. He probably felt just as uncomfortable with the protracted moment between us as I did. "What about the Het?" he said at last.

I told him about the antiviral drugs I'd injected into his carotid artery. He winced at the prospect of a kilogram or two of dead alien still being inside his body. It *was* an unsettling thought.

He noticed the electronic camera, sticking up out of my jacket's breast pocket. Probably just to get his mind on something—anything—else, he said, "Is that your night-sky photo? How'd it turn out?"

"Here," I said, pulling out the camera and the palmtop, which was still attached to it by a USB cable. I flipped up the little computer's screen and handed it and the camera to him. "Have a look."

He held the computer up to his face. "Can you see the two horizontal bands?" I said.

"Yup."

"Those are the tracks left by the two moons. But I'm puzzled by the stationary dots above them." I shrugged. "Maybe they're geosynchronous satellites put up by the Hets."

Klicks nodded once as he handed everything back to me. "They're the gravity-suppressor satellites," he said matter-of-factly.

"*What?*"

Klicks reached for the edge of the table, steadying himself. His voice quavered. "How did I know that?"

"That's what I'd like to know."

"Flatworms," he said suddenly, but this time it wasn't one of his little tests. It was a flash of insight. The instant he spoke the word, I knew what he meant. I'd done the Humphries-Jacobsen experiment myself as an undergrad, training a planarian named Karen Black—I called it that because of its cute little cross-eyed face—to contract when exposed to light. The flatworm stored the memory of that training in its RNA. I then chopped K.B. up and fed her to another flatworm, Barbra Streisand. Babs assimilated Karen's memories and immediately knew how to respond to the light. Klicks had apparently gained some of the dead Het's memories from the RNA it had left in his head.

"Gravity suppression," I said. "Fascinating. So the reduced gravity is caused by the Hets—"

"So they can comfortably move around here, yes. They've scaled Earth's gravity down to the same level as Mars's, cutting it to one Martian *g*—thirty-eight percent of what we consider normal."

I shook my head. "Damn, we were stupid. We never felt any movement when we flew in that Het spaceship—nor any weightlessness while we were in orbit, for that matter. They seem to be able to do all kinds of tricks with gravity. Ching-Mei would love these guys: their physics must be extraordinary."

Klicks frowned. "I don't think they're that much ahead of us," he said. "Yes, they have a better grasp on gravity, but they obviously don't have time travel. They want the *Sternberger* something fierce."

I scratched my beard. "Tell me more about the Hets."

"I don't know anything about them."

"Well, let's try a specific question. Tell me if there's free-running water on Mars right now."

He blinked. "Oh, yes. A complete water cycle, with rains and snow."

"And what else lives on Mars besides the Hets?"

"Nothing lives except us. All other things exist for our subjugation."

Talk about Manifest Destiny. "You're going to be in for one hell of a debriefing when we get back, my friend. Tell me: how do the Hets communicate?"

Klicks closed his eyes. "The individual viral units produce impulses like synapses that can travel short distances. All the units in one of those lumps we've encountered are acting together, like the cells of one brain. The bigger the conglomeration, the smarter it is."

"And what about the dinosaurs?"

Klicks's eyes were still closed, as though he were listening to an internal voice. "Well, without the low gravity caused by the Hets, dinosaurian giantism wouldn't have occurred. But, beyond that, the Hets have done some direct genetic tinkering recently, fine-tuning existing dinosaurs to be better suited for war. For instance, natural ceratopsians, like *Chasmosaurus*, had neck frills that were only for bluffing displays. They were just outlined in bone, with skin stretched across. That wasn't suitable for real battle, so the Hets tweaked them into the genus *Triceratops*, filling in the open spaces to produce a solid shield of bone."

"Okay, time for Final Jeopardy: who are the Hets fighting?"

"Good Christ! It *is* the natives of Tess." Klicks looked away. "I—I mean of the belt planet."

"Really? And what's this garbage about the Martian civilization being a hundred and thirty million years old?"

Klicks looked thoughtful for a few seconds, then his eyes opened wide in astonishment. "The civilization of the viral Martians did arise that long ago, back in what we'd call the early Jurassic. Ten thousand years later—nothing on the scale we're talking about—they put up the gravity suppressor satellites around Earth. Since the satellites can control gravity, their orbits never decay, and they're solar-powered, so they never run out of energy. They have indeed been in stationary orbit around Earth for one hundred and thirty million years now."

I shook my head. "That doesn't make sense. The Het technology is clearly more advanced than ours is, but it's centuries, maybe even tens of centuries, ahead of us, not a hundred-odd million years. I mean, the rosette-makers, whoever they are, they might have a million-plus-year-old civilization, given that they can move stars around, but the Hets aren't anywhere near that advanced."

"That's right," said Klicks, and then his face clouded. "Oh, shit, of course they left the dinosaurs alone until very recently. The Hets, the Hets died out, almost completely. It's—" Klicks was shaking slightly. "It's horrible. God, the destruction." He closed his eyes for a moment, then staggered toward his crash couch and held onto it for support. "Brandy, you were right. The Martians are inherently violent. They seethe with the need to conquer."

His breathing was growing ragged; his eyes were haunted, darting. "The original viral globs lived as parasites within different types of Martian animals. But eventually the viruses developed intelligence. They wanted to enslave creatures that had manipulatory appendages. In the Martian seas, there was a creature that looked kind of like a hand—five tubular extensions coming out of one side of a central disk. At the ends of each of their five finger-like tubes, the creatures had circles of extruded iron filaments controlled by sphincter muscles. They'd evolved these appendages to pop open a type of Martian shellfish, but the ancestral Hets enslaved the Hands and used the iron filaments as general manipulators."

Klicks's head was shaking back and forth, but he seemed unaware that he was doing it. "Eventually the Hands built spaceships for the Hets, ships that moved by polarizing gravity. The Hets visited Earth and the belt planet. On both, they found animal life that might indeed develop intelligence someday. The belt world was small enough for the Hets and their Hands to move around comfortably, but Earth was much too massive. A project was begun to—to *marsiform* Earth, to make it Mars-like and habitable. The first step was the installation of the gravity-suppressor satellites; as I said, they went into orbit a hundred and thirty million years ago.

"These early Hets saw, hanging there in their southern sky, the rosette, the cluster of arranged suns—yes, it's that old. They knew there were other creatures out there, somewhere. And they hated that fact—hated that there were minds that they couldn't reach, couldn't enslave. The Hets assumed that any intelligence would be as violent as their own, so they forced the Hands to build war machines, ready to meet the rosette-makers whom they felt were bound to come and try to conquer them."

Klicks's arms were trembling as he spoke. His voice had gone hoarse; sweat appeared on his brow.

"The Hands were small creatures, far too puny to accommodate enough viral material to constitute a very astute slaver mind. And the Hand children were far too small to contain any meaningful concentration of Het viruses and therefore couldn't be controlled at all. At last, the Hand children turned the war machines their parents had been forced to build against the entire planet. The holocaust was incredible. It wiped out almost all life, including every last one of the Hands and most of the proto-Hets. Both Hand child and Hand adult preferred death to a life of enslavement."

Klicks's fists were clenching and unclenching like beating hearts. I went to the tap and got him a Dixie cup full of water. He downed it in one gulp. "Mars was left almost completely barren after that uprising," he said. "Without animal vehicles, the viruses were scattered and lost their capacity for intelligence, although the memories of all this were still stored in their RNA. Earth was left unattended, the gravity-suppressor satellites still running.

"On Mars, something like forty million years—correction: eighty million Earth years—passed before the viral life re-evolved into intelligent creatures, the current Hets. But the

Hands had done their job well: the only animal life left on Mars was microscopic." He shuddered, his shoulders rising and falling with his ragged breath. "The Hets," he continued, "developed a remarkable bioengineering technology. Viruses, of course, have the innate ability to substitute their genetic material for the native DNA in a cell. Well, the Hets took that a step further. They can *selectively* substitute nucleotide strings, manufacturing replacement genetic instructions and snipping and splicing at will. They used this ability to directly modify animal DNA. Still, it took them almost fifty million Earth years to evolve new hosts large enough to use as vehicles. But this time out, the Hets resolved to use only biological devices that had to be controlled mentally; never again would they use machines that might be seized by their slaves and used against them.

"At last, intelligence did develop in the natives of Tess." He was so lost in the story that he wasn't censoring himself anymore. "The Hets set out to enslave those creatures, too. They returned to Tess in their living spaceships and began a terrible war against the natives, a war that still rages on."

Klicks was shaking from head to toe, like a man on an adrenaline high, rage coursing through his system. "God, Brandy, I feel like killing—something. Anything. *Everything.* It's such a strong urge, such a primal impulse with them. It's—" He bolted across the room, grabbed a red metal tool chest off the worktable, and heaved it through the air. It smashed against the curving bulkhead, pliers and screwdrivers and wrenches clanging to the floor. Klicks breathed in and out deeply, his eyes closed.

"Miles?"

He looked at me, a hint of calm returning to his face. "God, that felt good." A pause. "I'm in control now, I think. Do me a favor: don't ask me any more questions about the Hets. Even the memory of their hatred for life is enough to drive you out of your skull."

"Don't worry," I said. "I've—"

Something funny about the light levels from outside—

I started to turn—

Wham!

The *Sternberger* shook under a tremendous impact, the hull reverberating, the sound of water in the partially empty tank beneath our feet slapping in a giant wave against one side of the timeship. I staggered, trying to keep my balance. Through the glassteel over the radio console, I could see something dark and gray, like a flying wall, pulling back, farther and farther, bits of sky now visible above it, the brown of the mud plain starting to peek out below it, the gray wall retracting more and more . . .

A tail. A dinosaur tail. The part that had connected with the timeship was almost twice as high as a man. The tail was flattened from side to side, a giant tapering structure covered with wrinkled gray leather. It was still pulling back and back, until finally the creature it belonged to was fully visible.

A sauropod, a member of that giant quadrupedal group typified by what most people still called *Brontosaurus*, standing out there on the mud plain, perpendicular to the crater wall, its elongated tail balanced by a similarly long neck rising up and up into the sky, ending in a tiny block-shaped head. In between neck and tail, a vast gray torso like the Goodyear blimp supported by massive column-like legs . . .

Sauropods were rare in the Upper Cretaceous, and none had ever been found in Alberta—too wet for them, according to one school of thought. Still, at this time there was *Alamosaurus* in New Mexico, *Antarctosaurus, Argyrosaurus, Laplatasaurus, Neuquensaurus,* and *Titanosaurus* in Argentina, and a handful of others in China, Hungary, India, and elsewhere. I supposed that if the Hets needed a living crane, flying one in presented no problem for them. Although they'd been nicknamed thunder lizards, sauropods had massively padded feet. This one, despite its size, had obviously had no trouble sneaking up on us.

The tail had finished pulling back and now was reversing its course, slicing through the air toward us, zooming in to dominate the view out the window—

The first impact clearly had been just a warm-up. Klicks and I went flying when the tail connected with full force. He landed in a heap by his crash couch; I ended up smashing into the washroom door panel. I tried to rise to my feet and looked over at Klicks, who was bracing himself against the fake wood-grain molding around the edges of the radio console. His eyes were closed as he listened to that inner voice once more. "They're going to take our timeship one way or another," he said.

Countdown: 0

In one era and out the other...
—Marshall McLuhan, Canadian media philosopher (1911–1980)

A third impact by the sauropod tail again knocked Klicks and me to the floor, something neither of us was in any condition to endure. I put my hand to my face and it came away wet. My nose had started bleeding again. Two more blows from the giant's tail dislodged the *Sternberger* from its perch atop the crater wall. I'd thought it had been bad going down that slope in the Jeep, but at least I'd been strapped in and had had the benefits of the vehicle's shock absorbers. This time, loose pieces of equipment flew around the cabin as our timeship skidded down the crumbling earth. Klicks and I were tossed like rag dolls in a clothes dryer, bruising elbows, banging knees, twisting limbs. The *Sternberger* finally, mercifully, came to a stop on the mud flat, tilted at a bit of an angle. We staggered to the window.

Dinosaurs were moving in from every direction. A dozen dark red juvenile tyrannosaurs clustered along the shore of the lake, their bird-like feet giving them excellent traction in the mud. Seven triceratops tanks, garish in their blue and orange camouflage, lumbered in to form an arc to the southwest, heads bent low so that their mighty eye horns stuck straight out. Next to them stood the gargantuan gray sauropod with its skyscraper neck and a tail that seemed to go on forever. Thirty or so troödons milled about, hopping from foot to foot, their stiff tails bouncing up and down like conductors' batons. Goose-stepping in from the west were five giant adult females of the species *Tyrannosaurus rex*.

Standing behind the others, one duckbill reared up on its hind legs. It was a member of the genus *Parasaurolophus*, just like the famous specimen we had at the ROM, a meter-long tubular crest extending back from its skull. At first I couldn't fathom what that cow-like reptile was doing here. I'd imagined the Hets simply raised duckbills in herds to feed the fighting carnivores. But then the hadrosaur let out a series of great reverberating notes, its crest acting like a resonating chamber. The tyrannosaurs dispersed and I realized that the duckbill was calling out the orders of the Het general riding within it, the hadrosaur's thunderous voice carrying for kilometers.

I looked at our Jeep, over by the western base of the crater wall. The two tires I could see from this angle were completely flat—pierced open, I suspected, by triceratops horns.

A troödon stepped up to the window that Klicks and I were looking through. It stood on tippy-toe to see in, its pointed muzzle just coming to the bottom of the glassteel. The beast regarded us for a few seconds, gave its weird one-two blink, and then spoke, its raspy voice audible through the air vents around our roof. "Come out now," it said. "Surrender the timeship. Do these things or die."

The maximum a siege could last would be twenty-two hours; after that, the *Sternberger* was going home regardless. We could comfortably wait that long since we had plenty of food and water. But it seemed pretty clear that the Hets weren't just going to hang around outside until the Huang Effect reversed states. They intended to be on board when that happened, bypassing their own extinction.

Klicks ran to get our elephant guns but he shook his head as he passed one to me. "We could pump every bullet we've got into that sauropod and probably not even slow it down."

From outside, the troödon's gravelly voice shouted: "Last warning. Out now."

Klicks grabbed the red tool chest he had heaved through the air earlier and stood upon it, its sheet-metal construction caving in a bit under his weight. He jammed the butt of his rifle into the wire mesh that covered one of the air vents at the top of the curving outer wall, clearing the mesh away. Then he turned the weapon around and pointed the muzzle out. But despite his craning, there was no way he could see out the vent to aim.

"We could shoot out the main hatchway," I said, but no sooner had I done so than I heard the outside latch lifting. I leapt through door number one and skidded down the ramp that led to the outer door, hoping to jam it shut, but before I got there it was kicked open, swinging inward on its hinges. A dancing troödon jumped in, its sickle claws clicking on the metal ramp. I braced my rifle against my shoulder and fired into the thing's chest. It was blown backward out the door by the blast, but a moment later a second troödon jumped forward to take its place. I fired at it, too, winging it. But I was sure that the Hets had more dinosaurs than I had bullets.

While I was reloading, the second troödon made it through the mandrill's mouth, one three-fingered hand covering its wound. Klicks barreled past it, running down the ramp to the main doorway, trying to force it shut, but the arm of a third troödon scrabbled for purchase around its edge. Meanwhile, as I rushed to reload, the injured troödon that had made it inside scurried up the ramp and into the habitat. I followed it up. It tried to negotiate its way around the two crash couches to get at me. I fired both barrels into its torso. The creature slammed backward against our equipment lockers and slumped to the floor. The stink of gunpowder filled my nostrils.

I looked back. Klicks had managed to push the main hatchway almost shut, but a troödon arm still stuck around the edge. I heard the crack of breaking bone as Klicks threw his massive shoulder against the door, but the beast held on, its opposable claws snapping open and closed.

I ran for the equipment lockers next to the dead troödon and found the metal box containing my secondary dissection kit. I hurried down the ramp to join Klicks in the cramped accessway. While he continued to fracture the invader's arm with brutal body slams to the door, I used my bone saw to hack through the limb. Blood spurted everywhere. At last, the arm fell to the floor, twitching, and Klicks and I forced the main door shut. I then dashed up the ramp into the habitat proper and relayed boxes and pieces of equipment down to him. He rammed them up against the door as a barricade. It wouldn't hold for long.

The main doorway had been our one aperture for firing at the troödons. No—wait! I could shoot through the instrumentation dome. I scrabbled up the ladder into the cramped space. The vertical slit was still open. I rotated the whole thing to bring the opening around to face west, stuck the barrel of my elephant gun through the slit, and squeezed off eight rounds as fast as I could reload. The gunshots echoed deafeningly inside the glassteel hemisphere. Three of my shots missed completely. Three more found solid targets, killing the closest of the troödons. The last two injured a pair of the dancing beasts, hitting one in the right leg, the other in its left shoulder. Both collapsed to the ground.

The parasaurolophus was bellowing commands at the top of its lungs, the two separate nasal chambers that ran through its trombone-like crest each producing separate notes, harmonizing with itself. Apparently responding to the order, one of the triceratopses charged the *Sternberger*, its haunches pumping up and down as it ran. The ship rocked under its impact, and I was almost knocked off my feet. I tried to kill the horned-face, but my bullets just nicked tiny shards off its bony neck frill. Still, it was something of an impasse: no troödon could approach the ship without me picking it off.

The parasaurolophus barked again. Moments later the sky went dark. A great shadow passed over me. A huge turquoise pterosaur, its vast furry wings spanning a dozen meters, was flapping its way toward the instrumentation dome. Judging by the curving snake-like neck and the incredible size, this was either *Quetzalcoatlus* or a close relative, a genus known to range from Alberta to Texas at this time. I scrambled to reload, but in my panic sent the box of shells spilling across the floor, half of them rolling out the opening for the access ladder. By the time I was ready to fire, the dragon filled my field of view. My shots tore holes in its turquoise wings, but the pterosaur continued to swoop in, its claws sounding like chalk on a blackboard as they scrabbled for footing on the smooth metal hull of the *Sternberger*.

The head with its long narrow beak slipped through the observation slit, poking at me from the end of a serpentine three-meter neck. I scrunched myself back against the far wall of the dome. Holding the rifle in both hands, one on the painfully hot end of the twin barrels, the other on the wooden butt, I tried to ward off the creature. Fat chance. Moving with eye-blurring speed, it seized my gun in its jaws and twisted the weapon free with a sharp jerk of its neck. Before I realized what had happened, the beast had taken to the air again, the rifle clamped in its beak. My hair whipped in the breeze caused by the downward thrust of the immense blue-green wings.

There was no point in staying in the dome. I closed the slit, then backed down the ladder. Klicks was pushing the food refrigerator down the ramp that led to the exterior door. I guess he intended to use it to strengthen the barricade.

My heart jumped. "Oh God—"

"What is it?" Klicks said, looking up.

"Your leg."

A grapefruit-sized mound of phosphorescent blue jelly was throbbing on the shin of Klicks's khaki pants. It must have come from the troödon I'd killed earlier, the one slumped by the equipment lockers next to where the fridge had been. Klicks frantically undid his belt and pulled the trousers off, flinging them across the accessway. They hit the wall with a wet *splat* and stuck. But the Het had been having no trouble percolating through the cotton weave and some of it was still on his skin. Klicks was near panic. I grabbed a scalpel from my dissection kit and scraped the dull edge of its blade across his shank, gathering up pieces of Martian. After each stroke, I flicked the knife, sending dabs of blue jelly flying into the dissection-kit box. A minute later I looked up. "I think I got it," I said.

"All of it?" Klicks sounded desperate.

"Well . . . most of it, anyway. Let's hope there's enough Deliverance left in your system to prevent what did get in from interacting with your cells."

"What about that?" he said, pointing at his pants.

I got a pickax and used it to knock the trousers off the wall into a stasis box, then tossed in the dissection kit as well and slammed the silver lid shut. We went up the ramp and back into the main habitat.

Suddenly the ship rocked again as a pair of white triceratops horns burst through the side of the hull. The Hets must have learned from their brief mind-melds with us that the *Sternberger* was like a yo-yo, attached by a mathematical string to the Huang Effect generator 65 million years in the future. Even partially smashed, the timeship would still dutifully return to its launch point in midair between the Sikorsky Sky Crane and the ground. It didn't have to be intact, but they did have to be inside its walls.

The ship buffeted once more, its hull deforming where a second triceratops rammed against it. Moments later there was another impact, and another pair of horns pierced the wall, this time less than a half-meter from my head.

The parasaurolophus's call split the air again. Outside the window, the giant tyrannosaurs, looking like blood clots the size of boxcars, growled in response.

"We've got to do something," I said.

"Good thinking, genius," said Klicks. "*What* should we do?"

"I don't know. But we can't let them have access to the future. Christ, they'd take over the whole planet." The ship rocked again, another triceratops smashing into it. "Dammit!" I slammed my fist against the wall. "If only we had some weapon, or . . . or, hell, I don't know, maybe some way to turn off the gravity-suppressor satellites."

"A coded signal in binary," said Klicks at once. "1010011010, repeated three times."

"Christ, man, are you sure?"

Klicks tapped the side of his head. "The Martian may be dead, but his memory lingers on."

I was over to our Ward-Beck radio unit in two bounds and flipped the master switch on the black and silver console. "Do you think we can get a signal to the gravity satellites?" I asked.

Klicks squinted at the controls. "The satellites are obviously still in good working order," he said. "And the Hets do use radio in very much the same way we do."

"What about the satellites below the horizon?"

"The off signal will be relayed by those satellites that do receive it," said Klicks. "We only have to connect with one. That makes sense, of course; otherwise, there'd be no way to operate them all from a single ground station."

"Won't we need a password to access the satellite computers?" I asked, peering at the console, trying to remind myself of what all the buttons did.

"You said it yourself, Brandy. The Hets are a hive mind. The concept of 'passwords' is meaningless to them."

I reached for a large calibrated dial. "What frequency should the signal go out at?"

Klicks closed his eyes and tilted his head slightly, listening intently. "Let's see . . . three-to-the-thirteenth-power cycles per . . ."

"Cycles per second?"

"No. Shit! Cycles per unit of Martian time-keeping."

"And how long is one of those?"

"It's . . . uh, well, it's not long."

"*Great.*" The *Sternberger* shook under another impact. Triceratopses seemed to be using their horns to perforate a hole in one side of the ship. They were making damn good progress, too.

"Well, can't you program the radio to try a range of frequencies?" asked Klicks.

I looked at the controls. "Not directly. But I might be able to hook the radio up to my palmtop." There was a small patchcord bus running vertically along one side of the radio console. "I'd need the right cable, though."

Klicks picked up the electronic camera. "What about this one?" he said, unplugging the fiber-optic serial cable I'd used to connect it to my palmtop earlier.

"Well, that's the right type of cable, yes, but it's the wrong gender. The radio expects a female plug; that one has male connectors at both ends."

"I think I used a gender-changer when I hooked up my spectroscopes," Klicks said. He stepped over to the compact lab and started rummaging around. "Here it is." Klicks handed the little doodad to me, and we completed the connection between the radio and my palmtop computer. "Now can you send the signal?"

"Yes, but only in one frequency at a time, and—damn it. It would take all afternoon to send that binary sequence in even a small sampling of possible radio frequencies." I shook my head, discouraged. It had sounded like such a good idea. "Besides, we don't even know how long each of the binary pulses should be."

"One time-keeping unit each." Klicks paused, realizing what he'd just said. "That means if we get the right number for the frequency, we'll automatically have the right length for the pulses." He paused once more, straining to hear that inner voice again. "And don't bother trying to modulate the bits into the carrier wave. Just send them directly by interrupting the transmission for the zeros."

"Okay." I wished my nose would stop hurting. "I'll write a little program to try different variables for the length of the time-keeping unit." The cable wasn't long enough to reach back to my crash couch, so I had to type standing up, my palmtop balanced on the fake woodgrain molding that surrounded the radio console. "Any guess as to what value we should start with?"

Klicks closed his eyes. "Try . . . try four or five seconds. I don't know, but that *feels* about right."

The radio console could only accept instructions in CURB, a standard communications-processor language. It'd been ages since I'd programmed anything in that. I hoped I remembered enough; we certainly didn't have time for me to thumb through the on-line manual. My fingers danced, calling up a little calculator. I worked out three-to-the-thirteenth, the number of cycles per unit of Martian time Klicks had specified, then typed: *Set Frequency = 1594323. Frequency = Frequency + . . .*

Another ceratopsian head smashed against the hull, and this time it ruptured. I heard the roar of water rushing out of the tank beneath our feet. Bet that surprised them.

I decided to start a little lower than Klicks's guess. *Set Time-unit = 3.000 s. Goto Send . . .*

The ship shook again as a triceratops skull smashed against it. "Can't you go any faster, Brandy?"

"Do you want to do it, fathead?"

"Sorry." He backed away.

The horns had pierced the hull in enough places now to loosen a large piece of it. Through the glassteel, I could see the ceratopsian lumbering off.

I typed out the program's final line, then issued the compile command. One, two, three error messages flashed on the screen, along with the corresponding line numbers. "Boolean expression expected." "Type mismatch." "Reserved word." *Damn.*

"What's wrong?" said Klicks.

"Error messages. I made some mistakes."

"Did you want—?"

"Shut up and let me fix them, please." I switched back to the program editor and hit the key to jump to the first error. Ah, the Boolean problem was simple enough: just a typo, "adn" instead of "and"; serves me right for running with AutoCorrect turned off. I fixed the misspelling.

Crrack!

I swung briefly around. A boneheaded pachycephalosaur was ramming its skull against the perforated hole in the wall. It was now painfully obvious what the Het we had found inside the dissected bonehead had been up to: evaluating the dinosaur's potential as a living battering ram. How fortunate they'd been able to find an application for it so quickly. "They're almost through," shouted Klicks.

I tapped out the command that jumped the cursor to the second error. *Type mismatch.* What the hell did that mean in this context? Oh, I see. I'd tried to do a mathematical operation on a text variable. Stupid.

The self-harmonizing notes from the trombone-crested parasaurolophus split the air, presumably calling out for the bonehead to charge again.

The cursor jumped to the third error. *Reserved word?* That meant the name I'd chosen for a variable—FREQUENCY—was one the program didn't allow, because it used it exclusively for some other function. Okay, let's try a different name. Call it SAVE_ASS, and hope that it does. I almost cracked the palmtop's tiny case with the force with which I bashed out the compile command again.

I held my breath until the message flashed in front of my face: "Compilation successful. No errors."

"Got it!" I said.

"Terrific!" crowed Klicks. "Start transmitting."

I highlighted the program file name and held my finger above the Enter key.

"Hit the damn key!" said Klicks.

"I . . ."

"What's wrong?"

"You know what's going to happen," I said. "I'm not sure I can . . ."

"If you don't want to press it, I will."

I looked at him, held his gaze. "No," I said. "Failing to act is a decision in and of itself." I pressed down on the key. The program started running and the radio began transmitting.

Crrack! The pachycephalosaur skull with its yellow and blue display colors smashed the loosened section of hull inward. A circular piece of metal about a meter and a half across crashed to the floor with an ear-splitting clang. Before we could react, the bonehead was gone and a triceratops face was poking through from outside. Klicks cocked his rifle. This individual had only one eye horn. The other probably had snapped off while it was attacking our ship. In one continuous motion, Klicks flopped to his belly and fired up into the soft tissue on the underside of the beast's throat. It teetered for a moment, then slumped back, dead. Lucky shot: he must have severed the thing's spinal cord.

Through the jagged opening in the hull we could see two other ceratopsians shouldering the carcass aside. Klicks fired over and over, but these beasts weren't about to repeat the same mistake. They kept their heads tipped down, the bony frills shielding them. In short order, the path was cleared and a platoon of troödons danced into view. They waited for Klicks to lower his rile to reload, then charged, a scaly green wave of teeth and claws surging forward—

Klicks tried to rise to his feet, but instead slammed into the deck. My stomach seemed to drop right through my boots. The closest of the troödons slapped onto their bellies, two of them being impaled on the ragged edge of the hole in the *Sternberger* wall, most of the rest tumbling backward out onto the mud flat. Feeling like I weighed a million kilos, I ran as though in slow motion toward the edges of the impromptu doorway, leaning out over the two troödon corpses. Overhead, the great quetzalcoatlus, gliding in a wide circle, crumpled like a paper toy and began plummeting to the earth. Nearby, the sauropod's twelve meters of neck came crashing to the ground, hitting with a sound like a thunderclap. The tyrannosaurs staggered for a few moments, then, one by one, fell to their knees, their legbones snapping under their own massive weight. The earth vibrated and shook beneath our feet as gravity surged back to a full, normal g. Suddenly the mud flat began to ripple like the Tacoma Narrows bridge, great clouds of brown dust rising into the darkening sky.

I staggered away from the opening and dropped onto my belly near Klicks. The earthquake continued, the roar deafening, the constant heaving of the ground turning my stomach. Wind whipped through the openings in the *Sternberger*'s hull. There was much lightning, too, strobing through the glassteel, but the thunder was all but lost against the other noises, including a cacophony of animal screams.

On and on, the ground shaking, heaving . . .

I suspected fissures must be ripping open all across the Earth, spewing out magma rich in iridium and arsenic and antimony. The molten rock would spark countless forest fires and boil water in the seas. In places, clouds of poisonous gas would belch forth, and great tidal waves must be pounding the shores, sloshing ocean water into freshwater shallows, destroying coastal habitats. And, as the Earth compacted slightly under its newfound weight, quartz grains would be shocked and microdiamonds would form—two of the asteroid fans' favorite pieces of evidence for what they'd thought had been an impact.

My head pounded. I lifted my neck to look up through the opening torn in our hull. The sky had turned a bilious greenish gray, the clouds whipping along with visible speed. The *Sternberger* bounced like an egg frying. Each time it slammed back down, my chest was bruised, metal fittings on my jacket digging into my skin. My teeth rattled. I was afraid to open my mouth, lest it be slammed back closed by an impact, biting off my tongue. My nose bled steadily.

Eventually the screams from outside stopped, but the pounding went on and on and on, the ground heaving. Sheets of rain dropped out of the sky, as though buckets inside the clouds had been overturned all at once.

An hour went by, and another, the earthquake unrelenting. For a time, Klicks was knocked completely unconscious, his head smashing into the deck as we bounced again and again.

As the Earth's gravity increased, I imagined Luna must be reeling in its orbit. By the time it stabilized again, it would be showing the part of its face familiar to human beings. I suspected tiny Trick would never fully re-stabilize in its closer orbit, making its eventual disintegration inevitable.

At last the quaking stopped. We stayed put in the *Sternberger,* anticipating an aftershock. That came about twenty minutes later, and others followed for all the rest of the time we remained in the Mesozoic and perhaps, indeed, for years to come.

During one of the gaps between the quakes, we dared to venture outside. The sky, thick with dust, had cleared enough that we could see the blood-red setting sun.

It was a different world. Klicks and I were the only large creatures still able to walk around. Dinosaurs were everywhere, flopped on their bellies. Some still clung to life. The hearts of others had already given out under the hours of gravity 2.6 times what they were used to. Those that did survive would eventually starve, unable to move around to forage.

We saw several Hets. They had oozed out of their dead and dying dinosaur vehicles, but were flattened like blue pancakes, barely able to move. They seemed to be having trouble holding together in large, intelligent concentrations. In many places, we saw three or four smaller globs next to each other, unable to join up. Klicks set fire to all the ones we found.

Many of the small animals, including some tiny birds, tortoises, and a few shrew-like mammals, appeared to be doing all right in the full gravity, but broken bones, internal injuries, or cardiac arrest seemed to be killing or have killed almost everything else.

Death was everywhere and I took as much of it as I could. Finally, bone-weary, I sat down amongst the ferns next to a hapless duckbill, the creature whimpering slightly as its life slipped away. The beast's intricate crest had apparently been staved in when its head had slammed into a rock as the gravity surged on. The animal's dying breaths were escaping with ragged whistling sounds through its smashed nasal passages, and it regarded me, terrified, with an unintelligent eye.

It was the end of an era.

Stroking the dinosaur's pebbly flank, I let my tears flow freely.

EPILOGUE: CONVERGENCE

The oncology ward at the Wellesley Hospital is never a cheery place, but somehow this time it seems less oppressive, less a prison for both me and my father.

I sit in the uncomfortable vinyl chair next to him. It isn't important that we talk. There isn't much to say, anyway. Occasionally he does rouse himself enough to speak and I face him, looking as though I am listening. But my mind is thousands of kilometers away and millions of years in the past.

When the Huang Effect reversed, the mathematical string connecting the *Sternberger* to the present was reeled in. As the ship was hauled back up the timeline, the entire last 65 million years of history were rewritten. Reverse engineering: the future making the past what it must have been.

I'd killed the dinosaurs; I'd paved the way for the mammals.

Paved the way for my own present.

And the other Brandy? The other timeline?

Gone. There's only one timeline now; only one reality.

I suppose there is no reason to mourn. I *am* him, after all, and with Tess and me still together, perhaps he is content to hand off the timeline to me. Besides, it isn't as though he had never existed. I have some of his memories now, thanks to that strange swapping of diaries. Whether by quantum flux or deliberate design, I am grateful for those memories, for the small peek they afforded at what my life might have been. The time-traveling Brandy's diary reminds me of my neighbor Fred's tabby cat, appearing at his cottage up on Georgian Bay after it had supposedly ceased to exist. Sometimes the universe does care . . . just a bit.

And the universe has given me something else, too: proof that a future does exist for humankind, or whatever we become, for somehow that future gave Ching-Mei the knowledge needed to make the past what it had to be. The end *creates* the means.

But I do wonder what happened to the Hets, those bizarre alien conquerors who came and went in the dim past. Their ages-long war with the natives of the belt planet must have escalated into a devastating final battle, as the time-traveling Klicks had suggested, destroying the fifth world and laying waste to Mars.

The time-traveling Brandy didn't really have to make the moral decision about the Hets. There was only one possible course of action after he learned the truth about them. That's fitting, in a way, for the Hets themselves were inflexible chemical machines, driven to violence and conquest by their very nature. The other Brandy had no choice *because* the viral Hets had no choice.

But in the here and now, I do have a choice. We all do. For years, I've avoided making decisions. But the act of deciding is what makes us human, what separates the living from things like the Hets that only parody life. My father is experiencing a remission now, but if he asks for my help again, I know how I will answer.

I wonder about those Hets left on Earth after the resurgence of gravity. They apparently lost the ability to clump together into big enough packages to remain intelligent. But you can't really kill viruses, since they aren't truly alive. Would they survive somehow as part of Earth's ecosystem? Would we even recognize them, or their effects, 65 million years later?

It hits me. The Hets *did* linger on, dissolving into their constituent units. Their intelligence ebbed from them, their civilization reduced to nothing but chemically stored memories in their RNA. Only their hatred for things truly alive survives, their basic biological imperative continuing to drive them.

Influenza. The common cold. Polio. And, yes, the cancer that is killing my father. It seems that the Hets are still here.

ABOUT THE AUTHOR

Robert J. Sawyer is the bestselling author of twelve other novels, including *The Terminal Experiment*, which won the Nebula Award for Best Novel of the Year; *Starplex*, which was both a Nebula and Hugo Award finalist; and *Frameshift*, *Factoring Humanity*, and *Calculating God*, all of which were Hugo Award finalists.

Sawyer has won twenty-four national and international awards for his fiction, including an Arthur Ellis Award from the Crime Writers of Canada; five Aurora Awards (Canada's top honor in SF); five Best Novel HOMer Awards voted on by the thirty thousand members of the SF&F Forums on CompuServe; the *Science Fiction Chronicle* Reader Award; and the top SF awards in France (*Le Grand Prix de l'Imaginaire*), Japan (*Seiun*), and Spain (*Premio UPC de Ciencia Ficción*, which he has won twice).

Maclean's: Canada's Weekly Newsmagazine says Sawyer is "science fiction's northern star—in fact, one of the hottest SF writers anywhere. By any reckoning Sawyer is among the most successful Canadian authors ever." He is profiled in *Canadian Who's Who*, has been interviewed more than 150 times on TV, and has given talks and readings at countless venues, including the Library of Congress. He lives in Mississauga, Ontario (just west of Toronto), with Carolyn Clink, his wife of sixteen years.

For more about Robert J. Sawyer and his fiction—including a readers' group discussion guide for this novel—visit his World Wide Web site (called "the largest genre writer's home page in existence" by *Interzone*) at www.sfwriter.com.